ANTAGONIST:

Love and War, Book 5

R. A. STEFFAN

Antagonist: Love and War, Book 5

This book is a work of fiction. Names, characters, businesses, organizations, places, events and incidents either are the product of the author's imagination or are used fictitiously. Any resemblance to actual persons, living or dead, events, or locales is entirely coincidental.

ISBN: 978-1-955073-52-3 (paperback)

For information, contact the author at
http://www.rasteffan.com/contact/

Cover design by Ember

Second Edition: September 2022

INTRODUCTION

This book contains graphic violence and explicit sexual content. It is intended for a mature audience.

TABLE OF CONTENTS

ONE

"Well, that was two-and-a-half cycles of my life I'll never get back," Kade said, fussing with the fastenings at the collar of his formal gray suit jacket.

Ambassador Isadora Martinez of the planet Terra Nova walked next to her alien companion as they made their way down a nondescript corridor inside the Vitharan government complex, lengthening her strides to keep pace with his longer legs. She shot the Vithii a sidelong glance, privately enjoying the way the severely tailored lines of his suit accentuated his angular build. Despite her best efforts, she seemed to be doing a lot of that sort of thing in the weeks since they'd started working together—though none of it changed the fact that the man beneath the suit was a crusty, bitter old asshole most of the time.

He finally got the triangular lapel of the jacket unfastened and started in on the top buttons of the shirt beneath.

"You're fidgeting," she observed.

The look he gave her was jaded. "I've also got a freshly implanted neurotonin pump stitched into the skin above my collarbone. What's your point?"

Shirt and jacket loosened, Kade tugged the fabric away from his neck and stuffed his hands in his trouser pockets. Away from the meeting room full of Vitharan government officials, his shoulders curved into a comfortable slouch as they walked, making his two-meter-plus frame into something a bit less intimidating than it might otherwise have been. His gray eyes still snapped with the frightening intelligence he kept hidden behind a shell of sarcasm and grouchiness, though—their color accentuated by the nearly identical shade of the suit he was wearing. Dark brown hair stood up in the rough spikes common to his race, shot through with an occasional strand of gray here and there.

"If the pump's still bothering you, maybe you should visit the clinic and have them check it out," Martinez said mildly. "You could have taken another couple of days for the incisions to heal before jumping straight back into meetings, you know."

One of the first things she'd learned about Kade was that he was a long-term neurotonin addict. Without an injection every few cycles, his brain chemistry would fall hopelessly out of balance, with fatal effects if the withdrawal symptoms were left untreated for too long.

It had taken considerably more digging—including a candid conversation with one of his comrades from Ilarius—to learn that he'd gained the aforementioned addiction at the hands of the prison system on his home planet of Ilarius. There, the guards had apparently preferred to keep him drugged into compliance with neurotransmitter antagonists during his stay as a political prisoner. After the first few months, they'd grown tired of his continual legal challenges regarding the statutory basis of his incarceration, and decided he would be easier to deal with as a mental vegetable.

Frankly, it was rather amazing that he'd recovered to the degree he had.

Upon their arrival on Vithara—with its advanced medical technology—she'd managed to sell him on the idea of undergoing surgery to install a pump. The state-of-the-art Vitharan medical device was capable of delivering measured dosages of neurotonin as needed to keep his levels stable. She'd argued that, if nothing else, the pump would free him from the necessity of stopping whatever he was doing every few cycles to get an injection, thereby reducing the amount of time and energy needed to deal with his condition when there were more important things requiring his attention.

The surgery had been scheduled two days ago. He'd been back to work less than a day later, against medical advice.

For this reason, it was no real surprise when he shot her a dark look from beneath heavy brows and echoed, "Another couple of *days*? Sure, I mean… why not? I expect the humans facing genocide on Ilarius would be happy to wait for help while the redness and swelling around my surgical site go down."

She met his gaze with one equally as dark. "You're not the only person in this fight, you know."

He gave a quick, sharp shake of the head—the gesture replete with disgust. "No? Then why do I feel as though I'm constantly talking to a brick wall during these meetings? We're wasting time my planet can't afford."

She jerked her eyes away from him, facing front. "I warned you at the beginning that Vithara would be a hard sell when it comes to extra-planetary interventionism. At least Terra Nova is on board with us now."

"True," Kade allowed gruffly. "On both counts."

For some time, Martinez had been concerned about the situation on Ilarius. Anytime a hard-line nationalist government rose to power, there was the potential for things to turn ugly. A government like that needed an enemy in order to focus the populace's frustration outward, away from its leaders—and Ilarius had a human population ready-made for the task.

In fact, the planet had originally been a human colony, founded after the Great Diaspora, when Old Earth became uninhabitable. Ilarius had been settled by a much smaller group of colonists than Martinez's home planet of Terra Nova, but it had grown steadily over the decades and become relatively prosperous.

The humans already had a solid network of agricultural communities on the water-rich southern continent, and a small spaceport on the dry northern continent, when refugee ships arrived in the system, seeking asylum. The ships, as it turned out, carried thousands of Vitharans fleeing a civil war on their home planet. Vithara had always maintained cordial relations with the Seven Systems' human colonies, so the colonists on Ilarius were reluctant to turn them away. The fact that the refugees brought more advanced technology with them to offer in exchange for a place on Ilarius sealed the deal.

For nearly a century, the unusual arrangement seemed to work out well enough. There wasn't a huge degree of intermingling—perhaps not surprising given the rather stark cultural differences between the two races. Nonetheless, Ilarius thrived with its patchwork society of humans and Vithii, who'd altered their collective name to differentiate themselves from their Vitharan cousins.

Some twenty years ago, however, a group of Ilarian malcontents started a Vithii First movement, which had grown with startling rapidity. As more and more Vithii became convinced that they deserved a larger part of the colony's pie, sporadic violence against humans and those Vithii who were seen as human sympathizers grew increasingly common.

The real tipping point had come in the last election cycle, when all three arms of the Ilarian legislature fell under the control of the so-called Regime—an outgrowth of the Firsters led by a charismatic psychopath named Xandrie Kovak. With Kovak installed as the planet's Premiere, what had been scattered violence and unrest up to that point became institutionalized terror against half of the planet's population.

Genocide now appeared to be a real possibility, if Martinez and the handful of Ilarian revolutionaries she was helping couldn't garner some serious off-world support for the Premiere's ouster. Unfortunately, convincing Vitharan officials to commit troops and resources to dealing with the descendents of the people who'd instigated a civil war against them was, to put it mildly, an uphill battle.

Kade—real name, Ehkadian Finisterre—had arrived on Terra Nova several weeks ago with two associates; a human, Ashildir Purandhri, and a Vithii called Draven, with no last name. In addition to the mixed human and Vithii crew of the freighter they'd been flying, they'd also brought along the widow of a prominent Regime member… one whom Martinez was reasonably certain they'd kidnapped by force.

Of course, there was no way to prove it, since the kidnapping victim in question maintained vehemently that she'd come along by choice. Add to that the fact that she was also an old friend of Martinez's from their university days, and Martinez had decided to let it lie.

Basically, Jontalyss Lusivian had been a sweet girl who'd made a horrendously bad choice of bondmate, and gotten in way over her head. Now, she was trying to make amends for what she saw as her own complicity in the acts perpetrated by the government her husband had served. When Martinez and Kade left the planet to negotiate directly with the Vitharans on their homeworld, Jontalyss had stayed behind with Kade's two friends, arguing for Terra Novan intervention to save the humans on Ilarius. When they'd succeeded in gaining that support, Jontalyss had remained on Terra Nova to act as a liaison while Mr. Purandhri and Draven had joined Martinez and Kade on Vithara.

As she understood it, Kade had two other friends who'd traveled to the treaty world of Maelfius, seeking support there as well. If they could somehow get all three planets on board, it would present a powerful front against the Premiere in the form of opposition from Ilarius' largest trading partners. Martinez was convinced that with such an alliance to stand against it, Kovak's Regime could be stopped… or at least reined in.

They just had to convince the Vitharans to help.

"I think I finally detected a chink in old Trivaal's hardheadedness this morning," she said. "Hence my suggestion of a private consultation with him over lunch."

Kade looked at her with more interest. "I had wondered about the reason behind this meeting. The old fossil still sounded like he was banging the non-interventionist drum to me, but at this point I'm willing to take any grain of optimism I can get."

Martinez stifled a snort. From what she'd gathered so far, the words 'Kade' and 'optimism' didn't really belong in the same sentence. "You didn't see his face while you reporting on the agreement your comrades managed to strike with Terra Nova. He was definitely taken aback by the news."

Kade raised a speculative eyebrow. "Was he, indeed? Hmm. Sounds like I owe Ash and Draven another round of drinks to celebrate their accomplishment, in that case."

Martinez mirrored him with an eyebrow of her own. "But not Jontalyss?" she asked rather pointedly. Her tone turned ironic. "I gather she played some small part in gaining Terra Nova's support, you know."

Kade's expression closed off. "Frey Lusivian isn't here to collect on the debt. Besides, I would imagine she'd take more pleasure from throwing a drink in my face than consuming it."

There was no point in pushing the matter, so Martinez didn't. She had a pretty good idea that Kade had been the one to bully Jontalyss Lusivian into seeing the error of the Regime's ways. The human that the others called Ash didn't really seem the bullying type. And while Draven could no doubt play the heavy when the situation called for it, from what she'd seen, he lacked both Kade's innate vicious streak, and his Machiavellian one.

At any rate, *someone* had certainly reduced Jontalyss to a quivering wreck in the moments before the freighter they'd been on was surrounded and boarded by Terra Novan security forces in orbit. Martinez would lay credits on that individual being the one currently walking beside her.

Another person would probably have resented the fact, given her background of friendship with Jontalyss. Fortunately for Kade, Martinez could be a practical, cold-hearted bitch when circumstances called for it. The way she saw it, whatever Kade had said to Jontalyss resulted in the Vithii woman contacting Martinez and begging for her help with the situation on Ilarius. If it ended up saving tens of thousands of human lives from Premiere Kovak's mad plan of genocide, then a friend's tears and a bit of kidnapping could probably be overlooked.

"Yes," Martinez agreed. "I'm sure flinging a glass of alcohol in your face would be positively cathartic for her. Tell you what—if you can arrange it at some point, be sure to get someone to record video. There's an entire hypernet channel on Terra Nova dedicated to people getting splashed in the face with drinks."

Kade ignored her, his expression unamused. Like optimism, humor didn't really seem to be his thing. Perhaps that was why she secretly found it so satisfying to make him the butt of it whenever the opportunity presented itself.

Now, though, it was time to slip back behind the mask of professionalism. Really, she shouldn't have allowed that mask to slide with him in the first place. He wasn't *trying* to get under her skin, she was certain. His surly attitude toward those around him appeared to be universal, encompassing friends and political enemies alike. Also, she had a sneaking suspicion that his reaction would be complete bewilderment, should he ever discover that she frequently caught herself checking out his ass, or the breadth of his shoulders, or the insouciant curve of his spine leading down to a narrow waist.

In short, it wasn't Kade's fault that he simultaneously attracted and unsettled her. It also wasn't useful to their current objective of convincing Vithara to *act*.

She squared her shoulders and led the way to Councilman Trivaal Canutian's office, where their lunch meeting was to take place. The door intercom buzzed beneath her touch, and a tinny, female Vitharan voice replied, "*May I help you?*"

"Ambassador Martinez and Krau Finisterre of Ilarius to see the councilman. We're expected."

The door slid open silently, and Kade gestured her to precede him into the office. Above them, one of the ubiquitous motion-sensing security cameras that watched over the center of Vitharan government whirred softly as it tracked their progress inside. The door slid shut behind them.

At the front desk, Councilman Canutian's latest aide sat primly in her chair. The young Vitharan woman looked up from her data terminal with a polite smile. "Good afternoon. The councilman is waiting for you. Please go on through."

Martinez smiled back, equally bland. "Thank you, Frey… Venadiel, wasn't it?"

"Yes, that's right, Ambassador," said the aide. "And you're quite welcome. I'll be… *very interested* to hear the outcome of your meeting. The councilman has been unyielding in his position on Ilarian intervention up to this point."

Martinez's brows lifted in mild surprise. While her stint as the Terra Novan ambassador to Vithara meant she had more contact with the diplomatic corps than she did directly with the planet's government officials, she'd known Trivaal Canutian for a few years now. His aides weren't generally interested in much more than maintaining his schedule and keeping on top of his paperwork.

But, hey—maybe this one had aspirations of future elected office or something. Whatever the case, it would be up to Canutian to answer any questions the woman might have about the meeting, not Kade or Martinez.

"Yes. Quite so," she said pleasantly, and headed for the back room with Kade in tow.

The councilman was an elderly Vitharan with an upright bearing and snow-white spikes of hair topping a weathered face. He'd been in the military as a young man, and Martinez often wondered if his experiences there had informed his hard-line opposition to interventionist policies.

He rose to greet them as they entered, clasping them forearm to forearm in turn—the Vitharan version of a handshake. "Please," he said, "have a seat and make yourselves comfortable. There's flatbread and cheese on the tray if you're hungry, and *edelveen* in the pitcher."

"We're fine," Kade said, dismissing the offer of food and drink. "Honestly, I'm much more interested in discussing the new Terra Novan agreement in greater depth with you."

Once they were seated, Canutian returned to his chair and clasped his hands together on top of the massive *chik'taap* wood desk. "Indeed. I must say I was somewhat surprised to hear of that development."

Martinez tilted her head, regarding him shrewdly. "I imagine the fact that Vithara's largest trading partner is willing to commit troops puts a bit of a different spin on the situation, Councilman. So... why don't we talk about the things that are still holding you and your coalition back from a yes vote."

"That... could have gone worse, actually," Kade said in some surprise, after they left the office three-quarters of a cycle later.

"Hmm," Martinez agreed. "Like I've been saying, there's pressure building behind the scenes for the Council to act. I figured that with the right leverage, we'd be able to pry a few strategic bricks loose from the dam and let the tide of public opinion pour in."

Kade looked somewhat unconvinced, but Martinez trusted her instincts when it came to matters diplomatic. By unspoken accord, they turned in the direction of the wing containing the private quarters they'd been assigned for the duration of the talks.

"I have a deposition in an hour," Kade said. "And then there are some messages I need to answer, and others I need to send. But I would still like to speak with you in more detail about the Terra Novan developments before tomorrow morning's round of meetings."

She nodded agreeably, aware that logistics were going to become exponentially more complicated with multiple planets trying to organize a joint operation on a short timetable. "I'll come by your quarters at nineteen hundred or so. I'd offer to bring a bottle of wine to celebrate getting at least *one* planet officially on our side, but... well, you know. I'd hate to be responsible for killing any more of your brain cells than necessary."

He eyed her, visibly unimpressed by the reference to his medical condition. "I've been losing brain cells for years—mostly without the help of alcohol, thanks. Save the wine for when Kovak's either dead or incarcerated. When that happens, I'll get rip-roaring drunk with you, neurotonin addiction or no. And screw the lost gray matter."

She huffed a breath of amusement. "Deal. See you at nineteen hundred, then."

TWO

That evening, Kade sat in his quarters with two screens active on the desktop terminal. On one screen, Ash could be seen staring at his own computer, a frown marring his olive-skinned features. Draven stood behind his chair, one hand resting on Ash's shoulder, only half of his body within range of the camera pickup. He, too, was focused on the screen intently.

"I can't believe this," Kade muttered, as all three of them watched the grainy underground Ilarian transmission of a blonde human woman dressed in a practical black flightsuit speaking to the camera. "Are you two seeing this shit?"

"*Maybe they're still on the southern continent,*" Draven said uncertainly. "*Skye could be transmitting from there somehow, and routing it through servers in the Capital…?*"

"*She could be, but she's not,*" Ash replied, his voice tight.

"Look at the background," Kade said. "That's the fucking transmission equipment at Location Four. The idiots have gone back to the city."

On the second screen, Skye Chantrell—the human bondmate of Hunter Tarthasian, Kade's closest friend and the source of most of his ever-increasing collection of gray hairs—looked earnestly into the camera with large, summer-blue eyes.

"*... as the Premiere's strategy of imprisoning humans in the newly built internment camps grows ever more brazen, we can no longer rely on the rule of law to protect us*," she was saying. "*I call on every human and human-allied Vithii in the Capital to take to the streets in protest immediately. We must shut down the city by any means necessary, until the government agrees to pass legislation protecting all citizens of Ilarius from illegal imprisonment.*"

Ash scrubbed a hand over his face. "*We knew this was coming, Kade.*"

Of course, the human was absolutely correct in his assessment. They *had* known. And Kade, fool that he was, had selfishly hoped that the people he cared about would be smart enough to stay the hell away from ground zero until help arrived from the allied worlds.

He should have known better.

"All right. Do we think they have enough technological know-how to hide out right under the noses of the Regime like this?" he asked, resigned to the fact that he was surrounded by a bunch of noble imbeciles, most of them sporting martyr complexes the size of a small moon.

Ash looked unhappy. "*Between the two of them, Hunter and Ryder have a fair amount of experience at masking transmissions. Which isn't to say I wouldn't feel better if I were there to make sure the encryption they're using is solid.*"

"*Can we contact them?*" Draven asked.

Ash craned around to look at him. "*And do what? Tell them not to be heroes?*" He sighed, turning back to the screen. "*Good luck with that. Besides, it would be tricky. There are backdoors within the local Ilarian communications system, but all transmissions originating off-planet go through the network of orbital subspace comm arrays before being beamed to the surface. It's not really something you can hack.*"

Kade's door buzzed, announcing a visitor. He glanced at the chrono display at the top of the screen. Nineteen hundred cycles. "The ambassador is here," he told the others. "Hang on; she should probably know about this newest complication."

He abandoned the desk, Skye's crackling voice still inciting civil disobedience on one of the screens in the background. At his touch, the door lock disengaged. It opened to reveal Isadora Martinez holding a bottle of carbonated Vitharan *edelveen* packaged to make it look like wine.

She must have seen something in his demeanor, because her sly half-smile disappeared in a flash, replaced by a businesslike expression.

"What's happened now?" she asked, her eyes tracking past him to the terminal playing Skye's transmission.

"You'd best come in," he said tersely. "Sit down. There's been a development."

She did so with a brisk nod. He took the bottle from her as she passed, locking the door behind her before setting the *edelveen* aside on a table. Leaning around her chair at the computer desk, he rewound the recording and let it replay.

Martinez watched intently, saying nothing until the screen went dark. Then, she leaned back in the chair rather abruptly. "Well, shit."

"*Couldn't have said it better myself,*" Draven rumbled from the other end of the pickup.

Ash squeezed the bridge of his nose and rubbed at his eye sockets before letting his hand drop. "*Maybe this is actually the best option, in the absence of a fleet of allied ships arriving to save the day. Protest has been known to change things, on occasion.*"

The ambassador's jaw tightened. Her honey-colored complexion had gone pale, as though all the blood had drained from her face. "It's also been known to get thousands of people killed, when the guys with the army starts firing weapons indiscriminately into the crowd," she said.

Kade couldn't really find it in himself to disagree with the sentiment, much as he might like to.

On the other screen, Draven moved to clasp both of Ash's shoulders from behind, leaning down until he was fully in the frame. "*Speaking of fleets of allied ships arriving to save the day, what's the latest?*"

Martinez squared her shoulders, though she still looked wan. "Things are finally moving, I think. We talked to Councilman Canutian a few cycles ago, and I've sent out some feelers to other members of his coalition. Still no word from Maelfius, but they've always been bad about playing things close to the chest until they see which way the cards are falling."

"*Still, that's promising,*" Ash said gamely, straightening in his chair and drumming his fingers on the desk. "*Why don't you keep us posted, Kade, and in the meantime, I'll see if I can glean anything useful from this recording. It's a long shot, but I suppose it's always possible that the others could have included some encrypted information in the file, in hopes that we'd see it.*"

"Do that," Kade agreed. "The politicians have all gone home to their comfortable beds for the evening, but we'll be here working on potential strategy for the next couple of cycles, at least. Let me know if you come up with anything useful."

Ash nodded and signed off, leaving Kade alone in his quarters with the human ambassador who both intrigued and infuriated him by turns. Right now, she was throwing off a scent Kade couldn't quite identify, though the sourness of it spoke of some strong, negative emotion.

In a universe where Kade wasn't a broken-down shadow, grinding himself to powder against the millstone of a perpetual, unwinnable war, he might have asked her what it was that she thought she saw when she looked at him. Sometimes, he caught an expression that resembled speculation hiding behind those hazel eyes, shot through with threads of green. Other times, he saw a darkness reflected back at him that rivaled his own.

He told himself it didn't matter. They would either succeed in brokering some kind of an agreement here on Vithara, or they wouldn't. Either way, she would stay behind, doing her job as the Terra Novan ambassador. Meanwhile, he would hop on the next ship bound for Ilarius. There, he fully expected to be captured, killed, or otherwise brought low by the farce of a government that had defined his life ever since his parents were executed as political dissidents a decade ago. And even if he somehow managed to survive the Premiere's downfall relatively intact, he had perhaps another decade after that, until the long-term damage to his brain chemistry from neurotonin addiction finally put him in the ground for good.

In short, it was highly unlikely that he'd be following through on his sarcastically delivered vow to get rip-roaring drunk with the human ambassador in celebration of Kovak's ouster. Although, as dubious promises went, he supposed he'd made worse ones over the years.

"Glasses," said Martinez, pulling him from his dark thoughts.

She disappeared into the compact kitchenette and returned with a pair of tumblers, into which she splashed generous measures of the bubbly *edelveen*.

"Have you eaten?" he asked, dredging a basic level of etiquette from some dark recess of the past.

She waved off the question. "Yeah, yeah. I grabbed a sandwich earlier. Now, tell me the parts I don't know about what's happening on Ilarius. The human woman… she's the same one who made the broadcast a few months back about the siege at the water treatment plant, right?"

Kade leaned a hip against the edge of the desk and launched into a brief explanation of the context surrounding Skye's transmission.

Martinez listened intently, frowning over the rim of the tumbler clasped in her hands. "So your friends returned to the Capital, despite the fact that they've basically got giant targets painted on their backs. That's gutsy, I suppose. Not to mention stupid."

"And with two simple adjectives, you have perfectly described them as a group," Kade said, deadpan.

She saluted him with the quirk of an eyebrow. "Okay. So let's assume they're successful in bringing the humans and human sympathizers out in force to protest the internment camps. What does that mean for any off-world peacekeeping forces that might arrive at Ilarius in the next few days?"

Kade privately thought her assessment of the timeline was optimistic at best, but he fell into a discussion of the different avenues for approaching the situation anyway. A cycle or so later, they had an outline of various contingencies, taking into account different outcomes to Skye's call for action in the Capital.

Regarding her with a tilt of the head, Kade leaned back on his hands. "Your roots in the military are showing, Ambassador."

She lifted her chin, returning his stare measure for measure. "Ah. So, you've been checking my background on the sly? You could have just asked, you know."

He snorted. "I could have, yes. I figured it was easier to have Ash dig up your dossier, though."

Martinez held his gaze coolly. "I suppose that's fair, since I compiled dossiers on you and your comrades the day after we met. I do find it rather curious that while most of theirs were obviously fake… yours wasn't."

Since the important work for the day was done—to the extent it could be—Kade didn't bother to hide his reaction to the fact that the conversation had just gotten more interesting.

"Do you indeed? Hmm. While it's not precisely accurate to say that I've nothing to hide, Ambassador, large swathes of my past reside firmly in the public record," he told her. "I've never found any reason to try to change that fact."

That darkness he'd noticed on a handful of previous occasions sculled behind Martinez's steady gaze.

His brow furrowed. "Something about my past bothers you, though," he observed, and her expression of disquiet immediately disappeared behind a bland ambassadorial mask.

"What makes you say that?" she asked.

"The fact that you occasionally look at me like you're trying to peel my skin back and see what's underneath," he replied, equally bland. "You're doing it now, in fact. Normally, I'd assume that it had to do with the less-than-legal nature of some of my business holdings… but we both know that it's got a lot more to do with my last name."

Martinez rose from her chair with a bit too much haste to be casual, and started pacing around the room. She didn't look at him as she stopped to examine the nauseatingly impersonal knick-knacks and wall art decorating the temporary quarters.

"Well… for someone who's apparently trying to stop a violent and nationalistic regime, it *is* a last name soaked in quite a lot of blood, historically speaking," she said, directing the words toward a framed landscape painting hanging next to the door leading to the kitchenette.

"And your point is…?" he asked.

She turned, pinning him with that darkness as it bled past her mask of professionalism. "One of your ancestors is famous—or rather, infamous—for luring unsuspecting women and children to the site of a weapons depot with the promise of food when they were starving."

"And using them as human shields when the military showed up to destroy the weapons," Kade finished. "At which point a stray shot detonated a store of explosives and sent the whole facility up in a fireball, killing hundreds. Yes, I'm familiar with the story—from rather a young age, as you might expect."

They stared at each other for a beat. "I can't help wondering if your current crusade is some kind of attempt to redeem the family legacy, is all," she said.

He blinked at her, swallowing back a harsh bark of surprised laughter—because it wasn't actually funny, when you looked at it objectively. "Considering the fact that everyone else in my biological family is dead, and I'm permanently impotent as a result of long-term neurotonin dependence... it wouldn't be much of an attempt, even if that were my goal."

"Wouldn't it, though?" she asked, still watching him closely.

"No," he replied firmly. "It wouldn't. And while protecting the people I consider my family may in fact be part of my motivation, it's not remotely in the way you're thinking. For prophets' sake... what do I care about the fact that my great-great-great uncle was a fucking war criminal? He got his comeuppance when the explosion in the weapons cache blew him to smithereens. And when his brother and his brother's bondmate escaped to Ilarius, they were quick to spin cautionary tales for their children and their children's children about the dangers of warmongering."

"Yet, your own parents were dissidents, executed clandestinely by the government," she said, very intently. "And now you're a vigilante seeking the downfall of that same government. If the idea was to keep the family out of the ideological arena, apparently the lesson didn't stick."

He frowned at her, trying to follow her thought process. "Since my parents' only crime was to publicly support the opposition party during Kovak's rise to power, and since the government in question is legitimately evil, I fail to see the parallel. In case it's escaped your notice, *you're* currently seeking the downfall of the Regime as well."

She started pacing again, her faint pallor from earlier returning. "But I'm not the one urging thousands of civilians to throw themselves into the line of fire, in front of a military that's already shown a willingness to slaughter innocents wholesale."

Kade raised a sharp eyebrow. "Neither am I." Her implication finally penetrated, and he felt a flash of real anger... unexpected in its intensity. "Though even if my friends had asked my opinion first—*which they didn't*—I'd point out that there's a pretty fucking large difference between asking the populace to rise up against a government bent on killing them, versus luring starving women and children to a battle site with the promise of food."

She shook her head sharply, not looking at him. "If your *friends* had just waited a little longer, we might've been able to do this without significant loss of civilian life."

The words sounded tight... almost choked. Kade watched the human warily. There were broken edges hiding under the ambassador's smooth exterior, and the fact that he'd missed them up until now irritated him no end—he'd always hated being forced to rely on someone without knowing ahead of time what made them tick. He tamped down on his exasperated reaction with the ease of long practice, and pulled out a chair, sinking into it.

Despite the fact that he'd done nothing more strenuous all day than grind his jaw with impatience, every joint in his body ached, and every muscle groaned in protest. It was possible, the Vitharan doctors had told him, that the new neurotonin pump with its more nuanced dosage system would slow the damage being done to his body. If so, it clearly wasn't any kind of a miracle cure. In the back of his mind, he couldn't stop the small sense of relief that the endgame on Ilarius would be coming while he was still physically capable of doing his part.

Whatever that part might end up being.

He was pointedly silent until Martinez's eyes flickered to him in mid-pivot as she paced. When they did, he caught and held her gaze.

"This isn't professional concern over a peacekeeping operation," he said flatly. "The moment you learned about Skye's transmission, it became personal to you. Tell me why."

She stopped short. "It's not personal."

He kept her gaze pinned. "That's *greilo*-shit and you know it."

The tough-as-nails, ex-Special Forces mask slipped over Martinez's features. It was a mask that he'd seen her wear on a few occasions when her 'bland diplomat' facade faltered. She opened her mouth to speak, but her reply was cut off by the soft chime of the door intercom. Kade turned to look at it in irritation, and rose to answer it when it buzzed again.

"Are you expecting anyone?" Martinez asked, in lieu of whatever she'd been about to say before.

"No," Kade said. He thumbed the exterior camera control, revealing half a dozen uniformed Vitharan security forces standing in the hallway.

"What the hell?" Martinez muttered, having appeared at his shoulder with barely a rustle of sound despite the speed with which she must have moved.

Kade reminded himself firmly that this was Vithara, where the rule of law was a given. He opened the door, taking note of the twitchiness of several of the officers as their hands hovered near their stun guns.

Arms held at his sides to highlight his lack of weapons, Kade met the lead officer's eyes. "May I help you?" he asked, unable to completely bury the sarcasm in his reply.

"What's the meaning of this?" Martinez added, with noticeably more belligerence.

The officer kept a cautious eye on both of them as she said, "Isadora Martinez. Ehkadian Finisterre. Come with us, please—both of you. We've been ordered to take you into custody on suspicion of the murder of Councilman Trivaal Canutian."

THREE

Martinez allowed herself two seconds of shock. Then, she packed everything carefully away in a dark hole at the back of her brain, and squared her shoulders. Beside her, Kade stood cautiously neutral—the stance of someone who might know intellectually that they were not in immediate physical danger, but whose experience had still been shaped by a society where arrest by the police could easily mean imprisonment without trial, or a quick and mysterious death.

She stepped forward, hands half-raised. "We'll come quietly. Just to be clear, both Krau Finisterre and I are off-world citizens with full diplomatic immunity. That said, while we're innocent of this crime, we're more than happy to help with your inquiry in whatever way we can. What happened to Councilman Canutian?"

The Vitharan officer's businesslike expression didn't slip. "You can discuss the details with my Lieutenant, Ambassador Martinez. First, though, I'm afraid I must ask you to permit a weapons search before we take you into custody."

Martinez stepped back with a nod, lifting her arms and spreading her legs. The female security officer scanned her and followed up with a thorough but professional pat-down, while a male officer did the same with Kade.

"I need to contact my associates and let them know what's happening," Kade said gruffly, once the officer nodded that he was clear of weapons.

"You'll be permitted to make a call once we reach the station," said the group's leader, and gestured them out of the apartment with a brusque wave.

Kade's jaw worked, but he only nodded. The two of them fell into step, flanked by Vitharan security on both sides. Another pair walked in front of them, and a third pair behind, all of them with hands resting on their stunners. Wisely, Kade appeared uninterested in speaking as they were marched to a security hovervan parked outside the building. Martinez kept her mouth shut as well—thoughts racing at light-speed as she tried to put the puzzle pieces together with half of them still missing.

The van's door closed behind them, leaving them seated on one side of the vehicle with two stone-faced Vitharans guarding them on the other side. Martinez exchanged a brief look with Kade as the engine powered up and the van whirred into motion, but his expression was unreadable. Behind them, the government complex quickly grew smaller through the frame of the steel-reinforced rear window.

✦

By the time they reached the station, Martinez's circling thoughts were threatening to get the better of her despite all of her years of training. What evidence could they possibly have that would link her and Kade with a murder? How would Canutian's death affect the ongoing talks? Since *they* obviously hadn't done the grisly deed, who had?

She assumed that Kade's thoughts were traveling down similar lines, but his poker face didn't waver a millimeter during the journey. Upon arrival, they were booked in, and shown to an interrogation room with four chairs set on opposite sides of a heavy table bolted to the floor.

There, they were left alone for a good twenty minutes, presumably in hopes that one or the other of them would start babbling useful information as the pressure built. Of course, Martinez knew better than to do so. And Kade, meanwhile, might as well have lost the facility for speech altogether. From what she'd seen of him in the past few weeks, she sincerely doubted that whoever was in charge of this investigation had the capacity to out-stubborn him.

It took her most of the twenty minutes before she pulled her head out of her ass long enough to make the connection between what was happening to them, and the steel-corded tension in his shoulders. When she finally did, she felt like an idiot.

Ehkadian Finisterre had languished for nearly a year in an Ilarian prison—much of that time spent in a neurotonin-based hallucinatory nightmare, from what she'd gathered. At this point, he probably wasn't big on being incarcerated, even temporarily.

In her defense, the topic of conversation right before they'd been so rudely interrupted in his quarters was not one that she was remotely prepared to deal with. But even if Martinez *had* been ramping up for a frolic through her own personal PTSD playground, she should have connected those dots sooner. Feeling vaguely foolish—given the fact that

Kade's expression could have been carved from marble—she let her hand brush his where it rested on his thigh beneath the table.

He jerked as if she'd given him an electrical shock, piercing gray eyes flying to her face. That gaze cut like laser beams, and she thought how ironic it was that both of them had managed to stumble over separate psychological landmines in the space of a single evening.

Prophets. What the hell was she supposed to do if this mess ended up derailing the Ilarian peacekeeping effort altogether? Distantly, a little nagging voice from the days before she'd joined the military whispered that she ought to feel worse about Canutian's death. It was a raindrop lost in a hurricane, though. She'd known him, sort of. She hadn't liked him much, not because there was any-thing lacking in his personality or his moral character, but rather because he often seemed to stand in her way when she was attempting to get something done.

And now he was dead. She tried to think of who in his political coalition might step up to take his place within the Council, but the security force lieutenant's arrival interrupted her halfhearted at-tempts at strategic analysis.

The Vitharan officer was gruff, stoop-shouldered, and looked like he'd much rather be at home with his bondmate and children than stuck here in an interrogation room with her and Kade. His rank insignia flashed gold as he tossed a data padd onto the desk in front of him. A second officer entered the small room and closed the door behind her, joining her superior on the far side of the table.

"I'm Lieutenant Zetara, and this is Sergeant Rhone," the lieutenant said without preamble. "You stand accused of the murder of Trivaal Canutian. What can you tell me about your visit to his office at seventeen hundred cycles tonight?"

Martinez frowned. "I can tell you that there was no such visit. We had a lunch meeting with him at eleven hundred, which his aide can confirm, and left him in good health some forty-five minutes later. Which his aide should *also* be able to confirm."

"The security footage from the camera outside his office says differently," Zetara told her. "And my officers are currently seeking the aide for a statement."

An itch of unease skittered down Martinez's back—instincts prickling as the puzzle pieces failed to line up.

"What else?" Kade asked bluntly. "You've clearly got more than that."

Zetara leaned back in his chair, regarding them. "We have an energy weapon consistent with the wounds on the deceased, and registered to Ambassador Martinez. It was found near the body, with her prints on it and no one else's."

The prickle of her instincts roared into a klaxon, as the puzzle pieces fell into a pattern that screamed *frame job*. Martinez felt her expression close off like a blast door slamming down.

"Neither of us are prepared to discuss the matter any further without legal representation present," she said coolly. "Though I will remind you that both of us are duly appointed diplomatic representatives with full legal immunity from prosecution."

The lieutenant shot her a jaded look. "Oh, believe me, Ambassador—I'm well aware. And if you don't intend to cooperate, my orders are to transfer you to an orbital holding facility. There, you will have the option to arrange for legal counsel and dispute the charges, or to accept expulsion and return to your home planets."

"This is clearly a set-up," Kade said, scowling. "I mean, *come on*. Security footage altered, and the one eyewitness who could clear us mysteriously unavailable? Do me a favor."

"Means, motive, opportunity," the lieutenant said, still with the air of someone who was fantasizing about his comfortable armchair at home. "You were present at the time of death, you both have ample political reason to wish the deceased out of the way, and your weapon was found at the murder scene. Maybe I can't do fuck-all about it, thanks to your legal immunity—but that doesn't make it any less of an open and shut case."

"*Ample political reason*?" Martinez burst out. "Are you kidding? Canutian's death was the worst thing that could possibly happen!" She got control of herself and set her jaw. "If we're about to be expelled, I need to make a comm call."

"We both do," Kade said grimly.

"By all means," Zetara said, his voice flat. "The sergeant here will arrange it. As a courtesy, you will be allowed to keep your clothing and incidental possessions. Any other possessions may be shipped to the orbital facility via freight hopper."

"Krau Finisterre has a medical condition," Martinez said quickly, ignoring the dark look Kade shot her.

Zetara waved the words away. "As long as it's nothing urgent, the holding facility has a fully stocked medical bay and dedicated physicians."

"It's fine," Kade said tightly. "Let's make those comm calls."

———◆———

The grim professionalism of Martinez's higher-ups in the Terra Novan diplomatic corps upon receiving her call was in stark contrast to Ash's squawk of protest upon receiving Kade's.

"*You want us to* what?"

"You heard me, *leetha*. You and Draven will need to take point on the talks, assuming they can be salvaged now that the main opposition figure has been murdered. And if you can figure out who framed us and why while you're at it, that would be… helpful."

The silence on the other end of the voice-only comm call spoke volumes.

Eventually, Ash spoke again, not addressing the outrageousness of the request directly. "*You're… safe, though?*"

Kade huffed. "Vithara isn't Ilarius, Ash. We both have diplomatic immunity. Obviously I'm not pleased that the holding facility is located off-planet, but we'll still be able to send and receive communications from there. Report to me as soon as you have a feel for whether it would be more useful for me to stay and fight the charges or return to Ilarius and rejoin the others."

Another pause, briefer than the last. "*The timing of this is deeply suspicious.*"

With a snort, Kade shot back, "Oh, you *think*?" He shook his head in irritation. "Try tracking down the missing aide. Young, female, last name of Venadiel. She seemed overly interested in our meeting with Canutian earlier today. Watch your backs, though. I've got a sneaking suspicion this plot isn't home-grown, if you take my meaning."

"*I'm way ahead of you*," Ash replied, his tone grim. "*Watch your back, as well, Kade.*"

"I'll be in touch," Kade said, and ended the call.

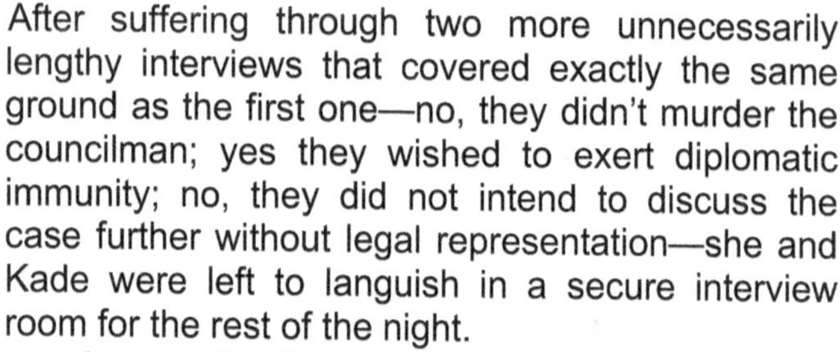

After suffering through two more unnecessarily lengthy interviews that covered exactly the same ground as the first one—no, they didn't murder the councilman; yes they wished to exert diplomatic immunity; no, they did not intend to discuss the case further without legal representation—she and Kade were left to languish in a secure interview room for the rest of the night.

Apparently, this was meant as a courtesy, rather than the alternative of tossing them in a cell while they waited. When it became obvious that they were being left to their own devices, Kade found a stretch of wall and wadded up his suit jacket to use as padding—sitting propped up on the floor, head back and eyes closed, ostensibly dozing. Martinez had claimed a chair at the bolted-down table, and was resting her chin on her crossed arms. She watched her companion in silence for some time, having seen enough people feigning sleep in her lifetime to recognize one... even if he *was* a different species.

The military was very useful for teaching one how to grab sleep whenever it was an option, regardless of the circumstances. So, she napped, ignoring the bright lights in the room… and mostly ignoring the tense line of Kade's shoulders. She woke to his hand on her upper arm, and sat up with a wince as her neck protested the uncomfortable position she'd fallen asleep in.

"Company," he said simply, as the door opened to reveal a Vitharan woman in a sharp business suit that screamed *lawyer*.

Martinez pummeled her wits into some kind of order as their visitor introduced herself. After a brief consultation, she left them each a card and agreed to contact them again, once they were checked into the holding facility. As she left, the reality of the situation started to sink in to a degree that it hadn't the previous night.

"This is a disaster," Martinez said.

If she hadn't already been aware that the observation wasn't helpful, the look Kade shot her would have clued her in pretty quickly. He looked rumpled in the way reserved for people entering their second day wearing the same clothing after a long, rough night with no bed. No doubt she looked the same.

For some reason, even civilized cultures seemed to take delight in such small, dehumanizing gestures when it came to those in official custody of the state.

Apparently, the lack of decent sleep had reduced Kade's vocabulary to grunts and one-word answers—not that he'd been all that chatty before. The two of them were allowed separate, supervised visits to the restroom. Martinez declined the offer of food, but accepted a cup of very bad coffee. The human fondness for the stuff might have bled into Vitharan culture over the decades, but the nuances of making it… hadn't, really.

Still, it was *caffeine*. Caffeine was good.

A short time later, a security cruiser with metal mesh separating the back seat from the driver delivered them to the orbital depot, where they were met by a fresh contingent of grim-faced guards. Vithara was nothing if not efficient, and within a cycle they were installed in the aft area of an orbital hopper, safely behind a clearsteel barrier separating them from the pilot's area.

"I'm not sure whether to be honored or not by the fact that we get an entire ship all to ourselves," Kade muttered, strapping himself into one of the half-dozen takeoff couches lined up in the secured compartment.

Martinez did the same, thinking that she might at least be able to catch another cycle or two of sleep on the reclining seat during the flight. "Better than being packed in with four other people who might or might not be dangerous criminals, I suppose," she mused.

At the front of the craft, two uniformed Vitharans entered through the side hatch, and stowed their flight bags in the cabin before beginning preflight checks. They spared her and Kade no more attention than if they'd been crates of supplies rather than sentient beings. Both were conspicuously armed, however, and had the hard cast of men who knew how to use a blaster when necessary.

"So, will you stay here to dispute the accusations against you, or return to Terra Nova?" Kade asked, once they were strapped in.

The engines fired up, a low rumble traveling through the contoured cushions beneath her. Martinez's eyes flew to her companion in surprise, before settling on him sharply. "I'll stay here and dispute them, of course," she said, unable to keep a bit of ire from creeping through. "What, did you seriously think I was just going to creep home with my tail between my legs after being *framed* for *murder*?"

He eyed her up and down. "You could still fight the charges from Terra Nova. It would be a lot more comfortable than being stuck in a pre-trial orbital holding facility, for one thing. Besides, it's not as though Ilarius was ever really your fight."

She blinked at him. "My *fight*? This is my bloody *career* you're talking about. Unlike some people on this hopper, being accused of murder isn't a regular occurrence for me!"

She realized after the words had passed her lips that they left something to be desired in the courtesy department, but Kade only raised his brows at her in a '*Who, me?*' gesture. Before she could decide whether to offer an apology—or at least walk that last sentence back a bit—the craft lurched into life, rising from the launch area.

"It's good that you're staying," he said, as though she hadn't just insulted him to his face. "Injustice should always be fought. And anyway, I'd feel better knowing you were still on the case, here on Vithara."

He thinks the talks are ruined, she thought, as the hopper accelerated smoothly into the atmosphere. G-forces pressed at her, the basic craft not equipped with high-end inertial dampening systems. *He thinks he's going to have to go back to*

Ilarius and fight without any support from the Vitharans.

The initial launch thrust moderated into something that felt a little less like having a boulder on her chest, as the ship began the shallow arc that would eventually propel them into orbit. Martinez was still trying to formulate a response to the unspoken words lying heavy across the silence when the copilot pulled his blaster out of its holster, and shot the pilot squarely through the chest.

FOUR

Kade's hands flew to the safety restraints holding his body in place against the seat, aware of the ambassador doing the same next to him. To his surprise, she didn't cry out or ask what was going on. She merely scrambled upright before grabbing him by the arm and dragging him behind the questionable cover of one of the launch couches.

Privately, Kade was skeptical of the utility of trying to hide behind the seat's bolted base. There was already a clearsteel barrier separating them from the pilot's area, and if the copilot wanted them dead, he could just don an e-suit and blow the craft's atmosphere once they reached the boundary of space. Martinez's reaction was the trained muscle memory of a soldier—nothing more or less.

"Not good," she was muttering, the words barely audible. "*Not good.*"

For his part, the murderous copilot barely spared them a glance as he shoved his dead companion out of the pilot's seat and slipped into it. The lack of sound carrying through the barrier to them made Kade think that asking the guy what the fuck was going on would most likely be a waste of breath… in addition to being a painfully predictable response.

He didn't bother trying.

Instead, he slid his cramped frame over until he was leaning against the base of another of the launch couches, rather than being jammed behind the same one as Martinez.

"Well," he said in a conversational tone, "I suppose this will at least be less boring than sitting around in a holding cell for days."

Martinez flashed him a glare. "Do you always joke about life-threatening situations?"

He held her gaze. "I wasn't joking."

The ambassador's jaw flexed with irritation, and Kade couldn't help thinking that she was rather attractive when her ire was up… for a human, of course. It was a somewhat surprising thought, honestly. Not the sort of thing he'd had much time or inclination for in recent years.

Her nostrils flared as she huffed out a breath and returned her attention to the copilot. "We need a plan. Though I guess we're pretty much stuck back here until we get to wherever we're going."

"Prison transports are tricky that way, yes," he agreed tartly.

Her glare didn't soften. "So, what are we thinking, then? Is this guy with the same group that engineered the frame job with Canutian?"

"Unless you're hiding any other mortal enemies I should know about, it seems likely," he said.

"Not that I'm aware of," she said, moving her attention back to the hijacker. He was still coolly piloting the hopper into orbit, though Kade was fairly confident he'd just felt their course change by a few degrees.

A disgruntled noise crept past his control. "This whole thing has the Premiere's stench all over it," he said. "He had to know that the other systems were watching what he was doing on Ilarius—

especially after the failed bioweapon attack in the Capital."

"You think he had spies embedded on Vithara."

He shifted, trying to find a more comfortable position before giving it up as a bad job and hauling himself back into his seat. "I've no doubt he's got spies embedded on Vithara. Canutian's overly curious aide was probably one of them. And apparently, what we were doing there was alarming enough to Kovak that it forced his hand."

Martinez nodded slowly. "Kill the opposition leader before he could change his vote, and pin it on the off-worlders who were trying to get him to flip his position on the issue. Makes sense."

"Then, hijack the aforementioned off-worlders and drag them back to Ilarius in hopes of prying information out of them," Kade said. "I'm sure he's *dying* to know how we're getting on with Terra Nova and Maelfius."

The idea that he might be on his way back to an Ilarian interrogation cell wasn't one Kade could afford to dwell on quite yet. He'd left a rather significant chunk of himself behind in the Capital prison system a decade ago, and he had no intention of ever returning to that place.

Particularly since he now carried far too much information about Hunter, Skye, and the others. If the Premiere's interrogators got hold of him, they'd eventually be able to extract everything he knew, by one method or another. For that reason, they would never be allowed to get hold of him alive. *Full stop.*

"How long until your neurotonin pump needs a refill?" Martinez asked quietly.

It took a moment for Kade to change mental gears and put the question into context. When he did, though, the seed of an idea began to form. He had no way of knowing if there was audio surveillance in the prisoner transport area, but it was probably best to be cautious with his reply. The ambassador had a mind like a steel trap; she'd be able to figure it out easily enough. He was confident he wouldn't need to spell it out for her.

"Not sure," he said. "It would have been fine to get to the orbital platform, but if this asshole is dragging us someplace else, things could get ugly."

Alarm crossed her face, quick as a flash. "*What*? I thought it was supposed to be good for more than a week at a time!"

He shrugged. "Yeah, sure—once it's calibrated. But the doctors wanted to check it regularly for the first several days. Apparently they didn't count on their patient getting stitched up for murder and hijacked off-planet."

And then, he winked at her, so brief that it would be almost impossible to see on camera, if there even was one in the holding area. Her lips parted, confusion clouding her eyes for only a moment before it cleared. He glanced down at his hand resting casually beside his thigh, and her gaze followed. When he flashed four fingers—*four days*—she nodded almost imperceptibly.

"Right," she said. "Well, I imagine the next few hours are going to suck pretty badly for you, in that case. Pity."

He shrugged. "If it's a choice between screaming seizures followed by death, versus going back to a Regime torture cell… I'll take the screaming seizures. Guess they'd better take good care of you, though—since you're going to be their only living hostage and all."

The look she was giving him was canny, as though with only that much information, she'd already figured out his half-formed plan in its entirety. The hopper they were on wasn't designed for interstellar travel, so assuming they really were in Ilarian hands, it seemed a near certainty that they'd be moved to a larger ship. If the two of them couldn't escape during the transfer, Kade would pretend to go into neurotonin withdrawal during the journey and attack Martinez in the throws of his imaginary breakdown. Since they obviously valued her enough to take her prisoner in the first place, whoever was guarding them would come in to drag Kade off her. That would—hopefully—give them a chance to overpower their captors using the element of surprise.

Or else their captors could decide to cut their losses and put a blaster bolt through Kade's heart, saving themselves the trouble.

That was another distinct possibility.

An unaccustomed feeling of regret assailed him at the idea of Martinez getting caught up in this clusterfuck with him. Despite appearances to the contrary, Kade did care about other people... at least, in the general sense of being willing to go up against a fascist government in an attempt to protect the innocent. But, on a more personal level, there were only a handful of individuals that he truly *worried* about.

People died all the time. They were injured. They were maimed. They were tortured by those who held power over them. If Kade felt emotional anguish every time something bad happened to a sentient being, he'd never be able to get out of his fucking bed in the morning. So it was a bit of a shock to experience visceral guilt at the thought of this human ending up in Kovak's hands—especially since Martinez was a woman who infuriated him more often than anything else.

"I'm sorry you were dragged into this," he said.

Her brows drew together. Then she snorted derisively. "*Dragged into this*? Seriously? I guess I must've missed that part somehow."

And… that was better. Now he was just irritated again.

"Never mind. Forget I said anything."

She climbed back into her seat across from him, managing not to look sheepish about it—though she did shoot the copilot another wary look as she settled. "You think your friends will be safe back at the complex?" she asked, changing the subject.

He took a slow breath and let it out through his nose. "Safe? Doubtful. But I gave up on underestimating those two some time ago. They're both certifiably crazy, but they can look after themselves."

"Apparently so, since they're still alive after what all of you have been through," she said.

That was veering dangerously back into emotional territory, so he didn't respond. She let the silence stretch, sitting tense and watchful next to him. Kade gave the holding area an incisive onceover, but another thing about prison transports—the designers were more than a little bit anal about not including anything that could be used as a weapon inside the prisoner area.

He debated the merits of retrieving the two items on his person that *would* be useful as weapons. Reluctantly, he decided that he'd be better off holding them back until he and Martinez were transferred to the—admittedly still theoretical—interstellar ship. For one thing, Kade wanted hard proof of who was holding them before he acted. And for another, their captors would doubtless be on high alert during the prisoner handover.

No… it was better to wait until they were underway for Ilarius. Then, if they could manage to get free and overpower the crew, they'd have a faster and more powerful vessel under their control. Additionally, no one else from Ilarius would be after them. Kade could return Martinez to Vithara, leaving her there to try and sort out the diplomatic mess with Ash and Draven's help. Then, he could hightail it back to Ilarius, and hopefully pummel some sense into Hunter and Skye before they succeeded in getting themselves killed.

Or, more likely, he'd get swept along in their wake as per usual.

Either way, Ilarius was where he should be, with the endgame barreling down on them from all sides. Perhaps, this way, some of them might still survive. Ash and Draven. Pax and Veila'ana.

Isadora Martinez.

But he was getting ahead of himself. Kade settled in to wait for whatever was going to happen next, his eyes fixed on their captor in the control cabin. Beside him, the ambassador waited as well, wary and pale.

———◆———

A couple of cycles later, the copilot started flipping switches and pressing buttons, preparing for something. Kade glanced at the ambassador to make sure she was still paying attention, and she gave a tight nod to indicate she'd noticed as well.

The familiar three-dimensional pitch and roll of imminent docking sent the stars sliding past the hopper's viewport. Kade caught a glimpse of the planet Vithara below them—gray oceans and green continents—followed by a glimpse of an unfamiliar interstellar transport as the two craft oriented their docking ports.

"Looks like our ride's here," Martinez muttered, giving their surroundings the same *is-there-anything-here-I-can-use-as-a-weapon* scan that he'd given it earlier. No conveniently sharp or heavy objects had appeared in the interim, and she swallowed a sigh, her jaw firming.

A few more minutes passed before a loud clang reverberated through the hopper's frame. More mechanical noises echoed through the small craft as the ports locked onto each other and the pressure equalized. A single Vithii entered the control cabin and nodded brusquely to the copilot before raking his gaze over the two of them through the clearsteel barrier.

Martinez rose to her feet. Kade followed suit, wondering now if he'd misjudged and this might, in fact, be their best bet for escape. Two on two—

The ambassador was ex-Special Forces… but she was also unarmed, human, and female. Her gaze played over the newcomer assessingly, no doubt taking in the blaster and shock wand hanging from his belt just as Kade had.

The Vithii thumbed a control, and an unseen intercom crackled to life. "Stand away from the barrier," he ordered, drawing his sidearm and pointing it at them.

They were already standing away from the barrier, so neither of them moved.

"Where are you taking us?" Martinez demanded belligerently. "You're in violation of several treaties, not to mention interstellar law."

If Kade still had any question about where they were being taken, it would have been answered by the newcomer's Ilarian accent. The Vithii sneered at her, making no attempt to hide his contempt for the human woman.

"That's not your concern."

The words were dismissive. At a nod, the copilot thumbed a control and the clearsteel barrier smoothly retracted toward the floor. As soon as it was low enough to provide for a clear shot, the new arrival pulled the trigger. A wide-dispersal stun beam slammed into Kade like a runaway hoverbus, and he was only peripherally aware of Martinez crumpling to the ground next to him as darkness swallowed his surroundings.

FIVE

Ash held Lieutenant Zetara's gaze, refusing to look away until he received the answer he wanted from the man. He'd come straight here from his and Draven's meeting with the joint military subcommittee of the Vitharan Council earlier in the day, and he wasn't in any kind of mood to hear the word 'no' for the dozenth time today.

The council was in an uproar after Trivaal Canutian's death—understandably so, perhaps, but they weren't *thinking*. Ash was holding out hope that someone who investigated crimes for a living would have a slightly more objective view of things.

"You *know* I'm right," he told the unamused officer, channeling absolute conviction into his tone. "Ambassador Martinez was discharged with honors after a highly decorated stint as a Major in Terra Novan Special Forces. She underwent some of the toughest and most intensive military training in the Seven Systems. Explain to me why an elite military specialist would panic and leave a registered weapon covered with her fingerprints at the scene of a murder."

Zetara—a grizzled old veteran of Vitharan law enforcement—frowned severely. He had at least done Ash the courtesy of listening to him without interruption, but Ash could see he'd still have more work to do before he found a chink in the detective's bland, by-the-book procedural bias.

"I have no idea why she'd panic and leave a registered weapon covered with her fingerprints at the scene of a murder," he said. "And I don't particularly care. I've got security video of her and her accomplice entering the Councilman's office shortly before the estimated time of death. I've got video of them leaving shortly *after* the time of death. I've got the weapon used in the attack. That's all I need."

Ash had some rather specific notions about the provenance of the security footage in question, but he wasn't quite ready to share his thoughts on that. Instead, he kept chipping away at the edges of the lieutenant's argument, looking for an angle that might break through.

"And have you found any trace evidence in the ambassador's quarters? Or in Kade's? Did they seem to be acting at all oddly in the footage of them leaving after allegedly killing a man... not to mention, being so rattled that they left the murder weapon behind? Your officers must have scanned them. Did the scans turn up any DNA from the victim?"

Zetara's frown deepened after each salvo, but Ash didn't let up.

"I can tell you right now that the answer is no on all counts," he finished. "Go on—convince me I'm wrong."

The lieutenant seemed to fight with himself for several seconds before he finally replied, "You're not wrong."

Tamping down any visible sign of relief, Ash nodded. "Of course I'm not. Lieutenant, you're giving an awful lot of weight to a motive that doesn't exist. To claim that Kade and Martinez wanted Councilman Canutian dead because he opposed a goal they were working toward ignores the reality of the situation. Canutian's death has practically ensured that Ambassador Martinez's cause is hopelessly discredited. *Think about it.*"

For the first time, Ash could see Zetara doing exactly that.

"Keep talking," the other man said gruffly. "I'm listening."

Thank the prophets for that, Ash thought with relief.

"In no world does the murder of a coalition leader by his political adversary convince his followers to mindlessly switch their views to the adversary's side," Ash continued. "In this case, exactly the opposite has happened—just as you'd expect. Council members that were leaning toward Ambassador Martinez's side of the argument are withdrawing their support left and right."

Zetara stared at him with the air of someone visualizing all the extra paperwork he was going to have to fill out if he pursued this line of enquiry to its logical conclusion. "If what you say is true, then we'd be looking for someone who benefited from the defeat of this political measure," he said flatly.

"And what group benefits most from Vithara staying out of Ilarian matters?" Ash asked. "The Ilarian Regime—that's who."

The Lieutenant pinched the bridge of his nose. "So you're claiming… what? That Ilarian spies have somehow infiltrated the innermost seat of Vitharan government and are murdering elected planetary officials? Framing off-world diplomats?"

Ash sat back in his chair and crossed his arms pointedly. "Tell me, have you located Councilman Canutian's aide yet?"

Zetara's expression closed off. "I can't discuss ongoing aspects of the investigation."

Ash raised an eyebrow. "So in other words—no. You haven't. Let me guess… her listed address is empty? Cleaned out? And there are no recent financial transactions logged under her name? It's like she's disappeared completely off the face of the planet?"

With each question, the lieutenant's expression grew stonier. "I told you, I can't discuss—"

"She's your killer," Ash interrupted. "An Ilarian mole, sent to make sure the council's most vocal proponent of nonintervention stayed that way. And when it looked like Canutian might be in danger of flip-flopping on the issue, she was perfectly placed to strike in a way that was as damaging as possible to the interventionist cause… after which she disappeared like smoke into a newly assumed identity."

"This is all pure speculation," Zetara accused in a dour tone.

"Let me have access to the security video files of Kade and Martinez," Ash shot back. "I'll bet you a hundred credits they've been altered."

"Department policy—" the lieutenant began.

"Is to *catch criminals*," Ash said. "Tell me it wouldn't be a huge deal for this department to uncover an off-planet spy ring in the heart of Vitharan government, Lieutenant Zetara. You'd be on the front page of every news site in the local cluster."

The detective's jaw worked. "I don't do this job for the fucking publicity," he growled.

Ash felt the moment the balance tipped in his favor, but he buried any reaction beneath an unruffled facade. "No," he said, more quietly. "You do it because you still believe in justice and the rule of law. The idea that diplomatic immunity meant justice wouldn't be served in this case must have irked you no end. *But what if it could be served*?"

Zetara's gaze drilled into his for a long beat.

"A copy," he said finally. "I'll give you access to a *copy* of the security footage—and only under direct supervision by a member of the electronic forensics unit."

"A *cloned* copy," Ash retorted. "Physical media, not digital."

"Fine." Zetara pushed away from the desk and rose. "Give me something concrete, and I'll take it to the intelligence agencies. Go see Dr. Fera'ano in the lab. I'll let him know you're coming."

"Thank you," Ash told him in relief. "Trust me when I say, you're doing the right thing, Lieutenant."

When Draven arrived at the station several cycles later, Ash looked up from the terminal he was sharing with Fera'ano. His eyes felt dry and gritty from staring at the screen for so long, but satisfaction dulled the mild headache threatening to erupt behind his temples.

The security force's forensic tech specialist was still scanning the source data with a furrowed brow, his gaze flicking back and forth between the raw video and the lines of code. "I can't *believe* you were able to find evidence of pixel alteration buried under all the compression artifacts. This is insane."

Ash shrugged. "Easier to see something when you already know it's there."

"So, got what you needed, then?" Draven asked, leaning over Ash's shoulder with a hand on the back of his chair. His forearm brushed Ash's back, as though by accident.

Even in the current circumstances, Ash couldn't help the flush of warmth that spread through his chest at the casual gesture. "Indeed we did. The time codes on this security video have been changed. That constitutes physical proof not only that Kade and Martinez weren't in Canutian's office at the time he was murdered, but also that someone wanted to make it look like they were."

Fera'ano finally managed to tear his gaze away from the screen. "And you really think an Ilarian spy did this?"

"I think it would be a hell of a coincidence if some other random person decided out of the blue to destroy the reputations of a respected ambassador and an Ilarian citizen who just arrived a few weeks ago," Ash replied with an arched eyebrow.

"But… it could have been someone from here on Vithara who had an interest in stopping the councilman from flipping his vote," the forensic tech shot back.

"It's possible," said Draven. "Your lot will just have to dig deeper and figure it out, won't you? Now that there's some hard evidence of the frame job."

"Too right we will," Fera'ano muttered, his attention sliding back to the video footage. "This place is going to be Mandatory Overtime Central for the next few days. I still can't believe you uncovered this."

Ash stretched, rolling his shoulders. "All part of the service. Now, it's late, and I still need to send out some strategically targeted comm messages tonight. Which means my associate and I will be leaving you to deal with the *fun-filled paperwork* part of things on your own, I'm afraid."

The tech waved him off. "Yeah, I'm on it. The lieutenant's gonna burst something when he sees this."

"I'll be sorry to miss it," Ash quipped. "Oh, and if you need anything, you can reach us through the communications switchboard at the government complex. Happy report-filing."

Afterward, Ash let Draven usher him out of the lab and through the warren of corridors to the station entrance. Outside, they fell into step side-by-side in the balmy Vitharan evening, arms brushing occasionally.

"Public transit's probably best," Draven said, gesturing toward the tube station at the end of the block.

"Agreed," Ash said absently. "Once we get back to our quarters, I'm thinking we should send one badly encrypted message regarding the surveillance video alteration to the head of the joint military subcommittee, and another one to the orbital holding facility administration office."

"Maybe send one to that lawyer, too, while you're at it," Draven said. "You never know who might be listening."

"Good idea," Ash agreed, as they headed down the steps to the transit station. "As you correctly point out, you never know. Though I must say... I do rather wish the government housing complex didn't have such tight restrictions on the possession of personal sidearms. I can foresee that becoming a logistical snag for us, once the wrong people get wind of what we've uncovered."

"Says the man who successfully assassinated a guy with bee venom once," Draven shot back. He grinned down at Ash, showing teeth. "But, hey—don't worry, little human. I'll protect you."

Ash let out an indelicate snort, and didn't reply.

In the small cycles of the following morning, Ash lay half-dozing on the sofa in the living area of the assigned quarters he shared with Draven, his hand tucked under the pillow he'd dragged in from the bedroom. The overhead lights were low—dialed down to five percent.

A faint sound reached his ears—something that might have been the scrape of a tool against the exterior locking pad of the sliding glass balcony door. Though it was barely audible, it was still enough to bring Ash to full awareness in an instant. He lay still, eyes half-open in the near-darkness… cognizant that he was in the direct line of sight of anyone entering from outside.

Shadows moved beyond the glass. Ash counted his breaths—heart beating in a steady but elevated rhythm. Minutes passed before a soft *snick* announced the surrender of the locking mechanism. The door slid smoothly open along its tracks.

"They should both be in here. Find the other one," said a female voice, pitched almost too low to be heard.

Ash watched through heavy-lidded eyes as the woman raised an arm, leveling the dark silhouette of a blaster at him. An instant later, Draven materialized from the shadows in the corner of the room, chopping a solid blow across the woman's wrist and sending the weapon flying from her grip.

The second intruder whirled, his blaster coming up to point at Draven. But Ash was already rolling upright on the couch, the heavy paperweight he'd been clutching beneath the pillow flying from his hand with force. It slammed into the side of the man's head in the instant before his female companion crumpled beneath Draven's punch to the jaw. The male intruder stumbled sideways and tripped over a table, going down hard—his blaster skittering across the tile floor.

After quickly making sure that the woman wouldn't be getting up anytime soon, Ash scooped up her sidearm and moved to cover the man, while Draven crossed his arms and looked down at the pair in satisfaction.

"Lights, fifty percent," Ash said, letting his eyes run over the two would-be assassins as the illumination smoothly cycled up. Both were dressed in black from head to toe, and both were Vitharan... or, more likely, Vithii. Determining which would require some rather nuanced medical tests, but the answer to that question would be of considerable interest to a number of people in the government and the security forces.

The man stared at them with cold brown eyes from his position sprawled on the floor.

"Well, now," Draven said cheerfully. "It looks like *someone's* been listening in on comm messages that were supposed to be private." He prodded the unconscious woman onto her back with the toe of one boot. "Bet the security forces are going to be real interested to talk to you two. Especially your girlfriend here—their people have been looking all over for her, for *days* now."

The woman moaned softly, just beginning to come around. Despite her freshly dyed hair, her face was instantly recognizable from the government I.D. badge photo Ash and Draven had examined earlier at the station.

Essler Venadiel—Councilman Canutian's missing aide—blinked open hazy eyes, glaring up at them.

⸻◆⸻

A little more than half a cycle later, Vitharan security arrived to take the pair into custody, hauling the two unsuccessful assassins off for questioning and blood tests to determine their planet of origin. Afterward, Lieutenant Zetara ushered Ash and Draven to a small conference room in the government complex where they could speak privately.

With a few short words, he briefed them on the latest developments. Ash felt a chill rush down his spine to settle—heavy and uncomfortable—in his stomach. Beside him, Draven sucked in a sharp, unhappy breath.

Ash frowned at the lieutenant in dismay. "What do you *mean*, 'the secure transport hopper never arrived at the orbital facility'?" he snapped.

Zetara looked like a man who had enough things to worry about without being interrogated by a human civilian, but Ash didn't back down beneath his fierce scowl.

Draven mirrored the Vitharan's expression with one equally as dark. "Yeah, that statement is definitely going to need some more explanation. Like… *right the fuck now.*"

"It means exactly what it sounds like," Zetara growled. "The transport didn't arrive on schedule, and when they sent out search ships, they found it drifting in a decaying orbit about fifteen hundred kilometers away."

A durasteel band tightened around Ash's chest, threatening to choke off his air. Beside him, Draven went very, very still.

"Survivors?" Ash asked hoarsely, because someone had to say it aloud.

"No idea," Zetara replied, still sounding mad enough to spit nails. "Except for the body of the pilot, it was abandoned. He died of a blaster shot through the chest. The engines had been powered down, and no one else was aboard. That class of hopper is equipped with emergency escape pods, but none of them had been deployed."

"They were intercepted," Ash murmured blankly. "Dear gods. Someone got to them. Someone who knew exactly who they were and where they'd be."

The lieutenant nodded, his face grim. "Your Ilarian conspiracy theory is looking less and less like a theory, I'm sorry to say. Anyway, I've forwarded the report on the hopper to the space force, and they'll be starting an investigation immediately."

Ash rubbed his forehead, trying to banish the fog of too little sleep and too much frantic worry. "If they're quick, the investigators may be able to determine a heading from the engine distortion trails."

"We'll need to meet with the council again and let them know about this," Draven put in. "The sooner, the better."

Zetara's lip curled in distaste. "Well, I sure as sin don't envy you that. But for what it's worth, I've forwarded copies of all the relevant reports to the council liaison. Taken together with the attack on you tonight, the evidence of Ilarian interference looks pretty damning."

"Let's hope it's enough to change some minds," Ash said.

"And some fucking *votes*," Draven added. "Maybe seeing evidence of an extensive spy ring in the middle of the government will finally get them off their collective asses."

Ash met his partner's eyes. "If this doesn't do it, we may have to give up on Vithara. We could make our way to join up with the Terra Novan forces heading for Ilarius. The clock is ticking, and if Kade and the ambassador were taken alive rather than simply killed, it seems likely that the Premiere would want them dragged back there for interrogation."

"Agreed," Draven said. "No guarantee we can do anything to help them if that's the case. But either way, it's past time to for us to go home and try to end this mess for good."

"Yes, it's time. One way or another," Ash murmured, his expression troubled. "First, though, there's a room full of clueless politicians waiting for us. This morning, you and I have some serious yelling to do."

SIX

On the interstellar transport ship that was presumably bound for Ilarius, Kade sat against the bare wall of the cell he shared with the unconscious ambassador, thinking.

It had taken him less than twenty minutes after he'd woken up from the stun beam to make a complete investigation of the stripped-down room. It had clearly been designed for the specific purpose of holding prisoners for transport. Heavy door with a clearsteel viewing port and a small hatch at the bottom for shoving food inside? Check. Exposed, functional latrine in one corner next to a motion-activated sink? Check. Recessed cameras in the two back corners to cover areas that couldn't be seen through the door? Double-check.

This was the extent of their world until someone came and got them out. There were no seams in the wall panels that might be pried open to get access to the ship's guts beyond. Even if Martinez sat on his shoulders to reach them, the cameras were safely covered with clear plates to prevent tampering. Kade would lay odds that the food, when it came, would be in biodegradable cellulose bowls with no cutlery.

Options, in other words, were limited.

And, *fuck*, he needed more options to use as a distraction, so he wouldn't start obsessing over the fact that he was *trapped* in a godsdamned *Regime cell*, just like he had been when—

With admirable timing, Martinez stirred and groaned, coming around from the stun beam that had hit her smaller human frame with more of a punch than it had hit Kade's Vithii physiology. Before setting himself to the exploration of their cell, he'd exercised the better part of valor by moving her limp form to the area right in front of the latrine and placing her on her side in the recovery position.

Now, he crossed to her and hefted her upright, not surprised when she fumbled for the rim of the toilet and emptied her stomach contents into it. Fortunately for both of them, forward planning had always been one of Kade's strong suits, and he'd harbored no desire to be stuck in a bare room with vomit splattered across the floor.

The experience of supporting her upper body as she tried to expel everything she'd eaten in the last six months was, at least, effective in distracting Kade from the sense of the walls closing in around him. It wasn't *quite* accurate to say that he'd never steadied someone over a toilet while they puked their guts out before. It was… reasonably accurate to say that he'd never steadied an attractive human female over a toilet while holding her hair back from her face because it had fallen out of its usual neat bun.

Somehow, that small detail made the connotations feel very different.

Martinez dry-heaved a couple more times and spit, before pushing herself away from the sanitized metal seat and looking around a bit wildly. Kade let her hair slip free of his fingers, but kept a steadying hand on her shoulder. Her eyes fell on the point of contact between them, and her eyebrows drew together in apparent confusion.

She eased away from his support an instant later, her attention returning on their surroundings. "Where—?" she rasped, climbing unsteadily to her feet and visibly shaking off the lingering disorientation from the stun beam.

Kade rose with her, feeling his joints creak and his muscles protest. "Prisoner transport ship, almost certainly bound for Ilarius."

Martinez scrubbed a hand over her face and scanned the inside of the empty box. "Cameras?"

Kade jerked his chin at the two back corners, just below the ceiling.

"Audio?" she asked.

"Probably," he said. "There's a small intercom speaker near one of the cameras, but no controls on our end. No one's been in here or tried to communicate since I woke up."

Some of the tension leaked out of her posture, and Kade mused that it was the first time he'd truly seen the Special Forces Major in all her glory, peeking out from behind the facade of *diplomat*. Not many humans her size would have bounced back from a stun weapon calibrated for Vithii physiology so quickly. She must have a headache like a supernova, at the very least... but she only nodded her understanding before crossing to the sink to rinse out her mouth and drink a bit of water from her cupped hands.

When she was done, she flicked the clinging droplets off her fingers and efficiently unraveled her ruined hairstyle, braiding the heavy mahogany tresses into a single plait and pinning it out of the way in a simple twist. Then she splashed water on her face, wiped her hands on her tailored trousers, and turned to face him.

"Right," she said, her tone matter-of-fact. "So, I guess we're kind of screwed, then. How much do I need to worry about your neurotonin withdrawal in the next few cycles?"

He hesitated—not completely certain whether he'd been effective in conveying his idea for a ruse back when they'd been on the hopper. He'd *thought* she picked up on it, but it was also possible that she'd taken him at his word.

Kade drew breath, but before he could frame his answer in a way that wouldn't garner suspicion from anyone who might be listening in, she winked at him. Her expression didn't waver otherwise, but the message was crystal clear.

They were on the same page when it came to an escape plan.

"I can already feel early withdrawal symptoms starting," he lied smoothly. "You shouldn't be left in here alone with me when they get worse."

She took a nervous step back from him, looking directly at the camera with the intercom speaker next to it. "Oh, *great*. Hey! Guards, or whoever's out there! You're hearing this, right? Someone come get me out of here before this guy loses his shit. He's a neurotonin addict, he'll get violent!"

Kade's jaw tightened—not because she was a bad actress, but because there was a second component to his half-baked plan that he'd had no good way to convey to her. If the guards showed up now, he didn't much like their chances.

Hopefully, they'd need more convincing before they could be bothered to act. He gave her the tiniest shake of his head, a frown touching his brow.

Confusion slid across her expression, and he mouthed, '*Wait*,' his lips barely moving.

Aloud, he said, "Prophets—I'm not a damned mental case yet. Don't overreact."

She narrowed her eyes, maintaining character. "Yeah, well pardon me if I don't want to still be stuck in here when it eventually hits you. *Gods*... I'm only in this mess because of you in the first place. I should've known better than to get involved with your crazy crusade."

He shot her a jaded look that required no acting ability at all. "Yeah... you're right. You probably should've." A quick look around, and he prowled over to a spot in the back corner that seemed like it had the best chance of being out of the line of sight of the cameras. It was in full view of the clearsteel door panel, of course, but that would only be a problem if a guard happened to look through it at the wrong moment.

"You stay over there," he snapped, injecting an extra layer of surliness into his tone. "I'll stay over here. Just... don't bother me, all right? I can't believe I'm stuck in a cell with a fucking *human* like this."

Martinez sputtered, and he had no idea if her outrage was real or feigned. But she retreated to a corner near the door and slid down the wall to sit on the bare floor, while he did the same in the opposite corner where the camera coverage was iffy. When a handful of minutes passed with no guards showing up to gawp at them, he quietly toed off the black leather loafers he'd been wearing as part of his now-ruined 'impress the politicians' ensemble.

The gray suit was exactly what it looked like. The shoes, not so much. If either the Vitharan security forces or the guards on this unnamed transport had been smarter or more thorough, his shoes would have been taken from him. But apparently, no one they'd dealt with in the past traded in deviousness to the same extent as an underworld businessman who dabbled in vigilantism and anti-government conspiracy on the side.

More fool them.

Her brow furrowing, the ambassador watched from her side of the cell as he picked up one of the shoes and pried open a small compartment in the inner part of the heel with the edge of a ragged fingernail.

⸻◆⸻

Martinez forcibly schooled her expression into something innocuous as the crazy Vithii bastard across from her pulled a small, unidentified item from the dark material of his shoe heel, and then repeated the process on the other shoe a moment later. Whatever the two items were, they were the same color as the shoes' soles. Before her eyes, they disappeared smoothly into his trouser pockets, as though he were a magician making coins vanish up his sleeve.

She blinked at the unexpected performance, but managed not to react otherwise. Had Kade seriously managed to sneak weapons past a Vitharan law enforcement scan and two sets of prisoner transport guards somehow? What the *actual fuck*?

This must have been why he shut her down when she started to play things up earlier for any guards that might be listening. He hadn't wanted their captors to show up at the cell door before he'd successfully retrieved whatever he'd been hiding in his footwear.

Martinez was gambling that they were on the same page with a half-baked plan conveyed on the strength of a couple of winks and head-shakes. The idea of trying to lure guards in and overpower them by making them think Kade was about to injure or kill her in the throes of neurotonin withdrawal became incrementally less suicidal if the two of them were armed… though she would have felt considerably better knowing what, precisely, they'd be armed *with*.

She assumed Kade hadn't survived the life he'd been leading for the past decade without being competent in a fight. For her part, Martinez hadn't been in a physical altercation in years. As a civilian, she'd kept up her fitness as much as her schedule allowed—but not through sparring. Fighting another person, even in controlled and non-threatening circumstances, had been too tangled up with… the rest of it.

She hadn't trusted herself to avoid getting pulled back into past trauma when feet and fists started flying, so she hadn't tried. *Gods and prophets*. She wasn't ever supposed to get dragged into this kind of shit again. She was a *diplomat* now, not a soldier.

The bare transport cell with its cameras and solid walls mocked her, as if to say, '*You're a prisoner now, nothing more. You can either wait to be handed over to a fascist monster with a penchant for torture and execution, or pull up your big-girl pants and try to kick some ass on your way out.*'

Somehow, she didn't get the impression Kade would be standing idly by when the guards eventually showed up. Men who carried custom-made concealed weapons in their shoes weren't generally the *sit-down-and-take-it* type. And—fuck it. Be honest—neither was she. Special Forces might have chewed her up and spit her out like a lump of crushed gristle in the end, but that didn't mean she was about to stand in the corner like a useless civvy while Kade took his chances with their captors alone.

So, it looked like they'd be biding their time for a bit longer. Her first salvo directed at the guards had apparently sailed wide, since no one had shown up to check on them directly. That might mean audio surveillance wasn't enabled in the cell, or it might mean they just didn't care enough to get her out.

She guessed that Kade would let a believable amount of time pass, and then up the ante in their little charade. Martinez had done basic research into Kade's condition shortly after his arrival on Terra Nova, but she'd certainly never had direct personal contact with an addict undergoing critical neurotonin withdrawal.

Mostly, she'd have to remember to play helpless. It wouldn't do to broadcast the fact that she had advanced hand-to-hand combat training, no matter how rusty that training might be. She wondered if the grunts on this ship knew about her military background at all. If they did, a bit of basic self-defense might not go amiss, especially if she could make it look ineffectual against a larger and more powerful opponent.

She shifted, trying without success to find a more comfortable position on the hard floor.

"Stop fidgeting," Kade growled. "You're making it worse. I already feel like I'm about to crawl out of my damned skin."

She shot him a look out of narrowed eyes, only to find him leveling a sharp grin at her out of view of the camera. The expression was wolfish, more a baring of teeth than anything else. It was the expression of someone who, given the choice between sitting around in a cell and risking everything in a life or death fight, would take the fight and go down scratching and clawing.

Martinez was entirely unsure in that moment whether she found that realization reassuring… or terrifying. Maybe, on further reflection, it was a bit of both. Warily, she settled back to wait for whatever he had planned next.

SEVEN

"Do you have to just... *sit there* like that?" The barked words broke a silence that had stretched for more than half a cycle, and Martinez didn't have to manufacture a surprised flinch.

"What the hell are you talking about?" she snapped right back. "I'm not even doing anything!"

Kade ran a shaky hand over his face and surged to his feet, pacing across the length of the cell before turning back and going the other way.

"Stay away from me," Martinez said, injecting a bit of anger into the words. "You said you'd stay over there. Don't you come near me while you're freaking out like this!"

She rose to her feet, using the wall as a brace, her shoulders pressed against it as Kade whirled on her, fists clenched at his sides. There was an edge to his expression that said he didn't much enjoy playing the role of 'addict,' even as part of a ruse. Martinez couldn't help the way her heart rate accelerated as he stalked over to the corner she'd staked out, looming over her.

Wow. Okay. He was... *tall*. How had she never noticed exactly how tall he was? Or how much heat his body threw off as he crowded her against the wall?

Probably because he's not prone to looming, in the normal course of things, noted a part of her mind that wasn't bogged down in the whole *big, male*, and *close* part.

He sneered down at her. "Stop bleating, little human. I can hear your damned *breathing* all the way over there. *In, out. In, out.* It's making me want to *punch* something."

She shoved him in the chest, figuring that maybe the guards would start to care about what was happening once things actually got physical. "*Get. Away!* Guards! Help! *Guards!*"

He barely moved, but an instant later, his fist flashed out and slammed into the wall a few inches from her head, shocking her. And… *damn*. That had been a pretty hardcore blow, from the look of it. She realized just *how* hardcore when she caught the flash of coppery Vithii blood welling from his knuckles.

"Shut. *Up*," he growled, getting right in her face.

A strange cocktail of adrenaline and excitement that she hadn't experienced in years bubbled up in her chest, in anticipation of a good old-fashioned brawl.

"Get. *Off*," she growled back, and pushed him again—harder this time.

That reckless and arguably somewhat unhinged part of her personality—the same part that had originally driven her into the arms of an elite military unit—whispered in her ear, asking what it would be like to go up against Kade for real. It was a part that had gotten her in a fair amount of trouble in her younger years, before the events of the Badlands Rebellion buried it beneath an avalanche of PTSD. That it was stirring from its long sleep today, of all days, was enough to seriously take her by surprise.

But there wasn't time to think about her ragtag collection of psychological baggage right now.

Rather than yielding to her violent shove, Kade grabbed one of her hands and pinned it against the wall. Martinez schooled herself not to react at the feeling of a slim object trapped between their palms. Whatever items Kade had pulled from his shoes earlier, one of them was now in her grip. She hadn't even seen him retrieve it from his pocket.

"You're testing my patience, little human," Kade snarled. "What do I have to do to get some *fucking quiet* in here?"

She jerked her hand free, and tried to ignore her body's reaction to the fact that they were basically pressed together from chest to hip, as he held her trapped in the corner with his body. She writhed against his hold; using the distraction to cover her movement as she slipped the slender object he'd passed her into her pocket.

"I said, *get off*!" she hissed.

Something hard pressed against the crease of her hip, twisting restlessly like a snake. An instant after she noticed it, Kade jerked back a couple of centimeters as though she'd burned him.

"And I said *shut up*," he shot back, though his cheeks darkened to a ruddy copper color as she watched.

It took a couple of seconds for her mind to catch up and make the relevant connections. When it did, her eyes widened. *Huh. Looks like I'm not the only one who gets off on a bit of rough and tumble,* she thought. *Now, isn't that interesting?*

With the mysterious object he'd passed her successfully hidden away, she took advantage of the small yielding of ground to shove him off-balance with a basic self-defense move and dart away from his hold.

"Fuck off!" she snarled. "Guards—damn it! *Guards*!"

With a frustrated cry, Kade punched the wall a second time before turning and sliding down it. In full view of the camera now, he covered his face, hands trembling. Martinez had to give him props for the performance. She took his previous position in the camera's blind spot and crouched down, bracing her back against the wall.

"Just… stay over there, okay? I… I get that this isn't really your fault, but you're seriously scaring me here," she said in a slightly calmer voice. He only grunted in reply, sounding utterly wretched.

There was still no sign of any interest from outside their cell, though if nothing else, one would expect a guard to show up soon with food—unless the two of them were being purposely starved.

Which was entirely possible, she supposed.

She was still buzzing with adrenaline, not to mention feeling a bit shaky after the sudden mental gear change from '*Kade is a bitter old revolutionary with a chip on his shoulder and a self-destructive streak*' to '*Kade has a big ol' alien cock which is apparently interested in female humans.*' Hadn't he said something to her once before, though, about being permanently impotent from his neurotonin addiction?

She shook her head sharply, dismissing the totally irrelevant line of thought. Sliding her hand into her pocket, she sized up the small object nestled inside. It was about six centimeters long—the length, unsurprisingly, of a large, male-sized shoe heel. Her first thought was *nutcracker*, which was obviously inaccurate.

There were two cylindrical posts arranged parallel to each other, with what felt like a hinge on one end and a latch on the other end. But something flat was held between the two posts. Her fingernail traced along it, and she could feel that the posts had channels on the insides to hold the edges of the flat piece.

Oh.

Cautiously, she flicked the catch free, allowing the posts to swivel around the hinged end. She eased one to the side, confirming that she held a very compact, very well designed butterfly knife, presumably made of some kind of polycarbonate that would have scanned as the same material as the rest of the shoe heel. When flipped around one hundred and eighty degrees, the two protective posts that shielded the blade when the knife was folded closed would form the handle.

The six-centimeter polymer knife wasn't the best fighting weapon, especially without any kind of a quillon or crossguard to keep her fingers from sliding off the handle and onto the blade. Speaking of which…

She feathered her thumb across the exposed edge of the knife. It was surprisingly sharp. Sharp enough to pierce flesh, without a doubt. Combined with the fact that the guards wouldn't expect them to have *anything* on them that could be used as a weapon, it was decidedly better than nothing. She only wished there was a way to get a few moments of practice with the grip, before she needed to use it for real.

No such luck, obviously.

Now that they were both armed and on the same page, she supposed there was no point in dragging out the addict withdrawal act longer than necessary. They needed to escalate things to the point that the guards came. Assuming, of course, that the guards cared if either of them appeared to be in imminent danger of death.

There was really only one way to find out.

"Are you all right now? Are you going to be able to keep it together?" she asked the huddled form on the other side of the cell.

Kade snarled—a wordless, animal noise. He raised his head, glaring at her. "Do I fucking *look* all right, human?"

"I don't know!" Martinez snapped. *Poke the bear.* "You tell me. I don't exactly have a long history of being stuck in a prison cell with an addict undergoing a meltdown!"

"I'll *tell* you… you irritating little creature," he grated, pushing to his feet and swaying unsteadily. "I'll *tell* you once I've got my hands around your scrawny gods-damned neck!"

Kade lunged for her clumsily, and she manufactured a startled yelp, scrambling out of his way. He was breathing heavily, his face pulled into a rictus. Idly, she wondered how much of his performance was true to life, and how much was for show. She sincerely hoped she'd never have a reason to find out.

They played that game for a while—him stumbling toward her, allowing her to dart out of reach at the last minute each time and run to the other side of the cell. He kicked and punched the wall in frustration when she escaped his grasp. Minutes passed, still with no sign of guards. Martinez was debating the merits of letting him catch her in hopes that it would shake the guards loose of their torpor, but then Kade changed tack.

Instead of chasing her, he hurled his body against the locked door, pounding on it. "Let me out, damn you!" he roared. "Give me a damned fix! I'll kill you all! *Let… me… out!*"

Martinez added her voice to the cacophony echoing off the cell walls. "Get him out of here! He needs help! Please, don't leave him in here with me!"

They continued to yell until they were hoarse, Kade punctuating the pleas and curse-riddled demands with more pounding against the door's clearsteel viewing port. When that didn't produce any result, he whirled on her with a final, slurred, "I'll tear you apart!" and stumbled in her direction, only to collapse dramatically to the floor in the center of the cell like a puppet with its strings cut.

Ouch, she thought, hiding a wince. *That had to hurt.*

She scurried away from his downed form until her back hit the wall, making certain to end up someplace where she could be seen both from the door and on the camera feed. Hopefully anyone watching would take Kade's sudden collapse as alarming, rather than seeing it as an excuse to leave Martinez to her own devices now that the direct threat to her was past.

Interesting that Kade had resisted getting any more physical with her than he already had. She'd assumed he would try to make it look like she was in imminent danger of being killed. And… he had to know that she was perfectly capable of absorbing a bit of manhandling, didn't he? Surely he must, since he was relying on her to help them overpower armed Vithii guards with a weapon that would have been better suited for use as a paring knife.

He lay there like the dead, and Martinez had a sudden, faintly hysterical vision of cycles passing with nothing happening, until he finally had to break character and tacitly admit to the ruse. On the scale of *one* to *humiliating*, that would rank pretty far along the *humiliating* end of the spectrum.

Fortunately, she didn't have to worry about it for long. Barely five minutes later, movement outside the cell drew her eyes to the door. She palmed the butterfly knife, arranging it in her grip so she'd be able to flip it open smoothly when the time came.

The intercom speaker next to the camera crackled to life, and a gruff, Vithii-accented voice boomed, *"Step to the back of the cell and stand against the wall. Do not move."*

She did as requested, her shoulders tensing as the door slid open and two guards entered the cell with blasters drawn.

EIGHT

Martinez pressed her shoulders against the smooth wall, the folded butterfly blade burning a metaphorical hole in her clenched fist. The heady buzz of an incipient life or death battle flooded her body like a drug, spurring her pulse into a staccato gallop as she stared down the muzzle of an Ilarian blaster.

Kade still lay unmoving. She wondered with a hint of worry if he'd thought to palm his own weapon before pretending to collapse. The second guard kept his blaster trained on his apparently lifeless form as he approached. Digging the toe of a polished boot into Kade's hip to roll him over, he examined Kade's lax features in the harsh overhead lighting.

Martinez's guard glanced away to see what was happening, and she had to stop herself from springing forward to try and take advantage of the moment's inattention. *Not yet.* Kade was the one with the element of surprise, here. It would be up to him to use it to best advantage.

"Don't waste your time—he's worm food," her guard opined, returning his bored gaze to her. "We're a long way out from Ilarius, and we don't have any neurotonin on board. Just drag him out of here and shunt him out an airlock."

Kade's guard nudged him again, still to no effect. "Nah. The higher ups might want to see his body as proof he's dead."

"Then shoot him to make sure, and leave him in here with the human bitch," the other guard said impatiently.

Fuck, Martinez thought, preparing to spring despite the weapon pointed at her. *Fuck, fuck, fuck—*

"Yeah, okay," said the first guard, lifting his weapon with intent.

Before his finger could tighten on the trigger, Kade rolled sideways and grabbed him around the knee, making a sharp slicing motion across the Vithii's hamstring. The guard cried out, a blaster beam erupting from his weapon only to sizzle against the deckplates a few centimeters from Kade's head.

The Vithii covering Martinez whirled sharply at the commotion, the muzzle of his sidearm sliding away from her. She launched herself at him, flipping the butterfly blade open in a smooth arc and catching the two halves of the handle in a solid grip. Her free hand knocked the guard's blaster further to the side at the same time she stabbed the tiny blade toward his groin, cursing mentally when he twisted just enough for it to bite into the top of his thigh instead.

She couldn't spare any attention for Kade's situation—not if she didn't want to end up very, very dead. The thud of flesh on flesh reached her ears as background noise, though… so he was at least still in the fight.

Her opponent grunted and tried to grab her by the hair as she ducked and spun. She winced as she felt a few strands rip free, but didn't allow it to slow her down. The blaster was the most immediate danger, so she went for the Vithii's wrist next.

She wasn't remotely strong enough to overpower him as he attempted to get the weapon pointed at her so he could fire, but she *could* hold his arm in place long enough to drive the tip of the polymer knife into the tendons of his forearm.

The guard let out a noise of rage as the weapon slid from his suddenly nerveless fingers and clattered to the floor. It was lying too close to their feet, though—she couldn't crouch down to get it without offering herself up for a kick to the head. Rather than chance it ending up in either of the guards' hands, she kicked it away, toward the space beneath the utilitarian sink.

Weapons fire sizzled past her shoulder, proclaiming the fact that the other blaster was still in play. She gritted her teeth and ignored it, knowing that she currently had no control over that aspect of the fight. A hard knee to her guard's groin was enough to gain her some space, and she twisted, using the grip she still held on his injured wrist to lever him over her shoulder in a standard martial arts throw. Prophets, she thought as her muscles strained against the load. Vithii men weighed a fucking *ton*.

Or you're just rusty as hell, said her helpful inner voice. *That might have something to do with it, too.*

Whatever the case, despite her protesting back, the guard was down—clutching his injured wrist and snarling up at her. She was just about to dive for the discarded blaster rather than risking trying to open his throat with the blade when Kade croaked, "Clear!" from somewhere outside of her field of vision.

She hit the deck without thought, rolling away. Blaster fire split the air, hitting the prone guard squarely in the chest. He convulsed and went limp, his limbs flopping to the floor. Martinez let her momentum carry her into a crouch, scanning the cell for any remaining threats. The other guard lay crumpled near the open cell door with a charred chunk torn out of his abdomen. Kade stood over him, blaster in hand.

Without thought, she scrambled over to the sink and retrieved the second blaster, checking that it hadn't been damaged and still had a charge. It was only when she straightened that she saw the coppery mess of blood soaking the left side of Kade's shirt beneath his collarbone.

"Kade!" she exclaimed, starting forward only for him to wave her off.

"It's not important," he said in a tight voice. "The rest of them will have seen all that on camera, and we don't know how many there are."

She jerked her brain back to practicalities. "Stay here and try to pick them off at the door?" she suggested.

He shook his head, wincing. "No, not enough cover. And they could just toss a gas canister in here or something."

"Right," she replied grimly. "Let's go, then."

She could only hope that Kade's injury wouldn't be enough to slow him down before they managed to take out the rest of the crew. They burst out of the cell, facing back to back to cover both ends of the corridor with their stolen weapons.

"This way," Kade said, loping off toward a T-junction perhaps thirty meters away.

Martinez had no idea if he was familiar with this class of interstellar transport, or if he was just taking charge because it was in his nature to do so. Either way, since she had no clue about the layout herself, there was no legitimate reason to question him. Leading with his blaster muzzle, Kade ducked left at the junction. It was clear, so they headed down it, but they only made it half a dozen paces before armed crewmembers appeared at the far end of the corridor.

Acting on instinct, she squeezed off two quick shots to send them scrambling for cover. With no other choice besides standing there in the open like a couple of marksmanship targets, she and Kade ran back to the corridor they'd just come from and ducked around the corner again. Martinez dropped to lie flat on her belly, easing her blaster out for a shot and peeking out just far enough to see the next junction.

"Draw them out somehow," she said. "Then get back under cover."

A short pause, and Kade tossed something down the corridor toward where the crewmen were sheltering. It clattered against the deck, and she recognized one of the folded butterfly knives. A crewman peered around the corner, weapon ready. Martinez fired at the same time he did, catching him in the side of the head even as his shot burst harmlessly against the bulkhead above her. He toppled to the ground, dead.

"They never think to aim low," she muttered, ducking back as a second crewman swung around the corner and fired at them. "How many crew does a vessel like this take, anyway?"

"Six, minimum," Kade said. "Not counting the guards. Piloting will require two people, since we're in the wormhole system."

She shot him a look. "You can tell that for sure, without access to a viewport?"

He returned the look, frowning. "Of course. You can't?"

The exchange was interrupted by more blaster fire scorching the corner of the bulkhead. When it stopped, Kade swung his head and shoulders out and returned fire.

"This is too slow," Martinez said, knowing they couldn't afford to be pinned down long enough for other crewmembers to circle around and pincer them. "Keep them occupied, okay?"

The blasters they'd taken from the guards were of a standard configuration, though not a model she was specifically familiar with. Still, there were only so many ways to wire up a phased energy weapon, and all of them could be tweaked to act in a way that the manufacturers wouldn't approve of.

Martinez levered the side panel loose with a fingernail, exposing the blaster's guts. What she was doing would have been easier with a multi-tool, but in a pinch, the edge of Kade's polycarbonate butterfly blade would have to suffice. After loosening the relevant connections and prying them free, she cross-wired the micro-dynamo with the power setting and snapped the cover panel back in place. A twist of the dial, and a low hum built inside the device, growing higher pitched by the second. The grip heated in her palm.

"Hmm," Kade mused. "That sounds dangerous. I'm impressed."

"Lay down some covering fire for me," she said. "Or else you'll be impressed *and vaporized* about five seconds from now."

He did, and she took advantage of it to step into the corridor and hurl the overloading blaster unit toward their enemies at the far end of the corridor.

"*Run*," she said, and suited action to word.

As the whine behind them reached a critical pitch, she grabbed Kade's arm and dragged him sideways, flattening herself face-first against the wall. Somewhat to her surprise, Kade plastered his larger frame against hers, sheltering her as the blaster exploded with a deafening screech. A wall of heat and light blew past them, making her exposed skin prickle.

"All right?" she asked, as Kade unpeeled himself from her.

"Never better," he grated out, already heading toward the scene of devastation at a brisk jog.

Three Vithii corpses lay burned and twisted in the corridor, near a section of bulkhead partially melted by the heat. There was no point in checking them for usable weapons; their blasters would be as melted as they were. Martinez poked at her reaction to the carnage as she and Kade hurried past, shoe soles bubbling against the heated deckplates. No sense of panic threatened her mind. The men had been armed combatants, bent on capturing or killing her. Nothing more; nothing less.

The distraction of her thoughts kept her from registering the guard appearing around the next corner until it was too late. Thankfully, Kade hadn't shared her dangerous inattention to their surroundings. He fired an instant before the guard did, drilling a hole through his opponent's chest and sending the man's beam wide.

She sprinted forward and scooped up the guard's weapon, dropping into a defensive crouch. No other crewmen appeared as Kade joined her, slightly breathless.

"That should be most of them," he said, the rasp in his voice reminding her of the blood staining his chest. "Let's get to the bridge and take over control of this bird."

"Roger that," Martinez agreed, following him through the maze of corridors.

A nervous-looking crewman guarding the entrance to the control room fell to a blaster shot from Kade. Approaching the now unguarded door, she drilled a beam through the electronic locking mechanism to fry it. It slid open, and they both dialed down their blaster settings to heavy stun, knowing they couldn't afford to hit something important on the vessel's control board with a full-strength beam.

Apparently, the copilot didn't share their concerns about damaging the bridge. A shot sizzled past Martinez's ear, even as she dove into a shoulder roll to avoid it and came up firing. Kade followed suit, leaving both the pilot and copilot slumped in their chairs, unconscious.

Kade had been right—they were in subspace, stars streaking past beyond the distortion of the wormhole tunnel. Martinez lunged forward, sizing up the controls in an instant and adjusting course to keep them from slewing into the tunnel wall.

Kade dragged the two Vithii out of their chairs and changed his blaster setting, drilling a neat hole through each of their heads without breaking expression. Then he joined her at the controls, calling up internal sensors.

"That's all of them," he said. "No other life signs aboard except us."

"Can we get back to realspace?" Martinez asked, fingers flying over the controls. "I need to look at that wound, and we can't exactly drift here in the wormhole system with no one at the controls."

Kade scowled at his readouts. "The nearest gate is a couple of cycles away. Looks like Space Station Beta-Four."

"That's the middle of fucking nowhere," Martinez said. "And besides, it's too far."

"There's a weak spot coming up a few minutes ahead of us. Still the middle of fucking nowhere, obviously."

"A smuggler's gate, you mean?" she asked. "Okay. Beggars can't be choosers. I take it you have experience getting through those?"

He snorted. "Yeah. You could say that."

She shot him a side-eyed glance. "Right, I sort of figured. In that case, match the intermix ratios and count it down for me."

He gave a single, tight nod and bent to the task, tweaking the frequency and amplitude of the transport's engine output to the frequency and amplitude of the weak area in the subspace tunnel.

Martinez kept an eye on everything else, and before long he said, "approaching the target in five… four… three… two… one… *now*."

She wrenched the ship into the barrier, her teeth juddering as they forced their way through without finesse and were dumped unceremoniously back into normal space. Once she was sure they hadn't suffered a hull breach or other catastrophic mechanical failure, she powered everything down and let the ship drift in the emptiness surrounding them.

"Let me see," she said, pushing away from the controls and rising. With a hand on the back of Kade's chair, she swiveled him around and started on the fastenings of his bloodstained shirt.

"Do you mind?" he snapped, batting her hands away and finishing the job himself. He peeled the fabric away with a wince, and Martinez felt her blood run cold. The compact marvel of medical tech that pumped a carefully calibrated supply of neurotonin into his body had been ripped out of his flesh at the top, its delicate components smashed by the impact of a fist or a blaster butt. She stared at the ruined remains, as blood oozed slowly from the torn stitches of the surgical site.

"Oh… *shit*," she said faintly. "That's not good."

NINE

"Thank you for your insightful commentary," Kade snapped, craning his head in an attempt to see the damage. "Can you tell if the reservoir is intact? Maybe there's a hypo-injector on board that I can use to deliver the contents the old-fashioned way."

Martinez peered at the device, but it was covered with blood in addition to being broken in several places. "I can't see a damned thing that's useful. Will taking it the rest of the way out of you tear you up anymore than you already are?"

Kade reached up and ripped the implant free of his flesh. She winced at the careless way he did it—even if it *had* only been hanging by a proverbial thread, that wasn't exactly the removal method she'd been envisioning.

With an exasperated growl, she grabbed the pump from him and gestured at the copper-colored blood oozing from his collarbone. "Get some damned pressure on that wound."

He raised an eyebrow at her, ignoring the directive. "Believe me when I say, a bit of blood loss won't be what kills me today."

She gritted her teeth and grabbed his shirttail to swipe the worst of the gore off the pump, ignoring the hard look he gave her. With a sinking heart, she examined reservoir at the bottom of the device before angling it toward him so he could see the cracked polymer shell.

"*Fuck*," he said with feeling, taking it from her and giving it a small shake to confirm it was empty. It would have been less than half-full to start with, but now its contents were nothing more than part of the bloody mess staining Kade's shirt.

Martinez chewed her lower lip, trying to think of options while knowing full well that there weren't any. Before her eyes, Kade wrestled with the same realization for the space of a handful of heartbeats before his expression smoothed to a stony facade.

"Maybe we could—" she began, even though she had no good way to end the sentence.

He cut her off with a sharp shake of the head. "Don't bother. We don't have time for any feel-good fantasy crap. I'm done for, unless there's a ship nearby miraculously stocking neurotonin on board—so discount my continued survival beyond the next few cycles. We'll need to get the communications system online and contact the Vitharans. Terra Nova, too, since we're probably still under investigation for murder on Vithara."

She swallowed hard—not as ready as he seemed to be to write off his own life just yet, but knowing he was correct about the need to contact their allies. "Right. Let's see what we've got to work with on this boat."

Kade gave a curt nod and settled into the copilot's seat as though he hadn't just been handed a potential death sentence. Martinez fought down the trapped, heavy feeling trying to clog her throat and re-took the pilot's chair. Over the years, she'd seen more than her fair share of death, both fast and slow. People had different ways of dealing with it. Some railed and begged and prayed to deities they barely believed in, while others went the stoic route, pretending to ignore the guillotine blade hanging over their heads.

It didn't surprise her one bit that Kade was part of the second group.

Fortunately, the ship's comm system was fairly standard for an interstellar cruiser. Kade was more familiar with its Ilarian tech than she was, but between them, it only took a few minutes to set up a subspace communications packet bound for Vithara. There was the usual lag involved with establishing a comm link over extended distances—compounded, no doubt, by the fact that the request was coming from an unknown Ilarian transport.

Finally, the comms speaker crackled to life. *"Ilarian vessel operator, please confirm your identity. Your ship's codes are not transmitting properly."*

Of course, the vessel they were on didn't have valid ship's codes registered in the first place. That would have rather defeated the point of being on an interplanetary kidnapping mission under the unofficial auspices of the Ilarian government. She and Kade exchanged a glance before she opened the mic and responded.

"Vitharan communications control, this is Ambassador Isadora Martinez of Terra Nova, aboard an unknown Ilarian transport ship. My companion and I were abducted from Vitharan custody while en route to an orbital holding facility. We were able to escape and overpower our abductors, taking control of their vessel. But we are currently drifting in open space, roughly two-thirds of the way along the route between Vithara and Ilarius. We have an emergency medical situation aboard. Please advise."

"*Standby, Ilarian vessel*," came the distant voice, after several seconds of subspace lag.

Martinez had to stop herself from grinding her teeth together as the speaker clicked off. To distract herself, she returned her attention to Kade. "How long do you have before you're unable to function?"

"No idea," he replied, his expression never wavering. "I'm used to undergoing wide swings in neurotonin levels—an injection that raises them just short of an overdose, followed by five or six cycles of slowly dropping levels, with the cravings starting somewhere in the middle. They gradually increase to the point where I'm useless until I get another injection."

She nodded slowly. "But the pump was feeding you a constant low dose, rather than a big spike followed by a gradual decline."

"Which means I'm most likely starting from a considerably lower baseline," he confirmed. "If I were you, I wouldn't count on my help for more than a couple of cycles. After that, you should stun me so I don't hurt you in the throes of withdrawal."

A shiver skittered down her spine. "We'll discuss that when it actually becomes an issue."

Kade let out an indelicate snort—the sound decidedly bitter. "Good luck with that. 'Discussion' and 'neurotonin withdrawal' aren't concepts that mesh well, generally speaking."

Before she could come up with a suitable reply, the comms panel lit up. "*Ambassador Martinez. We have confirmed your identity via voice-print.*"

"Thank the prophets for that," she muttered, too low for the mic to pick up. In a normal tone, she said, "We copy. How soon can a rescue ship be sent to rendezvous with us? We should be able to make our way through the wormhole system to the gate near Space Station Beta-Four before we're forced to return to normal space."

Another pause, shorter this time. "*We estimate a rendezvous at Station Beta-Four will take approximately eight cycles.*"

"Damn," she cursed, thinking fast. "Okay. Okay... is Beta-Four a manned station?"

"*Negative. Beta-Four is automated, but there is a self-service emergency medical pod on board.*"

Martinez squeezed the bridge of her nose between two fingers. "Is the pod stocked with neurotonin? Or able to synthesize it?"

"*Stand by.*"

Kade shot her a look. "Why the hell would you expect an unmanned space station to stock neurotonin?"

She shushed him with a gesture, knowing all too well that he was probably right. Confirmation came a few moments later.

"*Negative. The station stocks only basic medical supplies geared toward treating traumatic injury and common medical complaints.*"

Her stomach sank a little further. "Well... make sure the emergency ship is stocked with neurotonin, and get it headed in our direction ASAP. Can you connect me with someone in the governing council? Or, failing that, with Lieutenant Zetara of the security forces?"

"*I will attempt to do so, Ambassador. Rest assured that emergency services are scrambling a ship for immediate takeoff.*"

While they waited, Martinez attempted to plot their location relative to Ilarius. "It looks to me like we could maybe make it to Ilarius in six cycles, rather than eight to rendezvous with the Vitharan ship," she said.

Kade appeared unimpressed. "Why?" he asked. "I'll be a mental vegetable well before six cycles have passed."

She narrowly avoided pounding her fist against the edge of the control panel. Displays of temper wouldn't help, even if Kade's defeatist attitude *was* making her want to hit something.

It's not defeatist, her inner voice whispered. *It's reality*.

"*Ambassador Martinez?*" came a new voice. "*Is Krau Finisterre with you? This is Councilwoman Nebra'ath.*"

Martinez pounced on the mic switch, desperate for news about what had been happening on Vithara in their absence. "Councilwoman? Yes, yes he's here. Though he's been… er… he's been injured."

Councilwoman Nebra'ath had been a member of Trivaal Canutian's non-interventionist voting bloc. That she sounded so concerned about them was promising.

Kade pushed past her to get to the mic. "This is Ehkadian Finisterre. What is the state of the negotiations?" he asked without preamble, sounding far more invested in that question than he was in the fact that he might die soon.

"*Krau Finisterre—as you might imagine, things have been in considerable upheaval since the news of the Ilarian spy ring and the attempt to frame you and Ambassador Martinez for Trivaal's murder.*"

Kade met Martinez's gaze, sudden hope lighting his gray eyes. "The real murderer has been apprehended, then?" he asked.

"Yes, indeed! Two Ilarian Vithii infiltrators were caught trying to assassinate the other members of your contingent in the middle of the night, right in the middle of the ambassadorial residence wing. Shocking that they could have gotten into a secure area so easily."

At the mention of an assassination attempt on his friends, Kade's hand clenched convulsively around the edge of the console.

"Was anyone injured?" he asked tightly.

A nervous laugh. *"Well, according to the gossip, the would-be assassins ended up rather battered. Krau Draven and Mr. Purandhri are fine, though."*

Kade relaxed his death grip on the control panel. "And the talks?" he prompted.

Nebra'ath's voice grew somber. *"The uncovering of a network of Ilarian agents embedded at the deepest levels of Vitharan governance has put a considerably different spin on things, unsurprisingly. The council voted sixty-eight to thirty-two, in favor of sending Vitharan forces to join our Terra Novan allies in confronting Premiere Kovak."*

Martinez's eyes widened. "A veto-proof majority," she murmured.

Kade nodded almost imperceptibly. "What is the proposed timetable of the operation, Councilwoman?"

"Mobilization is already underway," Nebra'ath replied, static crackling across the connection. *"They should be less than a day behind their Terra Novan counterparts. Word is expected soon from Maelfius, as well."*

Kade's eyes slid closed. He leaned heavily against the console, his shoulder brushing hers for a moment before he straightened. "Thank you," he said, his voice hoarse with suppressed emotion.

Martinez wrapped a hand around his upper arm without thought—a wordless gesture of support. He didn't flinch or pull away, but she could detect a fine tremor running through his muscles.

"Yes—thank you very much for that, Councilwoman," she echoed. "As I'm sure you can guess, hearing such news is a considerable relief to both of us."

"*I apologize on behalf of Vitharan authorities for the false accusations leveled against you,*" said the Councilwoman, still sounding somber. "*I know we've been on opposite sides of the fence during this debate, Ambassador. But like many of my colleagues, our position of non-intervention was not intended as tacit approval of the events occurring on Ilarius. We're merely tasked by our constituents with protecting Vitharan interests first. But now that evidence has arisen of Ilarian interference here on the homeworld...*"

"Our interests align," Martinez finished, when Nebra'ath trailed off.

"*Indeed,*" the Councilwoman agreed.

Martinez thanked her again and signed off, feeling a sudden bout of nervous energy flood her chest. Things were moving. Their absence had sparked action on Vithara in a way their presence at the debate table hadn't managed to do. Such was the irony of the universe, she supposed. Now, she just had to figure out some way to ensure that Kade didn't end up paying for that outcome with his life.

She realized belatedly that her hand was still wrapped around his hard-muscled bicep. His eyes fell to the point of contact, staring at it for a moment before he lifted his gaze to meet hers. Still, she didn't pull away.

"We did it," she said quietly. "Even if it did take becoming accused murderers and getting kidnapped by interplanetary foreign agents."

The faintest hint of tired humor sparked behind his eyes before guttering like a spent candle flame. "As long as it got done. And at least this way, I won't have to put up with Ash and Draven's insufferable smugness over catching the Ilarian agents and convincing the council to act."

She raised an eyebrow at him. "Right. Way to find the silver lining, there. I'm impressed." With a final squeeze, she let her hand fall away from him. "I should contact Terra Nova and let them know what's happening, as well. Then we need to force our way back into the wormhole tunnel and get to the space station while you're still in any kind of condition to help me pilot."

TEN

The Terra Novan interstellar communications platform was businesslike and efficient as they confirmed Martinez's identity and routed her call. However—as she had known would be the case—they were even less help than Vithara had been, when it came to arranging for an emergency rendezvous. The closest available ship would take more than twelve cycles to reach them. By then, Kade wouldn't just be in a permanent coma with irreversible brain damage—he'd be long dead.

Martinez asked Terra Nova to notify her if any closer ships could be found, and signed off. Trying not to think about the hopelessness of their situation, she instead turned her attention to getting them to Station Beta-Four as quickly as possible. Subspace navigation of a ship this large and complex was definitely a two-person job. Fortunately, Kade appeared as focused and efficient as always—so far, at least.

"Doing okay over there?" she asked, cutting a sideways glance at him.

"No," he said. "But don't worry, I'll let you know when it becomes a problem. Just keep the engines running at maximum."

Silence fell, broken only by the occasional exchange of information relevant to flying the ship. That silence was becoming decidedly uncomfortable by the time Kade drew in a breath and held it, as though searching for words.

"I have a personal request," he said at length.

She turned to look at him properly, but his eyes remained stubbornly fixed on his readouts. "Yes?" she asked, not sure what to expect.

He took in a deep breath through his nose, and let it out slowly before speaking. "I'd hoped to live long enough to personally ensure that Kovak fell from power, and that his movement went down with him."

"The Regime's going down, Kade," she told him, meaning it. "There's no question about that. Not now."

But he only shook his head. "Last time I checked, they didn't hand out crystal balls in the Terra Novan Special Forces… or for ambassadorial assignments, for that matter. My point is, I didn't necessarily expect to *survive* the revolution, but I at least expected to be there. I'd… rest easier knowing that you were there in my stead… though I know that's a lot to ask."

She frowned. "*Hey.* Stop talking like your death is a foregone conclusion, please."

He scowled back. "In a few cycles I'm going to be a mental vegetable. A few cycles more, and I will, in fact, be dead. Those things are very much foregone conclusions, *Ambassador.*"

The choked, heavy feeling returned in force. "Look—if I agree to go to Ilarius, will you promise to stop acting like a dead man walking?"

Frustration clouded his strong features. "Sure, whatever. I'm more than happy to be a dead man sitting, instead. Less exertion involved that way."

She tried to tell herself that a short temper was one of the symptoms he'd be experiencing as his neurotransmitter levels fell out of balance. Which was true, though it didn't really address the fact that he was snappish even at the best of times.

"Honestly, you don't have to worry," she said. "I was already neck-deep in this crazy cause. That hasn't changed. If anything, I'm more invested than ever, now that I've been dragged halfway across the Seven Systems by Ilarian infiltrators."

He appeared to consider that for a moment before giving a short nod. "All right, then."

Quiet descended once more, broken only by the beeps and hums of the ship's systems. Pointless questions buzzed in her head, spurred by the idea that she might only have a handful of cycles to ask them before her chance was gone forever. What had Kade's childhood been like? What aspirations might he have held if not for the political cause that had consumed him after his parents' death and his imprisonment? Had he ever been in love? Wanted children? How had he met the ragtag collection of freedom fighters he called his family?

He wouldn't appreciate such questions, she knew. Yet, she was tempted to ask them anyway, just so she could know him a little bit better while she was still able to. She dithered uncharacteristically, half her attention focused on navigating through the wormhole system with the ship's propulsion systems pushed to maximum; the other half consumed with curiosity about his past.

Before she could give into the temptation to try and dig some of it up, he surprised her by speaking first.

"Before the security forces barged in and accused us of murder, you… were about to tell me why you reacted to Skye's speech the way you did," he said, not looking at her. "It was the same reaction you had to finding out I share a last name with a war criminal, which I find rather interesting."

She froze, taken by surprise—unwanted memories pushing in at a time when she could least afford them.

"This was personal for you, long before the goons on this ship kidnapped us," he continued. "Why is that?"

Her hands tightened around the ship's control yoke. "Let's just say that anyone who's pulled a few tours of duty in Special Forces has seen some shit."

She was proud of the fact that her voice stayed level. She was far less proud of the inner voice niggling her with a seductive little whisper. *You might as well tell him, you know. You were tempted to, back on Vithara. After all, who better to spill your guts to, than Mister 'Dead Man Sitting'? It's not like your secret will be out for long…*

She clamped her jaw shut, and tried to focus on not accidentally slamming them into the edge of the subspace tunnel. Unfortunately, the speed and ferocity with which her heart pounded against her ribcage wasn't really helping with that goal.

For his part, Kade only nodded, and let the silence stretch again. Martinez couldn't tell if something about his body language was contributing to the heavy atmosphere of expectancy that suddenly seemed to be smothering the bridge, or if that was all down to her brain playing tricks on her.

Whatever the case, it grew thicker and thicker until she could barely breathe.

"I was there when the Badlands Rebellion was put down," she blurted, after a small eternity had passed. And why did saying the words somehow make it easier to breathe?

Kade glanced at her. "Oh? I wasn't aware that Terra Novan forces were involved in that mess," he said.

She scrubbed a shaking hand over her face before determinedly returning it to the controls, her gaze fixed straight ahead. "Yeah, you weren't supposed to be aware of it," she muttered. "That's kind of the point of undercover ops."

"That colony was abandoned soon afterward, wasn't it?" Kade asked.

Her heart showed no sign of calming its frantic gallop, and she mused that being responsible for both of them dying because she had a PTSD flashback and crashed a ship in subspace would be a seriously humiliating way to go out.

"Yes. It was," she said, aware on some level that her voice had gone weak and reedy.

Godsdamn it.

"I'm not terribly well-educated on the background of the conflict," Kade said, as though they were talking about the weather, rather than the worst day of Martinez's life. "Something about a group of rebel Kritaani who tried to take over a settlement of humans and Maelfians? And... a religious sect, wasn't it?"

"Something like that," she agreed, the words still sounding breathy and strange. "The colonists... uh... they settled one of the unoccupied ringworlds because Maelfius and Terra Nova wouldn't make policy concessions regarding some of their more... controversial beliefs. I mean, they seemed pretty harmless for the most part, but they had some strange views on contraception, and some other stuff related to gender equality. So they left rather than being forced to live under laws they disagreed with."

"And the Kritaani rebels figured they'd make a soft target?"

An image of the forced labor camps wavered across her vision, blocking out the image of the controls before her for a dangerous instant before she wrenched her thoughts back to the present.

"I suppose. The Kritaani needed a base of operations, and a workforce to manufacture weapons and grow food for them. They... didn't much care what they had to do to get it," she said softly.

Kade let the words fade away, as though waiting to see if she'd continue. After a few moments of internal struggle, she did.

"The Kritaani government got tired of standing by while this upstart group was busy arming itself, basically thumbing their noses in the establishment's face while the rest of the Seven Systems watched. My unit was there as an intelligence-gathering team, infiltrating the imprisoned workforce and trying to find out if Terra Nova needed to take action. A big chunk of the settlers were still technically Terra Novan citizens, even though they'd emigrated voluntarily."

Kade nodded, the movement registering in her peripheral vision. "Terra Nova has always been protective of its own—even humans who *aren't* its citizens. I've had cause over the years to wish Vithara shared more of that philosophy."

She swallowed, the words piling up in her throat, eager to escape now that she'd started talking. With a start, she realized that she'd been seeing images from the past again, rather than reality, and the transport had veered a fraction to starboard without her noticing.

"You should… take over course control for a minute," she said faintly. "Are you well enough?"

She recognized the strange, detached feeling creeping over her. It made her pounding heart and the beads of clammy sweat popping out on her forehead seem distant and unimportant, but she knew from long experience that it was a warning sign. Kade wordlessly transferred control to the co-pilot's station, not commenting on her epic bad timing in losing her mental shit.

She swallowed, noticing with vague interest that her mouth was bone dry. "You've got control of the ship?" she asked, wanting to be sure.

"I do," he said. "I can handle things until the next system branch comes up." His eyes flicked to a readout on the console. "T-minus seventeen minutes and forty seconds."

Martinez leaned her elbows on the console edge and buried her face in her hands, digging the base of her thumbs into her eye sockets in an attempt to hold it together.

"So," Kade said, "you were there when the Kritaani government forces came in with orders to crush the rebels. I'm guessing, based on our previous conversations, that the rebels thought it would be a clever idea to use the human and Maelfian settlers as human shields."

"You'd be guessing right," she affirmed, not raising her head.

"And the Kritaani forces plowed right through them to get to the rebels?"

She pressed harder, pink starbursts flaring across the darkness behind her eyelids. It didn't stop the vision of the frightened human woman—barely more than a girl, really—lugging a baby on one hip and leading a toddler by the hand. Her hair had been a vibrant shade of reddish orange, and all Martinez could think was that she stuck out like a target.

"They're not exactly known for their diplomacy," she managed.

She'd seen the Kritaani forces approaching… seen the woman falling behind as the panicked mob of humans and Maelfians tried to get out of the way. Martinez was supposed to be rendezvousing with her unit commander in preparation for emergency extraction. But instead, she'd grabbed the woman by the arm and hustled her and the children in the direction of one of the holes that had been cut in the three-meter tall perimeter fence around the labor camp, blaster beams and heavier ordinance exploding around them like fireworks.

Afterward, she'd fought her way to the extraction coordinates with fists and boots and stolen weapons, only to find that she was too late. The others were gone. And when the dust settled after the rebels were beaten, she'd walked through the carnage left behind. Kritaani soldiers were hauling off corpses from a tangle of bodies that had apparently been mowed down while trying to get through the gap where Martinez had led the woman and her children.

She could still feel the terrible sensation of cold trickling through her chest as a body with a shock of red-orange hair was hauled off, followed by two more that were heartbreakingly small.

"I tried to save some of them," she said in a hoarse voice. "It… didn't work."

The words settled between them for a beat.

"And ever since then, you have no patience for those who would use civilians during a military conflict," said Kade. Another pause, and then, "I can't really blame you."

She tried to breathe through the visions of the past, knowing it would be pointless to attempt speaking until her body was done with its ill-timed panic attack.

Her commander had come back for her, returning to the extraction point after the battle was over and retrieving her. By rights, Martinez should have received a strongly worded reprimand at best, and a demotion out of her elite unit at worst. Instead, she received an honorable discharge, once it became obvious that the psychological fallout from what she'd experienced would prevent her from returning to her previous assignment.

It had taken years, but she'd eventually crafted a new life for herself, completing a master's degree at the largest university on Vithara—mingling with bright young minds like Jontalyss Lusivian that she found there, despite their age differences and the vast gulf between their life experiences. She'd like to think that she'd made an impression during her academic career. At least, between that and her military service, she'd managed to land a position in the Terra Novan contingent to Vithara. Which, in turn, had eventually led to her ambassadorship.

"If you don't want to watch a neurotonin addict attempting to fly a two-pilot ship through a wormhole junction without backup, you might want to come back to me now, Isadora," Kade said. The words were gruff, but not without compassion.

Martinez looked up, startled by the unexpected use of her first name. She felt dizzy and nauseated, weak as a kitten after a few minutes spent lost in the past, whereas the fight to overpower the transport crew had barely winded her. But she could focus again, and the tight band compressing her lungs had loosened enough for her to be able to breathe properly.

"Sorry," she rasped, looking down at her control panel to assess the situation.

"Don't be sorry," Kade said. "Just feed me some coordinates for the upcoming course change at the junction."

She thought she could detect a hint of strain behind the words, but it wasn't clear whether that was due to his growing neurotransmitter imbalance, or the rapidly approaching wormhole branch. After a moment spent double-checking the readings, she sent the numbers to his screen. The distorted view of subspace beyond the viewport twisted improbably, and their course settled again.

"Forty-five minutes to the station gate," Kade reported, still sounding a bit unsteady. "You should take over primary control again if you're able."

Gods, what a pair they made. Talk about the blind leading the blind.

"Okay, yeah, transferring control now." She checked the navigational readings. "Looks like a straight shot to Station Beta-Four from here, at least." Her mouth felt ridiculously dry. She swallowed, wishing she had access to a bottle of water or something.

Kade only grunted agreement.

Distraction. She needed a distraction. "You might as well tell me something from your past, to make us even," she said. "Fair's fair."

He was silent for a long moment.

"I got a girl pregnant when I was a teenager," he said eventually.

She glanced at him with interest. "Oh, yes? That's suitably scandalous to even up the score, I suppose. What happened afterward?"

He shifted in his seat. "My parents were still in good standing at the time. Wealthy, too. They paid off the girl's parents to keep it quiet, and the family moved away. I never spoke with her or heard from her again. Sometimes I wonder if she kept the child… if there's a person out there in the world who shares my benighted DNA." He made a low scoffing noise. "If so, they don't know how lucky they were—they avoided the family catastrophe a few years later, at least."

Martinez imagined that if he'd had a family of his own when Kovak decided to go after his parents, they might have ended up dead or imprisoned as well—or perhaps held as leverage against Kade, to secure his cooperation.

"Not knowing must be hard," she said.

"There are a lot of hard things to be found in this life, Ambassador," he said.

"Isn't that the truth," she agreed.

ELEVEN

Kade did his best to ignore the growing sensation of tiny insects scuttling through his veins as the wormhole gate to the isolated space station approached. The ambassador seemed to have recovered from her flashback, only the heavy circles under her eyes and the pinched skin around her mouth offering a visual reminder of her earlier mental lapse.

Sometimes he wondered if the whole damned galaxy was doomed to be a roiling mass of disasters for the rest of time, as sentient beings piled atrocity after atrocity on top of each other. Martinez hadn't given details about her experience in the badlands, but the mistake she'd made was obvious enough—caring too much in a situation where a tragic outcome was already a foregone conclusion.

It was a mistake he was all too familiar with, and if there was one upside to his imminent descent into madness and death, it was that he could try to delude himself into thinking that his friends would all survive in some kind of saccharine and totally unrealistic happy ending. And then he could let all of it go, so he could finally get some damned uninterrupted rest. An eternity of it, presumably.

He shouldn't have asked the ambassador to throw herself into the volcano for him by going to Ilarius in his stead. That had been unfair, not to mention irrational. If she were smart, she'd run back to either Vithara or Terra Nova and never give Ilarius another thought.

Kade knew she wouldn't do that, though. Just as he knew that Ash, Draven, Pax, and Nahleene wouldn't utilize the good sense the gods gave a snail, either. No, they'd all end up in the thick of it, because Xandrie-fucking-Kovak was destined to draw every single person Kade cared about into his all-consuming vortex of shit.

It was almost certainly due to the gradual un-raveling of his brain processes, but as they'd barreled headlong through the wormhole system, Kade found his thoughts turning more and more toward what-ifs.

What if he'd met Martinez under different cir-cumstances? What if he'd never been imprisoned, his mind and body broken on the wheel of Kovak's ambition? What if he and the ambassador had run across each other in peacetime diplomatic circles, without a planetary crisis looming over their heads? What if she'd showed up at his quarters one even-ing with a sly smile and a bottle of wine to share, when nothing else required their attention and no security forces arrived at the door to interrupt them with inconvenient murder charges?

He shook his head sharply, irritated with him-self. The answer was, that *nothing* would happen. Until *fucking Hunter* and his fucking insistence on falling for a human female in the middle of attempt-ed genocide, Kade doubted he would even have thought about the possibility of anything happening between them.

Did he have Hunter to blame for his gods-damned cock sitting up and taking notice of her without his permission? The embarrassing moment when he'd been playing at pinning Martinez against the wall in the holding cell hadn't been the first time it had happened, either.

The last thing he needed was his own body teasing him with what he could never have again. The way she'd looked up at him, though—speculation writ large across her face…

She didn't understand that he could no longer offer that kind of thing to her, or to any female. Not after what had been done to him in the prison. And that was its own kind of torture.

But it was too late now, anyway. Too late to have the conversation; too late to try and explain. Too late for anything except getting this bird safely docked at the station, and convincing her to aim a stun beam at his chest before he became a danger to her. To be brutally honest, he'd almost prefer a lethal blast at full power. But she'd never agree. He didn't dare try to do it himself, for fear his cravings would start whispering in his ear that she had neurotonin hidden somewhere, and the insanity would tempt him to turn the weapon on her instead.

Speaking of which…

He pulled the stolen weapon from his waistband with shaking fingers and proffered it to her, grip first. "Take this."

She glanced up from her readouts, confusion touching her features. "What? Why?"

He met her gaze and held it. "Why do you think?"

To his dismay, the words emerged noticeably slurred. They were too close to the gate for her to do more than take the weapon from him, with a look on her face that could only be described as distraught. He was losing control minute by minute.

Her continued safety in his presence was the only thing he had left to give her, and even that much would hinge on her willingness to act decisively once they were safely back in realspace.

The readouts in front of him were starting to blur and distort. His mind didn't want to untangle them... he needed a *fix*, damn it—not a bunch of wiggling numbers dancing across a screen.

"Kade." The word was soft, not at all like the ambassador's usual smooth, commanding delivery. He struggled to focus on what she was saying.

"Stay with me for a few more minutes, okay? I need you."

Lots of people had needed him for lots of different reasons over the years. Money. Contacts. Strategy. Well... mostly money, now that he really thought about it. They didn't generally tell him they needed him in such a sweetly desperate voice, though. He blinked rapidly until the readouts made sense again. Isadora Martinez needed him as a pilot. She needed him to help her navigate the wormhole entrance.

Cursing under his breath as his fingers fumbled at the controls, he sent her the navigational headings and time codes. And—*gods and prophets*—please let him not have made a mistake with any of them. Things went hazy for a bit, waves of heat and cold flooding through him. The jolt of the ship beneath him, combined with a heavy clanking noise, jarred every nerve in his overstressed body. He swallowed a growl of displeasure.

"We're docked," said the voice, still sounding unnaturally soft—like the speaker was trapped with a wild animal and didn't want to startle it. "We should go see if there's anything in the station medical pod that could help you."

Anger surged—had she not been listening to a word he'd said? Paranoia followed close on its heels. Was she trying to trick him in some way? Why was she suddenly so set on getting him off the ship? His thoughts ran in confused circles.

He shook his head sharply, clawing back an ounce of rationality. "No," he snapped. "You should stun me. Right now. It's not safe."

"I'm not stunning you." She sounded upset.

What the hell did *she* have to be upset about? *He* was the one who needed a godsdamned fix. But she continued before he could manage to moderate his response into something that wasn't rage.

"A stun beam would be a serious neural shock, Kade. It could speed the onset of brain damage. *I'm not stunning you.*"

He surged to his feet, dizziness making him stagger. "Either fucking shoot me or get me a fucking injection, damn you!" he nearly roared. Had he been right before? Had she been hiding neurotonin from him this *entire godsdamned time*? Was that why she wanted him off the ship, so she could keep it all for herself?

She raised her chin, not backing down despite the combination of fear and compassion in her hazel eyes. "I've got a better idea, so… come with me, okay? There's… there might be neurotonin inside the cell where they were keeping us earlier. Let's go look."

The possibility sent a fresh wave of cravings crashing over him, the feeling so powerful it nearly sent him to his knees. His vision tunneled for a moment, and when it spiraled out again, there was a small hand on his arm, guiding him down corridors that seemed to twist and warp around him.

If there was neurotonin in the cell, he was going to take every bit of it at once to make sure he never had to feel like this again. He hoped there were *buckets* of it. *Vats* of it. If he could just get *enough*, maybe this nightmare would finally end.

"Whoa, there," said the voice, and the grip on his arm tugged harder. He realized that he was listing heavily to one side, and made a concentrated effort to right himself. "Here we are," said the voice, and the gaping, tooth-filled maw looming in front of him resolved into a perfectly ordinary door.

He stumbled through it, desperate to get the fix that the voice had promised him.

"I'm so sorry, Kade," said the voice, and the door rolled shut behind him.

It didn't matter. He stumbled around, looking for his familiar time-release safe... for a cabinet... or a container... anything that might hold hypo-injectors for storage. There was nothing—where was it, *where was his neurotonin*? His movements grew frantic. Searching, searching. But the cell was just a blank box. There was nowhere that a hypo might be hidden.

Full-blown panic slammed into him like a runaway freighter. He couldn't be stuck in here without his fix. What had he been *thinking*, coming in here? *He needed a fucking fix*. Rage bubbled up like lava in his chest. *The voice*. It had told him to come inside—lured him here and trapped him, leaving him to die. A terrible, choked scream ripped free of his throat, scraping like sandpaper on its way out.

There was a figure on the other side of the door's viewing port. The rage turned outward, and

Kade flung himself bodily against the locked door. Mindless with desperation, he clawed and punched at the unforgiving metal. When that didn't so much as dent the barrier standing between him and the creature who'd sentenced him to this torment, he slammed his head against it instead, over and over, trying to quiet the maelstrom inside his brain.

Splatters of coppery orange blood smeared across the port, obscuring the horrified expression the creature wore. With each thump of flesh and bone against clearsteel, his view of his tormenter grew less and less distinct, but he knew she was still there. More screams of rage and agony echoed inside the bare cell, as Kade's world narrowed down to a burning point of absolute, single-minded *need*.

———◆———

Isadora Martinez fought desperately against her second panic attack in as many cycles, cursing herself for being the worst conceivable kind of fool. Prophets, what had she been *thinking*, ignoring Kade's directive to stun him as though she knew better than he did when it came to his own addiction?

Before her eyes, the self-possessed and carefully guarded man with whom she'd spent the past several weeks had been reduced to an injured animal, tearing itself apart to try to escape a trap. She'd been worried about the effects of a stun beam; now he was in danger of cracking his own skull open against the unforgiving clearsteel of the door panel.

With every horrible thing she'd seen in her life, this… *stripping away of sentience* might just be the worst. And it was her fault, for letting it happen. She had to act, even if doing so felt far too much like putting a rabid animal out of its misery.

"I'm sorry," she whispered. "Shit… *shit*. I'm sorry, I'm so sorry…"

Holding her breath, she readied one of the blasters, double-checking the stun setting. With her free hand, she unlocked the cell door. It rolled open and she retreated quickly, keeping the muzzle pointed at the expanding gap. Kade shoved his way through the instant there was enough space for him to do so, and charged at her with terrifying speed. The beam hit him high in the chest. His body seized in mid-lunge and fell to the deck, twitching.

Martinez stood frozen for long seconds, her heart threatening to pound right out of her ribcage. It took a moment to realize that the moisture dripping down her cheeks wasn't sweat, but tears. Her knees gave out, and she collapsed to the floor a few steps away from Kade's body.

She was alone, docked at an unmanned space station in the middle of nowhere. Safe, for a given definition—even if the thought made her want to collapse into hysterics and never stop screaming.

The uncoordinated spasms in Kade's arms and legs faded to stillness as she watched through tear-blurred eyes. Cautiously, she crawled to him, the blaster still held ready, just in case. The skin of his forehead radiated heat beneath her palm—he was burning up with fever, or perhaps just from the exertion of bodily attacking the door.

It felt… wrong to touch him like this, examining the wounds he'd inflicted on his face and hands in the throes of his delirium. As though she were stealing something from him. As though she didn't have the right to put her hands on him when he was unconscious and dead to the world.

It would be a struggle to move him, especially without risking further injury. He was simply too large and heavy for her. Maybe she could have dragged him when she was in active service, her muscles honed to hardness. But the years had leeched away that strength, which required more than a simple gym membership to maintain.

Dazed, she went looking for the nearest crew quarters, where she retrieved a pillow and blanket from the bunk. The bleeding from the split in his temple probably looked worse than it was, but she ventured onto the station and retrieved medical supplies from the pod. Against hope, she queried the AI for neurotonin, but of course the Vitharan communications liaison had checked the station's stores list thoroughly when they spoke earlier—there was none.

By the time she had Kade superficially patched up, his limbs straightened from their spider-like tangle and his head resting on the pillow, half a cycle had passed. It would be another five-and-a-half before the rescue ship arrived.

Too long.

Not good enough.

He'd be gone before they ever got here.

She had to do better than this. Kade deserved *better*, damn it.

As much as she hated to leave him lying unattended in the corridor, she knew she could do nothing useful for him by hovering. To do anything remotely proactive, she'd have to return to the bridge. She put one foot in front of the other like an automaton until she got there, aware that she was exhibiting several of the symptoms of shock—chills, shaking, disorientation, emotional withdrawal.

Fucking hell, how had she gone from being an elite soldier to being this... useless *thing*? It was *pathetic*. It was—

A light was blinking on the communications console, interrupting her self-flagellation—an incoming subspace message packet.

TWELVE

Martinez frowned, forcing her wits back into some semblance of functionality. The only people with the comm frequency for this ship would be the Vitharan and Terra Novan authorities she'd contacted earlier, presumably along with whoever had originally sanctioned the mission on Ilarius.

It seemed doubtful that the Ilarians would risk implicating themselves by initiating communications. Though if they had, Martinez thought she might get some emotional satisfaction from verbally ripping them a few new orifices. She flicked the switch to play the recorded message, still feeling oddly detached from her surroundings.

"N'komo to Martinez, please respond. Thought you'd given up pulling dangerous duty assignments these days, Major."

Surprise punctured the dullness of shock like a needle pricking a balloon, as the unexpected familiarity of her former commander's voice carried through the tinny speakers. She scrabbled at the controls that would allow her to respond.

"Commander N'komo? I'm here! How did you get this frequency?"

Back in the day, she'd have found herself scrubbing the latrine block with a toothbrush if she'd responded to a hail in such an unprofessional way. Bizarrely, the thought was comforting—a connection to simpler times, before everything in her life had gotten muddled and complex. She bit her lip as she waited out the lag time.

"It's Captain, now—and I may be part of the brass, but I'm still connected to the gossip vines, Martinez. A former aide of mine contacted me to let me know that you were in a bit of a scrape. Out by Station Beta-Four somewhere?"

Her heart gave an odd stutter she vaguely recognized as *hope*. N'komo wasn't the type to comm someone merely for the purpose of offering sympathy.

"Captain N'komo. Congratulations… and *by sin*, it's good to hear your voice, ma'am. Your information is accurate. We're docked at the station itself. I have a Vithii male here, suffering from advanced neurotonin withdrawal. I had to stun him to keep him from injuring himself. An emergency ship is on route to us from Vithara, ETA slightly more than five cycles. That won't be soon enough for him, though."

She held her breath while she waited for the message to go through.

"Hmm. Lucky I happened by, in that case. The lead ships of the Terra Novan contingent to Ilarius are approximately two cycles away from your location. I'll have one of the medical vessels rerouted to rendezvous with you as soon as possible."

Two cycles. Would it be soon enough? There was no way to know, but it was a lot better bet than the Vitharan rescue ship at this point. Her heart skipped and thudded, a counterpoint to the throbbing headache that had been building over the past few cycles.

"That would be... very much appreciated, ma'am. Can you confirm that the medical ship is able to treat neurotonin withdrawal?"

"*If it's a Vithii thing, they probably don't stock it directly, but all of the medical vessels are equipped with the latest technology. I'm sure they'll be able to synthesize it with no problems. I'll put the ship's chief medical officer in touch with you directly so you can describe the symptoms. Stiff upper lip, Martinez.*"

"Thank you, Ma'am," she breathed, sitting down rather abruptly in the pilot's chair as her knees decided to take another time out.

"*N'komo out,*" came the brisk reply. The owner of the voice had never been one for sentiment, even if she *had* come to Martinez's rescue twice now—once when N'komo had returned to the extraction point to retrieve her prodigal underling after the Badlands Rebellion, and once in the middle of deep space.

It made sense, even if it hadn't occurred to Martinez until now. Terra Novan forces were en route to Ilarius, traveling a day or so ahead of the Vitharan contingent. She and Kade had also been in the wormhole system, en route to Ilarius—albeit from Vithara rather than Terra Nova. They'd been traveling in parallel, converging through the convoluted subspace system.

The comm panel pinged with a new packet a few minutes later—a communication from the medical officer N'komo had promised her. Martinez forced herself to relay the history of Kade's condition calmly and succinctly, answering the doctor's questions as much as she was able. The woman signed off with the promise that she would have the best available treatment and be ready to receive her patient by the time the ship arrived.

"Looks like your friend has the honor of being the first casualty in the joint allied operation against Ilarius," the doctor said dryly, before excusing herself to go get things prepared.

The speaker crackled into silence, and Martinez was once more alone with an unconscious Vithii and her own misgivings. She knew she couldn't afford to stray from the comms station for long, lest she miss an important message from N'komo or the medical officer. Still, she couldn't stop herself checking on Kade—even though there was nothing she could do to help him until the Terra Novan ship arrived with its lifesaving neurotonin and medical equipment.

Would it be enough save his life, though? From what she gathered, it all depended on how much damage had been done to his brain by the time help got here. He looked far worse than when she'd left him to go to the bridge, his features appearing pale and sunken in the corridor's harsh lighting.

For lack of any more constructive options, she knelt next to him and took his long-fingered hand in hers. There was no response—not that she'd expected there to be, but his skin was disconcertingly waxy and chilled against hers. He'd been feverish before, and she hoped that wasn't a bad sign. He had calluses, she noticed, and not just on his trigger finger, either. They were the calluses of a man who worked with his hands. She wondered how he'd gotten them—this mysterious underworld businessman with a sideline in vigilante justice and revolutionary politics.

"Hey," she said quietly, having no idea if he would be able to hear her, or understand what she was saying. "Looks like the cavalry's coming after all. Hold on for me, will you? Help will be here way sooner than we thought."

<hr>

In the end, it took two cycles and ten minutes before a Terra Novan medical team entered the transport's airlock with an antigrav stretcher and a suitcase full of emergency gear. Five minutes after that, they were whisking Kade back to their ship, Martinez jogging along in their wake.

Being suddenly among allies and in safe surroundings was oddly disorienting. The medical vessel was exactly what its name implied—a dedicated site for battle triage and combat injury treatment. The chief officer was competent and efficient, but military medicine wasn't geared toward bedside manner. Particularly not for bystanders who weren't actually injured. Martinez found herself shunted out of the way, barely more than an afterthought.

It was a relief when N'komo contacted her via video feed to debrief her. Her old field commander gave her an incisive visual sweep through the screen.

"Not sure civvy life agrees with you, Martinez."

Martinez had to swallow a bark of laughter that would have come out sounding more than a little hysterical. One thing was certain—military life still suited N'komo, every bit as much now as it had back in the day. The shiny new captain's insignia did nothing to diminish the fierceness of her dark-skinned visage, marred on one side by a vicious scar running from the corner of her eyelid to the corner of her mouth. Martinez remembered the day N'komo had gotten it, during a hostage rescue mission in the mountains west of New Shanghai.

"I'm not sure it does, either," she replied after a short pause. With something like relief, she fell into the familiar rhythms of the debriefing, clarifying several points about the situation on Vithara, in addition to the events surrounding the kidnapping.

"*The Vitharans are a day behind us,*" N'komo said. "*And the Maelfians are following a few cycles behind them, if all goes to plan.*"

When do things like this ever *go to plan*? Martinez thought.

Aloud, she only said, "I appreciate the update, Captain."

"*I'm afraid I can't spare a ship to take you back to Vithara, Ambassador,*" N'komo said, using her current title for the first time. Martinez thought she detected a note of challenge behind the words.

"Doesn't matter. I'm sticking with the fleet," she said. "I made a promise to see the events on Ilarius through."

N'komo gave a curt nod of approval. "*Guess it works out well, then. I'll be in touch.*"

With nothing else to occupy her time, Martinez fretted. Kade was in critical condition and on life support, but beyond that, updates were thin on the ground. Cycles slipped by on the chronometer, the medical ship rejoining the Terra Novan armada and hurtling toward its appointment at the edge of Ilarian-controlled space.

It was apparent that her home world hadn't been messing around when they mustered their response—this was a massive military force. She wished desperately that Kade were awake to see it. Or, failing that, she wished she were at least allowed in to see him, so she could tell him about it.

Of course, that thought was her brain's cue to start worrying about how much damage Kade had suffered, before the medics had gotten to him and attempted to stabilize him. The words 'critical condition' and 'life support' made his situation sound dire, and she tried to ready herself for the reality that he might not be the same person she'd come to know over the past weeks… if he even survived.

Martinez tried to sleep for a bit, but only managed a bit of restless dozing—this, despite her usual ability to drop off anywhere and anytime, no matter the conditions. Eventually, a nurse came and got her, letting her know that Kade was stabilized as much as he could be, and that she would be allowed to sit with him if she so desired.

She swallowed hard as the nurse ushered her into the curtained-off area containing a medical cot and far too much beeping machinery. Kade was on a respirator, with IV lines running in both arms and sensors attached to every available bit of skin. He looked… like a corpse. A dead body that some mad scientist had hooked up to enough pumps and dripping chemicals to keep suspended in a cruel semblance of life. She came to an abrupt halt, just inside the flimsy barrier of the curtains—frozen in place.

Martinez had seen more death and carnage over the years than she cared to remember. Some of it had scarred her, perhaps permanently. All of it had been violent. Savage, brutal injuries from weapons. People blown apart by bombs, or with holes torn through them by blaster fire. She'd meted out that kind of death. Hell, she'd done so mere hours ago when she and Kade took the interstellar transport by killing its Ilarian crew.

By comparison, this was… clinical. Kade's injuries were healed. The doctors had repaired the wound above his collarbone where the pump had been torn out. There was barely a trace of the injury to be seen—the same for the splits and bruises on his face. Kade just looked… *absent*. Like he was a shell with nothing left inside to animate him. Martinez wrenched herself free of her paralysis and moved to the chair that had been placed next to the cot.

"The doctors have stabilized his neurotonin levels," the nurse said dispassionately. "There was quite a bit of ancillary chemical imbalance in the brain, and his blood oxygen levels were dangerously low. There's no way of knowing what the long-term effects will be. They intend to consult with Vitharan specialists once the fleet shows up, and possibly transfer him to one of the Vitharan medical ships."

"Thank you," Martinez said faintly, her gaze still fixed on the dark hollows beneath Kade's closed eyes.

The nurse left her to it, and Martinez made herself take Kade's hand—careful not to dislodge the IV line. As it had earlier on the transport, his skin felt waxy and chilled. He had a full sleeve tattoo covering his arm from wrist to shoulder—dark imagery of skulls and weapons intertwined in a macabre dance. She would never have guessed it was there, hidden as it had always been beneath his sober, buttoned down suits and shirts.

She wondered if there was a story behind it.

"Hey," she said softly. "Looks like we're both going back to Ilarius after all. You won't believe this—but we got picked up by the Terra Novan fleet heading there to kick the Regime's ass. They're not kidding around, either. This armada is *massive*. And that's before you add in the Vitharans and Maelfians. I wish you'd wake up so you could see it…"

<hr>

Twenty-eight cycles later, Kade had still not woken up. In fact, there had been no change whatsoever in his condition, beyond a brief scare when his readings had crashed and Martinez had been summarily chivvied out of the room for a cycle before being allowed back in again.

She'd done her best to stay on top of the tactical situation concerning the fleet's arrival at the edge of Ilarian space, but she was not an official part of the mission. She was also unwilling to demand information from those in charge—even N'komo—when doing so might interfere with their duties at a delicate time.

As was so often the case during military operations, so far the general sense of things was 'hurry up and wait.' They were here, and at last update, the Vitharans had joined them at the edge of the system a couple of cycles ago. Ilarian forces were gathering warily inside the planetary perimeter, both sides adopting a wait-and-see attitude toward whatever happened next. In the allies' case, she guessed they were waiting on the Maelfian contingent to arrive before making formal contact.

"This was always my least favorite part of an operation," she told Kade's comatose form. "The waiting, I mean."

"Yeah… mine, too," came a heavily accented Vithii voice from behind her.

Martinez whirled in her seat, not letting go of her grip on Kade's hand. Two newcomers entered the cramped space, one broad and heavy featured with amber-gold eyes and copper-colored spikes of hair; the other lithe and olive-skinned with worry clouding his dark, human gaze.

"Hello, Ambassador," Ashildir Purandhri greeted in a somber tone, his eyes sliding past her to land on the figure in the cot.

THIRTEEN

"Mr. Purandhri," she said in surprise. "Krau Draven. I...wasn't expecting to see you here." A sudden wash of irrational guilt tightened her throat at the realization that these were Kade's friends, and she hadn't managed to keep him safe in their absence.

"Just Ash and Draven if you please, Ambassador," Ash said. "No need for formality on our end of things. How's he doing? We weren't able to get any detailed information beyond the fact that you'd been picked up, and that he was in critical condition."

The lump in her throat grew worse, and she swallowed to clear it. "He's been... upgraded to serious but stable condition. We were kidnapped by Regime operatives en route to the Vitharan orbital holding facility. We managed to overpower the guards and take control of the ship that was transporting us to Ilarius, but Kade's neurotonin pump was destroyed during the fight."

She realized she was worrying the skin on the back of Kade's hand with her thumb, and stilled the nervous movement.

"He went into withdrawal before you could get help?" Draven asked.

"Yes," she said quietly. "I... had to stun him to keep him from hurting himself." The words came out like a reluctant confession.

"You did the right thing," Ash said without hesitation. "As you can imagine, with the life he leads, it's not the first time something like this has happened."

"He'll be all right," Draven added optimistically. "He's stubborn as hell, always has been. Besides, I don't think he'd miss the next few days for anything."

Martinez envied Draven his faith.

"What are you two doing here, anyway?" she asked, to change the subject.

Draven gave a rueful snort. "Well, it's not like *we* were gonna miss the next few days, either."

Ash moved to the far side of the cot, looking down at Kade with a furrowed brow. "Ilarius is our home," he said absently. "Our friends are risking their lives there as we speak. Our place is with them."

"We'll be making for the Capital as soon as it's feasible," Draven added.

Rather than asking if they'd cleared that plan with the allied commanders, Martinez merely said, "When you do, I need to go with you." Her hand tightened on Kade's, and she saw Ash's eyes track the small movement before lifting to hers.

"Are you certain?" he said. "It's likely to be an armed free-for-all down there, and someone should be up here to watch over Kade."

She held the human's eyes evenly. "I promised him I'd go in his stead, and make sure Kovak got taken out."

Draven gave a low whistle. "He really asked you to do that for him, huh?"

Ash was still watching her closely. "He must have quite a high opinion of you, Ambassador," he said. "Kade's not generally prone to making requests of people. Especially not ones like that."

"Please," she said, "call me Marti—" She paused. "Call me Isadora. As you correctly point out, these aren't really professional circumstances."

"As you wish, Isadora," Ash said graciously. "Thank you for getting him help before it was too late."

A nurse bustled in—one Martinez recognized from the group that had retrieved Kade from the Ilarian transport. "Excuse me, you three. Krau Finisterre is to be readied for transfer to a Vitharan medical ship. I'll need all of you to leave now."

"Of course," Ash said. He leaned down and clasped a hand on Kade's shoulder. "All right, you bitter old reprobate. Looks like they're kicking us out. If you can hear me, you need to wake up in time to see the fireworks kick off. After all we've been through to get here, I'd hate for you to miss the denouement."

"He'll wake up. You'll see," Draven said, with the same determined optimism as before. "Come on—let's go, you two. We can head back to the Vitharan command ship and get the details of where they're taking Kade from that side of the aisle. I just hope Pax shows up soon with the Maelfians."

Draven and Ash did not share Martinez's problem of being unaffiliated with the official mission. Apparently, they'd finagled themselves into consultant positions, due to some combination of their knowledge of the situation on the ground on Ilarius, and, she suspected, Ash's silver tongue.

Whatever the case, the three of them were currently on the bridge of the Vitharan command ship. There, they stood watching with the rest of the crew as the Ilarian defense forces advanced from their defensive positions in planetary orbit, to meet the allied ships at the boundary of the system.

The Vitharan fleet commander, a no-nonsense man in his early sixties, ran his gaze over the bridge crew as he got up from his chair. "Look sharp, everyone. It appears we won't be waiting on our Maelfian allies before making contact, after all. Ensign Graath, send a message fleet-wide—hold position, take no offensive action. Then hail the lead Ilarian vessel."

Martinez stood at the back with Draven and Ash, staying out of everyone's way as the comm officer carried out her orders. A few moments later, the viewscreen resolved into the image of a square-jawed Vithii in his early thirties, with dark hair set in aggressive spikes and muscles bulging beneath his brown military uniform. An instant later, a smaller inset appeared, showing Captain N'komo standing on the bridge of the Terra Novan command ship.

The Vithii commander spoke. "*Outworlder fleet, this is Lieutenant Commander Makeem of the Ilarian Defense Force. You are infringing on sovereign Ilarian space. Desist and return to your own territories.*"

For cultural reasons, Martinez knew that the Vitharan commander had been tasked with taking the lead in any negotiations, since he was more likely to be taken seriously by the Regime than a human female like N'komo.

He squared his shoulders and lifted his chin. "There has been no territorial infringement, Lieutenant Commander, as you are no doubt well aware. Not *yet*, at any rate. On behalf of the allied forces of Vithara, Terra Nova, and Maelfius, I wish to negotiate a direct meeting with Premiere Kovak. The location of the meeting is open for debate—we will accept safe passage to the Ilarian Capital for a combined Vitharan and Terra Novan contingent, or the Premiere may choose to meet us at a neutral off-world site within the next three Standard days."

The Lieutenant Commander narrowed his eyes, like a young lion sizing up an older male for a fight. *"The Premiere does not recognize the legitimacy of Vithara's attempt at intimidation tactics,"* he said, not even giving Terra Nova or Maelfius the courtesy of a mention. *"There will be no meeting. My orders are to repel this unlawful enemy incursion by whatever means necessary."*

Martinez saw the Vitharan commander's shoulders rise and fall almost imperceptibly on a tired sigh.

"Son," he said, "the other members of the Seven Systems aren't enemies to Ilarius unless you plan on *making* them enemies, right here and now. Vithara and Terra Nova together represent your planet's largest trading partners. For that reason, we *will* speak with your Premiere regarding the serious concerns that have been raised about his recent policies. We can do it the easy way, or we can do it the hard way. Now go send a message to your superiors, and let us know what you hear back."

With that, he made a cutting-off motion with one hand, and the comm officer ended the transmission. N'komo remained on the screen, and she gave a rueful snort once it was clear that communications to and from the Ilarian ship had been terminated.

"*I can't deny that was satisfying to watch, Commander,*" she said. "*Though I'll wager there's an ambassador on your bridge right now who's cringing so hard she's likely to strain something.*"

It was true that Martinez had winced a bit at the bluntness of the Vitharan officer's ultimatum. However, like N'komo, she also couldn't deny that a part of her had found it rather satisfying.

The Vitharan commander turned to look back at her, raising an eyebrow.

She met his gaze head-on. "Yeah… so, honestly? When it comes to Kovak and his Regime lackeys—after being kidnapped and framed for murder, I'm pretty much over the whole diplomacy thing."

Beside her, Ash's huff of amusement was quickly stifled, but Draven didn't even try to hide his low rumble of appreciation.

"*I already tried to tell her she wasn't cut out for civilian life,*" N'komo quipped over the screen. Then her expression sobered. "*Look lively, now. They're on the move over there.*"

Martinez looked at the holographic tactical display over the weapons board. The Ilarian forces were scrambling into a hemispherical deployment, a move that would allow them to flank the allied armada. She frowned as several of the Ilarian ships near the edge of the phalanx crossed the border into unaffiliated space.

The screen crackled into static for a moment before reforming into the image of the Ilarian Lieutenant Commander.

"*Outworlder fleet*," he said in an icy tone. "*My orders stand. Retreat now—the Ilarian Regime will brook no interference in its internal affairs from other planets.*"

"Stand firm, everyone," the Vitharan commander told his crew in a low voice, before toggling open the comms mic. "Lieutenant Commander Makeem, your fleet is entering unclaimed inter-system territory. Any act of aggression outside of Ilarian-controlled space would constitute an act of war. Consider your next actions carefully."

Makeem's lip curled. "*On the contrary, it is you who should consider your actions. Our glorious Premiere has claimed all territory within two parsecs of the blessed homeworld as being under Ilarian control.*"

Several people on the bridge glanced at each other in consternation at the unmitigated gall of the claim.

Yeah…that's not how it works, Martinez thought. *That's not how any of this works. Fucking prophets, why didn't someone manage to get rid of this Kovak asshole before he went full-on psychotic dictator?*

Apparently, the outrageous claim was also too much for N'komo. Her scarred visage darkened like storm clouds. "*Your 'glorious Premiere' is still part of a multi-system negotiated alliance, and in the Seven Systems, we don't annex neutral territory just by claiming it's ours. Make a move outside of established territorial borders, and you'll be starting a war that won't end well for you.*"

The tactical display lit up with amethyst warnings as more Ilarian ships approached from the planet, ranging in a second rank behind the first group.

"Why do I get the feeling we're about to regret the Maelfians being late?" Ash asked, in a tone laced with irony.

No sooner had he finished speaking, than one of the Vitharan ships altered position to protect a medical ship that had come into direct line of fire from the edges of the expanding hemisphere of Ilarian vessels.

"*Damn it!*" N'komo cursed, as someone on the Ilarian side succumbed to an itchy trigger finger—a beam of phased energy shooting out at the ship that had broken position. "*Battle stations, everybody! Time to stop jabbering and get this shit done.*"

"All hands, prepare to engage," said the Vitharan commander. "Fighters, ready for scramble."

At Ash's touch to her elbow, Martinez looked around and found a seat to strap herself into. Ash and Draven did the same, all three of them turning to watch the tactical display with tense expressions. The scene quickly descended into chaos as the rest of the Ilarian fleet took the first shot as an excuse to engage.

The allied fleet broke formation to evade the Ilarian attempts to further flank them. Draven was watching the display closely. His brows furrowed, and he let out a sharp curse.

"Commander! The squadron of new arrivals with the beta-six-four ID codes are from the cyborg division—don't let them get close enough to attempt boarding!"

Martinez felt her stomach dip in a way that had little to do with the command ship's sudden defensive maneuvers. Everyone in the Seven Systems was aware of the Ilarian cyborg program. It was feared for a reason. Fighting the tech-enhanced Vithii super-soldiers ship-to-ship would be bad enough, but if any of them managed to get aboard the allied vessels, there would be a slaughter.

"Understood," the Vitharan commander said grimly, before relaying the information to the rest of the fleet.

She couldn't help sparing a thought for Kade, helpless in his coma aboard one of the medical ships. At the first sign of hostility, the hospital vessels had all been surrounded, retreating to the middle of the fleet for protection. But they were also unarmed, and while purposely attacking them would be a war crime, Martinez wasn't at all sure that would act as a deterrent for the Regime at this point.

Orders and reports buzzed around the bridge, a constant low murmur of communication. It was clear that neither N'komo nor the Vitharan commander were the type to lead from the rear. The ship vibrated with the low roar of the phase cannons firing, and torpedoes spat from the weapons tubes in a regular pattern as they blazed away at the Ilarian forces trying to hem them in.

The Premiere had obviously been busy behind the scenes with Ilarius' shipbuilding facilities. Martinez wouldn't have credited the little colony planet with having the kind of manufacturing capacity to expand their fleet to this extent. They must have been throwing everything they had at the allied armada, too, because the collection of Vitharan and

Terra Novan ships that had so awed her with its size was beginning to struggle against the Ilarian defensive forces.

"Hard to port!" the commander snapped. "Z-minus ten thousand meters, thrusters on full!"

Martinez saw the line of torpedoes coming at them an instant before they struck, tearing through the shields and exploding against the hull with a deafening shudder of protesting metal. The inertial dampeners gave up the fight to absorb the shock wave, and Martinez was thrown hard against her restraints as sparks and electrical explosions erupted around the bridge.

The sounds of screaming could be heard, as well—attenuated against her battered eardrums. For a terrifying moment, everything went dark, only the sputtering electrical fires providing a surreal, flickering illumination. The air was choked with the smell of ozone and burning duraplast. Moments later, the emergency lighting painted everything violet, and the automated fire suppression systems smothered anything that was still sparking.

"Medics to the bridge!" the commander barked, supporting an arm that was clearly broken with his free hand.

Several of the bridge officers lay slumped in their seats or on the deck, thrown clear of their restraints. Martinez fumbled at her straps until they popped free, ignoring what was likely going to be some spectacular bruising across her shoulders and torso where they had dug into her flesh. Beside her, Ash and Draven were doing the same.

"We have flight experience, Commander," Draven said. "Ambassador—can you man the weapons station?"

"Yes," she said and turned to the injured Vitharan in the center chair. "Orders, Commander?"

He nodded. "Do it. I'll get replacement crew up here as soon as I can."

The bridge doors hissed open, and several medics rushed out. Ash and Draven were already easing unconscious crewmembers out of their chairs so they could take over the controls.

"Helm or navigation?" Ash asked.

"I've got navigation," Draven said promptly. "Your reflexes are better on helm."

Martinez slid into the seat at the weapons station, running her eyes over the console for a moment before she set to work rerouting things past damaged controls. "Looks like we've still got phase cannons and starboard torpedoes. Port tubes are damaged, though."

The commander settled himself back into his chair with a grimace, waving off the medical officer who tried to approach him. "Protect the port side as best you can. Covering fire with the phase cannons. Engineering?"

The intercom speaker spit static for a moment or two before a Vitharan voice came through. "*We're shaken up a bit, Commander, but no serious damage to the engines. Port shields are down, and thrusters on that side are at fifty percent; everything else is holding.*"

Martinez laid down a pattern of fire toward the approaching Ilarian vessels, while Ash slewed the vessel around until their damaged port side was protected by other allied vessels in the area. Her eyes flicked between the controls and the sputtering holographic tactical display. In the background, she was vaguely aware of the medics carting the injured and dead crewmembers off the bridge.

"Cyborg vessels approaching in an attack formation," she reported.

"Well, *that's* not good," Ash observed grimly.

"Torpedoes, full spread," the commander ordered. "Hit them with everything we've got left."

Martinez did, knowing it wouldn't be enough. Around them, allied ships were trying to reorganize to come to their aid, but most of them had their own problems to deal with. The Vitharan's and Terra Novan's attempts to avoid appearing excessively confrontational during the initial contact with Ilarian defense forces not only hadn't worked, it had put them at a serious tactical disadvantage once the shooting had started.

They'd been gambling that Ilarius wouldn't risk a full-on war by firing the first shot in what was widely recognized as neutral interstellar territory. Unfortunately, as gambling losses went, this one was shaping up to be kind of a biggie.

The cyborg attack wing was closing in at blazing speeds from below them, dodging their fire with inhuman agility. Martinez raked a phase cannon beam through the mass of fighters, feeling a wash of vicious satisfaction as one ship was too slow to evade, its wing vaporizing in a shower of exploding gas. The damaged ship spiraled out of control, taking out two of its neighbors in the process.

Later, Martinez would take time to wonder how she'd slid so softly and easily back into the role of *killer*. At that moment, she was too busy trying to come up with some way to stop the remaining mass of ships bearing down on them. Nothing useful presented itself.

"Those Ilarian fighters were faster than this ship, even before we lost full power on the port thrusters," Ash said in a tight voice. "If the cyborgs get aboard, tell security to aim for the head—and even that may be an iffy proposition. Body shots will barely slow them down."

The ship shuddered as it took another glancing strike. The emergency power flickered, then stabilized. When the tactical display came back online, new ships were approaching.

Just what we need, Martinez thought. "More ships incoming," she reported, peering at the ID codes. A jolt of surprise caught her. "Wait—it's the Maelfians!"

"Oh, good," the Vitharan commander muttered. "The peaceniks are here. All of our problems are solved."

Martinez shared the commander's opinion of Maelfius as a military power—namely, that it wasn't one. However, at this point she was more than willing to be proven wrong. The viewscreen lit with a pixelated view of Captain N'komo, her bridge looking somewhat better off than theirs.

"Fresh troops incoming," she said tersely. "Hang tight, we're swinging around for a strafing run from the sunward side."

Martinez sent another wave of phase cannon beams into the approaching cyborg formation, but they were almost too close now for ranged weapons to be useful. Ash sent the ship into a dive that threatened the already strained inertial dampeners, making her stomach swoop. At the same instant, the combined Maelfian and Terra Novan forces descended into the melee.

A heavy clanking noise proclaimed that one of the cyborg ships had managed to match Ash's frantic maneuvers and latch onto their hull for boarding.

"Sidearms," the commander ordered. "Sub-lieutenant Kristaal, make sure everyone on the bridge has a weapon. Quickly, now."

Martinez accepted the blaster she was handed, giving it a quick once-over to check the settings. Around them the battle raged on, as the Maelfians plowed into the fight with more skill and aggression than she would have given them credit for.

The intercom crackled. "Security reports two cyborgs intruders on level three. Several dead and injured reported during the initial skirmish. They appear to be making for the bridge."

Because of course they fucking are, Martinez thought ruefully, setting the blaster on her lap with the grip within easy reach of her right hand.

"Man your stations," the commander ordered. "Kristaal, Shenrath—with me."

Martinez glanced up just long enough to see the commander set himself with a clear line of sight to the bridge doors, the other two crewmen flanking him. The wrist of his broken arm was shoved carelessly into his belt to keep the useless limb from flopping around, and she felt a surge of fresh respect for the guy. It took a real leader to put himself in death's way so his people could continue to do their jobs while he protected them personally.

The doors slid open and a cyborg staggered out, its face expressionless and its torso riddled with blaster craters. Even with the horrific wounds, the thing fired its weapon with deadly accuracy at the three defenders standing between it and the rest of the bridge crew.

FOURTEEN

Kristaal fell under the cyborg's deadly assault, even as the other two defenders aimed for the cyborg's head and let fly. There was an explosion of bone, gristle, and metal implants as half of its skull disappeared. Terrifyingly, the thing's body continued forward for a few more steps, its weapon still firing with eerie precision, before it collapsed to the deck, twitching.

Martinez kept her grip on her sidearm with one hand, and kept firing the ship's phase cannons with the other—trying to split her attention between the doors and her contribution to the space battle. Sure enough, no sooner had its comrade fallen, than the second cyborg emerged uninjured through the doors, having used its damaged partner as a sacrificial distraction.

The Vitharan commander and the other defending crewmen fell under fire from the creature's weapon in the first instant. Martinez, Draven, and the remaining crew who could do so without immediately causing the ship to crash rolled out of their chairs, seeking cover and a clear line of fire toward the doors. Ash hunched over the helm as blaster beams crisscrossed the bridge, unable to abandon his post lest they ram another ship in the melee surrounding them.

Draven shot a lightning glance at the human before placing his body between Ash and the cyborg, firing wildly at the intruder as he did so. The cyborg was so fast it was terrifying, dodging and ducking even as stray beams from the remaining bridge crew tore chunks out of its body. More crewmen fell, and a shot from the creature's weapon heated the air next to Martinez's ear before exploding part of the console behind her.

Ignoring the close call, she took a deep breath and let it out—allowing the thing's movement to slide past her conscious mind to the part of her that acted on instinct. Steadying her weapon, she fired at a place several centimeters to the left of it, relief flooding her when its erratic movement took it right into the path of the beam. Brain and skull pieces exploded in a messy splatter. As the first one had, it stumbled forward a few more steps, still firing at them even with a massive chunk blown out of its head.

When it finally fell, she straightened from her crouch and looked around. Several people lay dead. Ash was still clinging to his controls, piloting the ship through the chaos of ships and debris surrounding them. Draven was already sliding back into the navigator's seat, ignoring the blackened patch on the shoulder of his flightsuit—the result of a near miss from a blaster beam set on full strength.

"Who's next in command?" Martinez asked hoarsely.

"The Chief Engineer," said one of the handful of surviving crewmen.

"Get him up here," she ordered. "Then contact the rest of the fleet."

"Looks like the fleet's finally got the Ilarian defense forces on the run," Draven said, flipping through sensor readings one-handed.

Martinez checked the tactical display to confirm it, relief flooding her as she took in the battlefield. Allied forces had succeeded in hemming in the remaining planetary security vessels, and were picking them off as she watched. The Ilarian command ship floated in a lazy spiral—unpowered, with its atmosphere venting from a massive rip in the hull.

"*N'komo to Vitharan command vessel,*" said a welcome voice from the comms.

Video was non-functional, but Martinez routed the audio to her station and answered.

"Captain N'komo, this is the Vitharan command vessel," she said. "The ship's commander is dead, and we've taken heavy damage and casualties. Need assistance ASAP."

"*Copy that. The acting leader of the Ilarian forces has just surrendered. We'll send you some support staff just as soon as all of the enemy ships are secure.*"

"Understood," Martinez said. Unable to help herself, she added, "Are the medical vessels all right? No damage or casualties?"

She could feel Ash and Draven's eyes on her as they waited for the answer with as much impatience as she felt.

"*Two of the Terra Novan hospital ships took light damage, but that's it,*" said the captain. "*Help will be with you soon. N'komo out.*"

As soon as the news that none of the Vitharan medical transports had been damaged and Kade was safe penetrated her brain, so did the adrenaline crash. Post-battle shakes had always afflicted her during the years spanning her military career, but for some reason they seemed even worse than usual this time.

"Out of practice," she murmured, not realizing she'd spoken aloud until Ash glanced over at her.

"All right over there, Ambassador?" he asked, not sounding at all like someone who'd just kept his back turned to a deadly cyborg firefight, so he could continue piloting a damaged ship through the middle of a chaotic space battle. In that moment, Martinez kind of hated him for his preternatural calm.

"Fine," she said. "And I told you before—call me Isadora."

Draven gave Ash a pointed look. "What... you're not gonna ask if *I'm* all right, then? Careful, you'll hurt my feelings."

Ash snorted. "Since I can smell the burning flesh from here, I figured the 'no' was rather a foregone conclusion. Maybe you'd better get down to medical before the battle high wears off and you actually start to feel that shoulder wound."

"I will in a bit," Draven said. "I expect they've got more serious stuff to worry about than a blaster graze. Isadora, can you see a fighter somewhere in that mess with call sign epsilon-four-two-eight-delta? Assuming he came here in Hunter's fighter and managed to avoid getting vaped during the battle, that'll be our friend Pax."

Martinez nursed the damaged display into showing the ships' ID codes, searching for the string Draven had given her. The crewmembers that were still ambulatory made the rounds, checking for others who were still alive. Someone must have given the all-clear via intraship communications, because a fresh round of medics swarmed onto the bridge and started work to stabilize the injured survivors.

Eventually, Martinez found the right fighter in the chaos outside. "I've got your friend located, gentlemen. Hailing him now."

Draven—now sporting a cooling bandage around his upper arm—crossed to her station and leaned over her shoulder to flip on the mic as Pax responded.

"*This is allied fighter epsilon-four-two-eight-delta*," came a flat, faintly mechanical-sounding voice. Martinez tried to hold back her instinctive shudder at the idea that the voice belonged to a cyborg not so very dissimilar to the two currently lying on the deck with their heads blown off.

"Pax!" Draven exclaimed. "It's Draven. I'm on the Vitharan command vessel with Ash and Ambassador Martinez. Thanks for bringing the cavalry—though we could have used you a bit sooner."

"*It is gratifying to hear your voice, Draven. Ion storms at the edge of the Maelfian system required a detour that delayed our arrival, unfortunately.*" A slight pause. "*Is Kade not with you there?*"

"He's down for the count," Draven told him. "Critical neurotonin withdrawal. They've got him on one of the Vitharan hospital ships. Where's Nahleene?"

"*She is on one of the medical vessels that took minor damage, but she reports that she is unharmed. I will collect her and come to you.*"

Martinez perked up. "No, wait. Not here. Meet us on the hospital ship where Kade is. I'll transmit its ID and coordinates."

Draven gave a nod of agreement. "Good plan."

"*Ambassador Martinez, I presume?*" came the vaguely disconcerting cyborg voice. "*Very well, I will await the information and meet you there.*"

"At which point we need to figure out the best way to get to the surface and meet up with the others," Draven added.

"*Indeed. Pax out.*"

Martinez acknowledged, and sent the coordinates for the ship where they would meet. "A cyborg of few words, I gather?" she observed, still trying to wrap her brain around the idea of such a being as an ally.

"Not necessarily," Ash replied. "At times, he can be quite loquacious."

"As long as he's got some good ideas on how we can find Hunter and the rest of the Shadow Wing, he can talk my ear off as much as he wants," Draven put in. "We need to get down to the Capital. Once word of what's happened here leaks on Ilarius, it'll be complete chaos."

"If it isn't already, you mean," Ash finished in a bleak tone.

Martinez turned back to the comms and started the process of calling replacement crew to the bridge, so they could leave.

———◆———

Oddly enough, Martinez was already acquainted with Nahleene Veila'ana. In fact, they'd met on more than one occasion over the years. The diplomatic corps in the Seven Systems was not so large that the Vitharan ambassador to Ilarius and the Terra Novan ambassador to Vithara wouldn't rub shoulders now and then.

Of course, there *was* the small matter of Veila'ana having recently been outed as both an unregistered telepath and a spy for Maelfius. Martinez couldn't help replaying every handshake, every friendly clasp of an arm or shoulder—wondering if the other woman had, in fact, been reading her mind in search of intelligence to send back to her Maelfian handlers.

Veila'ana and Pax had beaten them to the medical ship, and were already inside Kade's room when Martinez, Ash, and Draven arrived. Talk about a disturbing pair… between the one who could see inside her mind and the one whose emotion centers had been ripped out and replaced with tech, it was going to take a bit of an adjustment period before she felt comfortable letting her guard down around either of them.

She swallowed the irrational surge of worry at the sight of them looming over Kade while he was helpless, and greeted the pair with a curt nod, hanging back near the door.

Ash and Draven appeared to have no such compunctions regarding the reunion. Something unpleasant stirred in Martinez's chest as she realized that *she* was the interloper here. These people were Kade's longtime friends, while she was just the random person who'd ended up in a crisis situation with him… and the one who'd failed to protect him from harm, despite her extensive military background and training. Any connection she'd convinced herself might exist between the two of them could easily have been one-sided on her part—a result of the circumstances into which they'd been thrust, and nothing more.

So why did that idea burn and ache behind her breastbone like acid?

"Ash. Draven. It is most agreeable to see you both," the massive cyborg was saying. The bright overhead lights glinted off his facial implants.

"Right back at you, big man," Ash replied. "Hello, Nahleene. Looks like you two made it to the party just in time."

Draven crossed the room and clasped Pax forearm to forearm in greeting, with every indication of genuine affection. Meanwhile, Ash accepted an embrace from Veila'ana.

"Thank goodness you're all right," she murmured, then pulled back and looked from Ash to Draven in surprise. A genuine smile lit up her face. "And… I gather congratulations are in order?"

Ash's return smile was wan, though when his eyes drifted to Draven, there was a certain softness in his dark brown gaze that hadn't been there before. "Hello, Nahleene. And, yes—on that particular front, they are indeed." Then his attention moved to the figure on the medical cot, and he sobered. "Were you able to detect anything telepathically from Kade?"

With a jolt, Martinez realized that Veila'ana must have the ability to sense Kade's mental state, even when he was unconscious. She joined the others as they gathered around the bed, looking down at Kade's unmoving form. The ache grew sharper. He still looked… *absent*. Empty.

The telepath drew in a slow breath, and Martinez braced for the worst.

"I should preface this by saying that I'm not a healer. But his mind is struggling to recover from intense trauma, on top of his existing chronic, low-level chemical imbalance. His thoughts are confused, and until his brain is physically able to function in a more normal manner, there is little to be done for him from the outside."

"But he still *has* thoughts?" Martinez blurted. "He's still… in there?"

"He isn't brain dead," Veila'ana said. "Of course, the doctors here had already confirmed that fact with scans. I can't really judge if he was aware of my mental touch, and if so, how well he was able to process that awareness."

That wasn't exactly the reassurance Martinez had been hoping for. She looked down, and a faint thread of surprise cut through her worry when she saw that her hand had crept over to cover one of Kade's without her even noticing that she'd done it.

"Vitharan medical science is well respected in the local cluster," Pax said, in his eerily inflectionless voice. "I will offer the doctors here a sample of my bots before we depart, in the event they might become useful in Kade's treatment plan. Perhaps Ryder can consult with them on the case, once we have completed our current mission."

Draven heaved a heavy sigh, visibly switching gears. "Speaking of which—have either of you had any contact with Hunter and the others recently?"

"Not since they abandoned the lunar base and returned to Ilarius," Veila'ana said. "Though of course we saw the leaked transmissions of Skye inciting demonstrations in the Capital."

"That was a hazardous strategy on her part," Pax complained.

"But not a surprising one," Ash retorted. "Can you honestly picture the people we left behind standing by while the human population is rounded up and shipped off to internment camps?"

"No," Pax said. "But it is still hazardous."

"So is flying back to the Capital in the middle of large-scale rioting," Draven pointed out. "And isn't that what we're getting ready to do?"

Veila'ana shot the cyborg a rueful half-smile. "He's got you there."

"Right. Next question," Ash said. "I assume the allies will be escorting the defeated Ilarian security forces into planetary orbit imminently, if they're not already underway. Do we have access to a ship we can use to get to the surface? Because Hunter's two-seat fighter isn't exactly going to cut it for all five of us."

"Five?" Veila'ana echoed with a frown.

Martinez jerked her awareness back to the matter at hand. "I'm coming, too. I made a promise."

Veila'ana's frown deepened. "You won't be doing your career any favors if you head off on a rogue side-mission during an interplanetary military intervention, Isadora." Her expression turned rueful. "Voice of experience speaking here, in case that wasn't obvious."

Visions of human and Maelfian bodies piled in the streets of a doomed Badlands colony threatened to block out the sterile white medical bay, and Martinez blinked rapidly to dispel them. "Told you— I gave my word. Also, what the hell good is an ambassadorship if it can't stop things like this?"

Veila'ana held her gaze with pale green eyes. "Funny—that's exactly the same question I asked myself, right before I agreed to start spying for Maelfius."

A fragile thread of understanding passed between them—an unspoken acknowledgement of the parallel paths that had brought them here to this ship… to Kade's bedside.

"Let me have a quiet word with someone I know in the fleet," Martinez said, thinking of all the ways this could backfire if her gut instinct about her old commander was wrong. "I'll see if I can get us a ship."

FIFTEEN

Captain N'komo raised a scarred eyebrow, her skepticism clear even over the grainy video feed. *"Off the record, Martinez? This sounds like a good way to get your civvy ass killed."*

Martinez didn't break eye contact. "In the last few days, I've been framed for murder, kidnapped, nearly crashed a ship inside the wormhole system, and been on the wrong end of a cyborg attack. And *that* was when I was playing by the rules. So your point is… what, exactly?"

N'komo snorted. *"You know I can't just hand you and your merry band of vigilantes a ship, Am-bassador."* The title still held the same faint air of challenge as the last time she'd used it. *"The fleet took heavy damage in that battle. We need every undamaged ship we've got."*

The words hung in the air for several seconds before they clicked in Martinez's mind. "Every *un-damaged* ship," she repeated slowly.

"That's what I said," N'komo agreed, and Martinez was sure she wasn't imaging the flash of approval that touched her former commander's ex-pression—even if it was only there for an instant before it disappeared beneath a professional mask. *"All of the vessels in need of repairs are moored at the system's edge. Some of them are in worse shape than others, obviously."*

"Copy that," Martinez said, her mind already spinning with plans and logistics. "Thank you for taking the time to speak with me, Captain. I know you must be busy."

"*Never too busy for an old colleague, Major,*" N'komo replied. "*Go on, then—go and put your ghosts to rest. Just try not to die while you're doing it.*"

"Fair winds, Captain," Martinez said, not willing to make a promise she might not be able to keep. "You try not to die, either. Martinez out."

As the connection clicked closed, she straightened from the medical ship's comms panel and turned to look at the others. "Okay. It looks like I've got us a ship," she told them. "Though we might have to patch it up a bit first."

———◆———

Pax ferried the group one at a time to the least battered looking of the abandoned allied fleet vessels, using Hunter's fighter for transport. The temporary ship graveyard had been left to deal with later, since the high number of casualties on the allied side meant no crew could be spared to work on the damaged craft at the moment.

Before she'd left the medical ship, Martinez had returned to Kade's room alone. The others had already said their brief goodbyes to their unconscious comrade, with varying degrees of emotionality. Veila'ana had touched his face again in an attempt to contact him telepathically, but shook her head afterward, indicating that there had been no change in his mental condition.

Martinez looked down at him—this man who'd broken himself against the rocks of the Regime's downfall. It seemed so unfair that he should have come this far, only to miss the culmination of everything he'd toiled and bled and suffered for over the years. She took his hand again, knowing he probably couldn't feel the tenuous connection to the world beyond his damaged mind.

"Hey," she said softly. "Like the others said, we're going now. We'll find the rest of your friends and make sure this mess ends the way it's supposed to. I don't know if my presence there will make any difference or not, but I'll be acting in your stead, just like we agreed."

There was, of course, no response.

She swallowed and continued. "So… here's another proposal for you. I'll try not to get killed in the process, or to let the people you care about get killed. In return, you have to fight your way back from wherever you are right now. Because you and me, we need to talk about… some things. Afterward, I mean—when we're not in the middle of a crisis. I think we've both been dragging around a bunch of really heavy shit for a really long time, and I'm not sure either of us will know what to do with ourselves if it's not there anymore."

The door slid open, admitting a nurse with a tray full of vials and medical instruments.

"Right," Martinez told Kade's silent form. "I'm going. But I intend to be back. Get better, so we can have that talk."

She let his hand slide free, sparing the nurse a brusque nod as she ducked out of the room. Blinking back the unaccustomed burning sensation behind her eyes, Martinez headed for the medical transport's hangar, where Pax would be waiting for her with the fighter.

The others were already hard at work when she and the cyborg arrived. They'd chosen a modestly sized ship with atmospheric capabilities. It had taken heavy damage in the area of the crew quarters and weapons systems, but been largely unharmed when it came to the propulsion and computer systems. Emergency bulkheads had successfully contained the atmosphere in most of the ship, leaving the vessel functional for basic navigation. If anyone wanted to lie down somewhere comfortable, or shower, or take a piss, they were pretty much S.O.L., but it would be good enough to get them to Ilarius.

Pax insisted on escorting them in the fighter, since there was no way of knowing what the conditions would be planet-side. The fighter, at least, was armed with functional weapons. Draven nominated himself as Pax's copilot, leaving Martinez and Ash to pilot the patched-together transport with Nahleene as a passenger.

No one raised the alarm as they navigated the ship out of the jumble of allied wrecks, though it was unclear whether that was because they simply weren't considered a priority, or because N'komo had quietly mandated that they be left alone. In the distance, the heavily armed allied convoy was beginning its trek toward Ilarius, heading for the government complex at the center of the Capital.

It was unclear what they would be likely to find there. The first transmissions from the surface were beginning to leak out, and the situation on the ground was unsurprisingly chaotic. Martinez and the others weren't headed for the government center, however. Instead, they would be looking to hook up with Hunter Tarthasian, Skye Chantrell, and the rest of Kade's allies.

Pax seemed quite certain that faced with such overwhelming oppositional force, the Premiere and his inner circle would attempt to flee the Capital—perhaps to establish a government in exile somewhere as they attempted to rally Vithii support for a fresh coup. Their hope was that Hunter and Skye's resistance movement would be in a position to better track any Regime officials trying to escape the city, and be able to act more nimbly in response than the cumbersome outworld alliance.

They arrived to find the orbital defenses already neutralized by the allied convoy that had preceded them. Ash had programmed their borrowed transport ship with counterfeit ID codes, but his efforts ended up being completely unnecessary. The planetary border was wide open, with commercial and private vessels alike fleeing the chaos below.

The Capital itself hadn't quite given up it defenses, however. Ground to air weapons split the gray sky with beams of sizzling energy, and a few loyalist fighter ships still patrolled the airspace. Most were engaged in battle with the incoming allied ships, but one peeled off to intercept them. It managed a glancing blaster strike across one of the stabilizers on their borrowed ship before Pax and Draven swooped in and disabled it, sending it limping off for an emergency landing.

The transport slewed as Martinez and Ash struggled to compensate for the lost stabilizer. After a few moments, it steadied.

"You're way too good at that," Martinez said, shooting Ash a sidelong glance.

"I've had more practice lately than I care to think about," he replied, grim-faced.

"Haven't we all," Veila'ana agreed, clinging to the arms of her seat with both hands.

Between them, they got the craft down safely inside the hangar they'd been aiming for, while the fighter hovered overhead, covering them. Pax and Draven set down a few moments later inside the echoing structure, landing a short distance away.

The hangar was surrounded by crowds clogging the streets—Martinez had gotten a good look at the mob outside as the ship approached for landing. Plumes of smoke rose lazily into the air throughout the city as buildings burned. Above them, the hangar roof rolled closed, cutting off their view of the sizzling energy weapons lighting up the sky.

She and Ash efficiently powered down the ship's systems. With Veila'ana in tow, they exited onto the hangar floor. Martinez and Ash were still armed with the blasters they'd been given earlier, when the cyborgs had boarded the Vitharan command ship. The building was quiet, though, despite the chaos beyond the walls—apparently the crowd hadn't managed to get inside the structure, which Ash had explained belonged to Kade.

Draven and Pax dropped down from the fighter's cockpit ladder, their sidearms also held at the ready.

"Plan?" Draven asked.

"Get to Location Four on foot," Ash said. "That's the last place where we know the others were staying. First, though, I want to use the communications equipment in Kade's office."

"You intend to check the underground news sources for intelligence on the Premiere's movements?" Pax asked.

"Just so," Ash replied. "There should be quite a bit more information available locally than what makes it past the orbital communications arrays. I'm willing to bet someone down here has got eyeballs on the top officials."

"You do that," Draven said, "and I'll see if anyone's monitoring the comms at Location Four."

As it turned out, someone was—a human kid named Jonah, who sounded excited beyond measure when he realized who was calling.

"*Can you believe all this*?" The voice across the staticky connection sounded painfully young. "*It's really happening, man! You need to get over here as quick as you can… but be careful, yeah*?"

"We're on our way," Draven said—steady in the face of Jonah's unbridled enthusiasm. "Tell the others."

At the other station, Ash straightened. "A small hovercar convoy was seen leaving the government complex a few minutes ago. Heading west, which suggests a few possible destinations."

"We will rendezvous with Hunter at Location Four. There may be more information available by then," Pax said. "As both of our groups are situated west of the complex, we will have a head start in reaching any of the convoy's likely destinations."

Martinez wasn't deeply enamored of the 'traveling on foot' part of the plan, given the scale of the mob clogging the Capital's roads. However, she recognized the logic. They'd already seen how dangerous travel was through the city's airspace, and ground transport would be too slow with the streets blocked by people.

"How far is it?" she asked, resigned.

"Slightly less than one kilometer," the cyborg replied.

An insignificant distance, in the general scheme of things—but one that took them nearly a full cycle to negotiate, even with the threat of drawn blasters to open a path through the crowds. As they traveled through the city, Martinez was able to get a feel for the protests. It seemed that every human still free in the Capital had taken to the streets. There were an encouraging number of Vithii among them, as well. Almost all of the protesters were wearing white—white shirts, white bandanas tied around their heads, white armbands. She gathered it was some kind of identifying mark to show that they were anti-Regime, since there were also occasional bands of Vithii without any white clothing, engaging in scuffles and shouting matches with the main group.

Pax took point, leading them with uncanny precision around the skirmishes. Interestingly, the Regime security presence in the area seemed almost non-existent. She saw a couple of official looking vehicles in the distance as they rounded a corner once, but that was about it. Had the police and military been recalled to the government complex in the face of the allies' arrival, or were they simply overwhelmed by the scale of the mob?

Whatever the case, the five of them arrived at their destination without suffering any injuries or major confrontations. Perhaps unsurprisingly, something about an armed group led by a two-and-a-half-meter tall Vithii cyborg seemed to put a damper on people's desire to start anything with them.

The building ahead was largely unremarkable except for the blaster-toting humans flanking a door in the side alley. A cryptic sign hung over the guarded entrance. It was hand-drawn in white paint on a red background—a messy circle that didn't quite close at the top, with a horizontal line beneath it. A skinny human male was lingering in the doorway, scanning the alley as they approached. His slate-blue eyes lit up when he saw them, and he gestured for the guards to lower their weapons.

"You made it!" he said, waving them toward the door excitedly. "Man, it's good to see you guys! Come on in—mind the gurneys."

The kid's expression split into a wide grin as Ash and Draven approached, his eyes still sparkling. Ash gave him a friendly nod, and Draven clapped him on the shoulder good-naturedly as he passed. The teenager's smile grew more tentative as his gaze landed on Martinez, but he stuck his hand out for her to shake.

"Hey, I'm Jonah. Welcome to the Haven."

"Isadora," she said.

His eyes widened. "Isadora… as in, Ambassador Isadora Martinez of Terra Nova?" he asked.

"Well… probably not anymore. Not after this stunt," she said, poking at her reaction to the idea. "But it's still nice to meet you."

Once inside, it became immediately apparent what Jonah had meant about the gurneys. The building had been set up as an informal clinic, and the dim hallway was like a maze of them—many occupied by human and Vithii protesters sporting injuries of varying severity. She eased past patients awaiting triage and volunteers in stained scrubs, trying not to take up any more space than necessary as she followed the others deeper into the building.

They entered a stairwell and jogged up a couple of flights to a floor that seemed quiet and free of patients. Jonah gave a complicated series of knocks on a door that looked identical to all the other doors in the hallway. It opened a moment later to reveal a blonde head.

"Jonah? Are they here?" asked the woman, who Martinez recognized immediately as the infamous Skye Chantrell. Her blue eyes slid past Jonah, falling on their ragtag group. A small noise escaped her throat, and then she was bounding forward, practically throwing herself into Ash's arms.

Martinez watched, bemused, as Ash staggered back a step with a startled *oof* noise. He caught Skye's body against his an instant later, his arms closing around her to return the embrace.

"I know Draven told Jonah you were okay," she said, the words muffled against Ash's shoulder, "but that was weeks ago, and then we didn't hear anything else after Kade went to pick you both up, so we just weren't *sure*—" Her voice wavered, the words choked off as she clutched him tighter.

Ash's eyes slid closed, and he let his face rest against Skye's blonde hair to hide his expression. His voice, when he spoke, held a hint of unsteadiness that Martinez had never heard from him before.

"I'm sorry, Skye. I truly am. I couldn't see another way."

Skye made another choked noise and pushed away, in favor of punching Ash in the chest with a half-hearted blow. There were tears in her eyes as she said, "I don't care. Don't ever do that to us again! Not *ever*, damn it. No matter what you think is at stake!"

"Yeah," Draven said, "we've already had that conversation, actually."

"Good!" Skye moved to hug Draven, who looked a bit surprised by the display. He patted her awkwardly on the back.

"Thanks for being right about him being alive," Skye added, squeezing tight before letting go to greet Veila'ana and Pax.

A new figure had appeared in the doorway during the emotional reunion—one Martinez vaguely recognized from intersystem newscasts. The Rook; real name Hunter Tarthasian. The de facto leader of this unlikely group of revolutionaries, and a man who—if Kade and the others were to be believed—had been unfairly vilified as a violent criminal by the same government whose existence he threatened.

Feathered black tattoos peeked from the neck of his shirt and covered the backs of his hands, but it was his eyes that Martinez found most striking. Vibrant green, they played over the group in the hallway, incisive and piercing. Satisfaction shone in his gaze as he took in those present, only to be replaced by a haunted look as he registered the one who was notably absent.

"Kade," he said, with the resonant tones of someone accustomed to command. "Where is he?"

SIXTEEN

Martinez's throat tightened at the leader's question, but Draven saved her from having to answer.

"Bit of a long story. Short version—he's on a Vitharan medical ship in orbit, after undergoing a critical bout of neurotonin withdrawal."

Hunter's haunted look grew bleaker, but he only nodded. "I see."

"I attempted to touch his mind," Nahleene offered. "While there's been significant damage done, he's still in there. The Vitharans are cutting-edge when it comes to medical science, and Pax left them some of his bots to work with, as well. They'll do everything possible to aid his recovery."

Martinez watched as the powerful Vithii leader forced aside his personal worry for his friend, and focused on the people who *had* made it back.

"He's strong. Not to mention, stubborn," Hunter said. "Draven... it appears I owe you a sincere apology. You've retrieved our wayward *leetha* from beyond the grave, despite all odds. And he, in turn, appears to have brought us another ambassador for our growing collection. Isadora Martinez, I presume?"

Martinez tore herself free of her reverie and moved from where she'd been hanging back, watching the reunion unfold. "That's me." She reached out a hand and clasped forearms with him in greeting. "Though I'm afraid I'm only here because Kade asked me to come in his stead if he was unable to do so—not in my formal role as Terra Novan ambassador to Vithara. Neither my home planet nor my host planet would approve of what I'm doing right now, I'm sorry to say."

"Hmm. We should start a club," Veila'ana said wryly.

Hunter gave Martinez the same look of surprise Ash and Draven had given her when she told them Kade had asked her to come. Apparently, the request truly *had* been out of character for him. The Vithii leader recovered quickly, though, and gave her a terse nod.

"Whatever the case, your assistance in procuring Vitharan and Terra Novan support can hardly be overstated, Ambassador. Welcome to the heart and soul of the Ilarian Resistance, such as it is."

"Where are Ryder and Temple?" Pax asked. "We did not see them on the way in."

"That's because we were busy in surgery, trying to patch someone back together after he tangled with a stray blaster beam," came a new voice—female, Vithii, and irascible. "The 'heart and soul of the Ilarian Resistance' is currently where people come to get patched up when they're too scared to go to a government-run hospital. I swear, it's like I've come full circle—back to my days as an unlicensed back alley sawbones."

The speaker was a middle-aged Vithii woman with hair dyed a vibrant shade of fiery red, wearing doctor's scrubs that had recently seen some action, based on the array of interesting stains covering them. She was accompanied by a tall, dark-skinned human man with a hint of epicanthic folds over his heavy-lidded eyes, who Martinez gathered, by process of elimination, must be Temple.

"All of which is Ryder-speak for 'hey, good to see you, glad you're back safe,'" the dark-skinned man said in a wry tone. Then he stopped short. "Wait. Where's Kade?"

This time, Pax recapped Kade's whereabouts and condition. Both of the newcomers looked increasingly grim as he spoke.

"I need to consult with the doctors who are treating him," Ryder said immediately. "Especially if they're considering using bots on him."

"I'm afraid it will have to wait, Ryder," Ash said softly. "The allied forces are taking control of the government complex, but it looks like Kovak may be on the move—trying to get out of the Capital."

Ryder's gaze fell on him and hardened, though it also looked pained.

"*You…*" she said sharply. "I'm not speaking to you just yet, *leetha*. Not until I'm more confident I won't say things that can't be taken back."

"I understand," Ash said. "And for what it's worth, I truly am sorry."

"You should be!"

Temple looked between them. "Well, *I'm* still talking to you. And it's really good to see all of you again. Now, can we go make sure Kovak gets what's coming to him, before he manages to scurry off and hide under a rock somewhere?"

"First we need to determine where he's going," Pax pointed out reasonably.

"The freighter terminal," Hunter said, and everyone's attention centered on him. "I've been monitoring the underground forums, and a small convoy of official-looking hovercars has just been sighted in that area. I was getting ready to make my way there when you arrived."

Skye's eyes widened, then narrowed. "Alone? Yeah… that's a no. In fact, it's a great big *hell no*."

"Seconded," Ash said. "While I'm aware of the irony, take it from me that you'll never hear the end of it if you try to sneak off on your own."

"Our chances of success increase significantly if we work as a group," Pax said, the words as emotionless as ever. "We should leave now, however. Ryder, do you need to stay behind for your patients?"

"Not on your life," Ryder replied without hesitation. "I'm not the only medic here. We have a full rota of human doctors who lost their licenses in the last round of anti-human crackdowns. They're perfectly capable of watching the patients."

"Very well," Hunter said, taking charge. "We'll get weapons on the way out. Anyone who wishes to stay behind should do so. This is likely to be dangerous even by our standards. Jonah—"

"Oh, no," said the kid. "I'm coming. Ilarius is my home, too."

Hunter nodded in acquiescence, and directed them down the hallway toward a room that was apparently being used as an armory of sorts. In the corner of her eye, Martinez saw Ryder stop Ash with a grip on his arm as they left. Ash paused, covering her hand with his as their eyes met and held for a brief moment. Then she did the same to Draven, and her look was one of gratitude. Draven smiled at her like the sun coming out, despite the grim circumstances.

There was a story there, beyond the bare bones that Kade and the others had sketched for

Martinez when they'd first met on Terra Nova. She hoped they'd live long enough for her to ask about it.

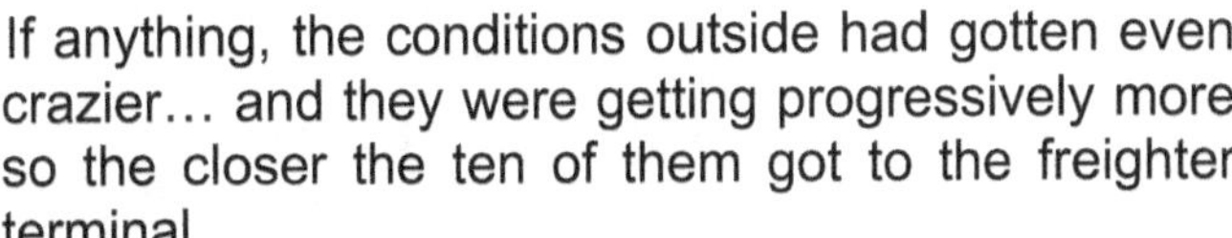

If anything, the conditions outside had gotten even crazier… and they were getting progressively more so the closer the ten of them got to the freighter terminal.

In addition to sidearms and stun wands, the members of the group who weren't already wearing something white had gotten bandanas or armbands. The streets were completely choked with people, many of whom seemed to be trying to get to the same place they were. Martinez was finding it increasingly difficult not to be reminded of a different mob in a different place and time—something she definitely could *not* afford to focus on right now.

"It's been like this in the city for days," Temple told her, raising his voice to be heard above the din. "Shit's been crazy since Skye got back on the airwaves and started riling people up."

They were traveling in a tight formation, with Pax at the front and Hunter watching the rear. Martinez was fairly sure that the massive structure she could see over the tops of the nearest buildings was the freighter port, and if so, they were now only a few blocks away. The appearance of the first organized police response they'd seen since arriving further solidified her suspicions that they were on the right track.

A line of armored vehicles was plowing through the crowd on the street running parallel to theirs, one block over. It came into view each time they reached a cross street. *"Disperse. This is an illegal gathering. Disperse. Disperse,"* blared from speakers on top of the lead vehicle. Protesters were jeering, throwing rocks and bottles at the security forces.

"Stay alert," Pax called from the front, just as several canisters arced through the air from one of the armored tank-cars on the next block. Clouds of white spewed into the air—gas grenades. The fitful breeze would carry it away from them, Martinez knew, but Pax was already leading them another block over, putting more distance between their group and the ugly police confrontation.

The reason for the detour became clear when the crowd surged in their direction, attempting to flee the gas. The ten of them clustered together, trying to let the panicking protesters slide around them, and occasionally grabbing someone who was in danger of getting trampled and setting them back on their feet. It seemed for a few moments as though they would escape the mess unscathed— they were only two blocks away from the freighter port now, as best as Martinez could tell.

Then, a second surge of frightened people came at them from the front. She caught a brief glimpse of black helmets and riot shields in that direction, and suddenly they were in the middle of a firefight.

Police were firing indiscriminately into the crowd.

Her mind went blank for a critical instant, while around her, the others ranged into defensive firing stances, taking any opening through the thinning crowd to lay down return fire. As if in a dream, sizzling energy crackled past Martinez's shoulder and slammed into the freckled teenager who'd greeted them with a grin at the door to the safehouse-slash-emergency clinic. Jonah crumpled silently to the pavement, a smoking hole through his chest.

Distantly, she heard Draven cry out in denial, and Temple shouting, "No! Damn it, *no!*"

But all she could see was orange-red hair… a body lying unmoving on the pavement as the past and present blurred into one.

Other people around them in the crowd were falling, too. But rather than continue its retreat, the mob *roared*, a sound like a ravenous beast. Others in the throng were armed, as well. More return fire erupted toward the riot squad. As the protesters at the front either fled or were mowed down, she could see that the crowd was closing around the line of police from the sides and rear, cutting them off, pelting them from all sides with crude projectiles as well as energy weapons.

Uselessly, she stood there with her blaster hanging in numb fingers, her heart beating triple-time as she relived the utter helplessness of watching the death of innocents unfold around her, unstoppable. It was only when she saw one of the last riot police still standing take steady aim at Skye, that Martinez was able to get a signal from her brain to her muscles. She plowed into the taller woman, sending them both to the unforgiving concrete an instant before a deadly beam sliced through the place where Skye had been.

For long moments, there was only the confusion of legs moving around them, and Jonah's wide-open slate-colored eyes staring into hers from a meter away—no life behind them. Then, arms were lifting her back to her feet, though she couldn't feel the pressure of hands against her skin properly through the numbness. She looked around, everything seeming oddly flat and monochrome.

The weapons fire had stopped. No black helmets or riot shields were visible. The crowd around them had thinned out. Some had no doubt fled, while others lay on the ground like Jonah. Draven and Temple crashed to their knees on either side of the dead boy, the desperate hope in their eyes fading as they got a look at what had happened to his chest.

Temple covered his face with one hand, curling forward, while beside Martinez, Skye covered her mouth to hold in whatever sound was trying to escape. Hunter, Pax, Ash, and Ryder were covering the rest of them as best they could, ranged around like points of a compass with weapons still held ready.

Martinez was aware of this on some level. She knew she should be moving… acting. But her eyes kept sliding back to the dead boy lying on the street. The arms that had lifted her jostled her with a sharp shake, and someone was talking near her ear. All of it was distant, though—like something happening to someone else.

A slender hand rested on one side of her face, fingers seeking. An instant later, a sharp jolt echoed through her consciousness, like someone had slapped her, but on the inside. She blinked in surprise and staggered back a step, the hand sliding away from her face as she did. When she blinked again, Nahleene Veila'ana was in front of her, blocking her view of Jonah's body. The telepath's pale green eyes peered into hers with an expression of worry.

"What—" Martinez croaked, and gave her head a sharp shake. Her left elbow throbbed, scraped and bruised after impacting the pavement when she pushed Skye down. She hadn't even felt it until now.

"I apologize for the presumption," Veila'ana said, still watching her closely. "But you looked like you were someplace else entirely, and we can't really afford that right now. Are you back with us?"

The present crashed back into focus, blocking out the echoes of the past. "Yes, I…" She trailed off and swallowed hard. "Thanks."

Ryder had backed up a few steps until she was at Temple's side, half of her attention still on their surroundings as she clasped a hand on his bowed shoulder. "We need to go," she said in a voice caught between sympathy and worry.

"We can't just leave him lying in the middle of the road!" Temple snapped.

Draven clambered to his feet, his face set in haggard lines. He hooked fingers around Temple's bicep and half-dragged him to his feet, then rummaged in his pockets.

"Would you rather we hang around here while Kovak hops the first freighter off-planet?" he growled. Coming up with a scrap of paper and the stub of a pencil, he started scribbling. "I'll leave his name, and the name and address of his aunt and uncle tucked in his shirt pocket. He's gone, Temple. Nothing that happens to his body now is gonna make him any more dead than he is already. So let's go find the bastard responsible for all this and make sure he pays."

Temple's chest heaved, an ugly noise escaping as he scooped up the blaster he'd dropped when he ran to Jonah's side. "I'm fucking *done* with this shit," he snarled. "I want this *over*."

"Come," Hunter said, his voice carrying over the sound of fresh weapons fire erupting from the area around their destination. "The mob has closed in on the entrance to the freighter terminal. We need to leave."

Martinez spared a last look at the fallen boy as they left, swallowing against the lump rising in her throat. Skye slowed her with a gentle grip on her wrist, and she looked into blue eyes wet with unshed tears.

"Thank you," Skye said. "They would have taken me out, too, if you hadn't pushed me out of the way of that shot."

But Martinez could only shake her head, her throat still too thick for words to get past.

SEVENTEEN

The freighter terminal was a compound under siege. Word had obviously gotten out that high-level Regime officials were attempting to use it to escape, and those who'd been trodden underfoot by the Premiere's corrupt government had swarmed here to vent their anger.

An intense assault was underway at the entrance to the main building. Still, every guard Kovak had been able to muster was defending the place, and the layout gave them a distinct tactical advantage. They just had to pick off anyone who got too near the door, and no doubt they'd erected barricades for added protection as soon as they arrived. Martinez was confident the defense would eventually fall beneath the force of numbers, but—

"This approach will be too slow," Pax called over the roar of the crowd. "We'll have to find a different entrance, or make one."

"Agreed," Hunter replied. "Skirt the edges of the mob. Make for the south side of the complex."

Around them, heads turned—eyes catching on Skye. She'd been a public figure in the resistance of late, and it was clear she was being recognized. People from the crowd started to follow them, in a trickle at first, but then by the dozens. Ash gave Skye a nudge and tipped his chin toward the growing retinue when she looked at him.

Her eyes widened, but then she composed herself and caught Hunter's eye. He nodded, his gaze flicking over the growing group.

Skye cleared her throat. "We're going to look for a side entrance and try to get inside that way," she called. "It's still likely to be guarded, but we need to find a way in and make sure that Kovak and his cronies don't make it to a ship. We can use you, especially if you're armed, but you need to follow Hunter and Pax's orders—not make it into a free for all."

Expressions of agreement came from within the group. They rounded a corner, separated from the main building by a chainlink fence topped with coils of razor wire that defined the boundary of the freighter port. Pax's blaster moved too fast for Martinez to follow, and two Regime guards who'd been flanking a nondescript door on the side of the building fell to the ground, dead. The cyborg's shots had struck home in less than a second flat; the pair never even had time to react to the threat.

"That's our way in," Hunter said.

Martinez was still covered in clammy sweat, a distracting buzzing in her ears as she fought not to succumb to another PTSD episode. But she clutched her blaster in her hand and strode up to the fence, dialing the beam to narrow and starting work on the chain link. Other people joined her efforts, sparks flying as a metallic burning smell filled the air.

In less than five minutes, they'd opened a gap large enough for people to squeeze through one at a time without getting singed. No more guards had swarmed to replace the two Pax had killed, so apparently it was 'all hands on deck' at the main entrance, where the bulk of the mob was trying to get in.

Pax prowled up to the unprepossessing employee entrance and broke the lock with a single, powerful kick. Hunter, Ash, and Draven swarmed through the gap as the door squealed open on bent hinges, weapons held at the ready. Martinez castigated herself for her uselessness and followed them in, her training finally coming to the forefront and beating back the intervening layers of psychological bullshit that had been stifling it.

She slotted herself in among the men, scanning her quadrant of the echoing interior—weapon poised to fire. Hunter gave her an assessing glance.

"She's ex-Terra Novan Special Forces," Ash said in a low voice.

The Vithii leader graced her with a terse nod. "You saved my bondmate earlier."

Martinez kind of wished everyone would stop making a big deal of that—but she'd been a diplomat too long to say something churlish, like 'it was nothing.'

"I'm glad I could help," she said instead.

A noise came from deeper inside the building, and Hunter's attention returned to their surroundings. "Take the left flank, between Ryder and Draven," he told her. "The Regime officials will be making for the docks, trying to find a ship to commandeer."

The rest of the group gathered inside the building, forming up with the most heavily armed protesters and members of the Shadow Wing arrayed in a narrow wedge at the front, sheltering the less battle-ready individuals behind them. As they approached the loading areas where the freighters docked for cargo transfer, sounds of activity could be heard ahead of them.

The roar of the crowd outside of the main entrance was only distant background noise here, but Martinez could make out voices much closer, barking orders.

"We'll try for the element of surprise," Hunter said, keeping his voice low. "Take out the guards as quickly as possible. If anyone gets a clear shot at the Premiere or any other officials, take it."

As the order filtered its way to the people at the back, there were quiet acknowledgements and nods of agreement. It was a risky approach. They would simply be following the sounds of activity and barging in, with no idea of the layout of the battle zone or the number of combatants involved. It was clear to Martinez that the people gathered here were willing to give their lives to ensure that Xandrie Kovak didn't escape, potentially reappearing in the future to sow more havoc on Ilarius.

Unexpectedly—and perhaps inappropriately—she spared a thought for Kade, back on the Vitharan medical ship. His future was uncertain as he battled to recover from the massive chemical trauma to his brain, but at least he wouldn't die here in a run-down freighter terminal. She only hoped he didn't wake to find that all of his friends had perished in this last-ditch firefight, attempting to bring down the Premiere he despised so passionately.

The group of vigilantes moved quickly but quietly along the echoing corridor connecting the terminal gates. Many of those berths were empty, the pilots presumably having fled with their ships to avoid the conflict when the allied forces arrived.

Some of the loading docks were cleared of cargo; others were still piled with crates and containers, abandoned in the face of a falling government and an angry mob.

Their confirmation that they'd found the source of the voices came in the form of a startled shout, followed immediately by blaster fire. Thankfully, the dock in question was one of the ones still packed with cargo, and the group of rebels scrambled for cover, returning fire. Martinez ended up sharing space behind a pile of metal crates with Temple, who wore the fixed and stony expression of a man dead-set on revenge at any cost.

Closer to the ship, the Regime guards were also taking cover. She tried to tally up the various angles of fire coming at them, and frowned.

"I don't think there are more than a dozen enemy combatants in here," she said, raising her voice to be heard over the sound of weapons fire.

Temple leaned out long enough to squeeze off a couple of rounds before ducking back. "I'll take your word for it. If so, it looks like Kovak must be scraping the bottom of the barrel when it comes to loyal defensive forces."

"Most of the ones that are left are probably tied up at the main entrance," Martinez said, still frowning. A flash of vibrant blue drew her attention to a half-concealed corner near the ship's loading ramp. "Wait... did you see that?"

"See what?" Temple asked, peering around to look in the direction she indicated, only to pull back when more blaster fire erupted.

"I saw a flash of blue. It was roughly head-height for a tall Vithii."

Temple looked again. "You think Kovak's holed up back there?"

Dyed hair was a common fashion statement among Vithii—male and female both. But Premiere Kovak had long used a particular shade of striking blue as part of his personal branding. While Martinez had no doubt that the color had gained a following among Kovak's more ardent supporters, its presence here and now seemed like fairly reliable evidence that he had, in fact, come here hoping to abandon his sinking ship of a planet.

"It's a pretty big coincidence otherwise," she said. "I'm going to try to get closer."

She dropped down to the hangar floor, ignoring the protest of her injured elbow as she belly-crawled to the next pile of cargo containers. Temple was right behind her, as weapons fire flashed above their heads.

They really never do think to look down at ground level during a firefight, she mused. *Why is that, anyway?*

With the guards outnumbered and largely pinned down by the motley collection of armed protesters, she and Temple were able to make their way around the edge of the cargo area until they had a clear view of the hidden corner where Martinez had noticed the suspicious flash of blue.

It was definitely Kovak. He was hunkered behind cover with a drawn blaster, wearing his ridiculous military-style uniform. It was a navy-blue monstrosity, complete with epaulettes and medals. And it had always pissed Martinez off something fierce, because everyone knew Xandrie Kovak had never performed a day of military service in his miserable life.

The uniform was an affectation, nothing more—just like the dyed hair, and the paternalistic 'glorious fatherland' rhetoric.

Briefly, Martinez worried about the optics of an offworlder being the person to assassinate the bastard, wondering if it would be better for Temple to do it. But under these circumstances, it would be fairly easy to spin the death ambiguously. *'Killed during a firefight between protesters and loyalist forces.'* In the end, even if it were practical to capture Kovak alive, the spectacle of a trial and the prospect of him becoming an ongoing focus for discontent argued against letting him live.

Her decision was cold-hearted.

It was calculating.

It was the way she'd been trained by the military to assess things when lives were on the line. She lifted her weapon, sighting along the barrel, only for Kovak to shift further into the shadows, ruining her angle for a clean kill-shot. She swallowed a curse.

Next to the Premiere, something shifted in the shadows. It was low to the ground, half-hidden. Martinez frowned as what she had at first taken as the top of a dark plastic bag resolved into a cascade of long, black hair, falling forward like a curtain across the profile of a bowed head.

There was a female human kneeling at Kovak's side. Temple must have seen her at the same moment, because he caught his breath. At the barely audible noise, the woman's head whipped around, searching for the source of the sound.

Next to Martinez, Temple froze. "*Stella*?" The word was infused with shocked disbelief, and he rose to his knees, breaking cover.

"*Shit*," Martinez hissed, as Kovak turned glittering eyes on the human slave kneeling at his feet. Then his gaze followed hers, right to their hiding place.

She raised her blaster at the same moment Kovak did, searching for a shot as clear as the one Kovak currently had at Temple. Before she could fire, though, the human woman let out an enraged shriek and lurched to her feet. Her hands were shackled with a length of chain running between them. She slung the metallic length over Kovak's head and jumped on his back, still wailing like a crazed banshee.

The chain tightened across the front of Kovak's neck. His blaster shot at Temple went high, hitting the pile of crates above their heads. The Premiere twisted and turned, trying to reach behind him to tear the screaming human off his back. Martinez held her fire, aware that she was as likely to hit the woman as the Premiere if she tried to make a shot while they were struggling.

Temple was on his feet, as though he was about to lunge toward the armed Vithii. Martinez gritted her teeth and latched onto his arm, dragging him back down behind the pile of cargo.

"Let me go!" he hissed, pulling against her hold. "That's my *stepmother!*"

EIGHTEEN

Martinez twisted Temple's wrist into a pressure lock, keeping him down. "You'll break cover when he drops the blaster and not before," she said.

"Godsdamnit—" Temple cursed.

But in front of them, unforgiving metal chain was winning the war against unprotected flesh. Kovak gave up trying to tear the woman off his back in favor of scrabbling at the links cutting into his windpipe. He choked and coughed, blood erupting from between his lips as he crumpled to his knees. The dark, glittering eyes that had graced a thousand vidscreens with their inner light of fanaticism widened in shock... then dimmed as the life bled out of them.

The Premiere's weapon fell from his nerveless fingers, and Temple jerked free of Martinez's grip. He vaulted over the crates they'd been using as cover, running fast and low across the space separating them. Martinez followed, her heart thudding painfully against her ribs.

They arrived an instant after Xandrie Kovak toppled onto his side and lay still, his eyes open, staring at nothing. The whites of his sclera were coppery orange with burst blood vessels, and his tongue protruded thick and ruddy between his bloody lips. The human woman went silent behind him, flopping onto her rump with her shackles still tangled around Kovak's ruined throat.

Martinez yanked her attention to practicalities, repeatedly bitch-slapping her stunned brain until the neurons started firing in some sort of useful fashion. Temple was still staring down at the grisly scene in shock.

"Stella?" he said again, his eyes turning toward the woman's haggard features. She didn't respond, her gaze growing distant to the point that she was staring right through both of them, unseeing.

Thinking fast, Martinez slipped the chain free of Kovak's head. "Use your blaster to cut this chain free from her shackles," she snapped. "Melt it to slag to destroy the blood evidence, and then get her out of here. Hide in the next cargo bay over."

Without pausing to think too much about what she was planning, Martinez aimed her blaster at Kovak's bloody neck and fired, vaporizing the ruined flesh.

"What in the prophets' names are you doing?" Temple asked, aghast. He grasped his stepmother's shoulders and lifted her carefully to her feet, backing them away a few steps. Stella followed the movement like a posable doll, her eyes still far away.

"Kovak was killed in the firefight," Martinez told him firmly. "We didn't see who got him; he was like this when we found him. Someone's stray blaster bolt must've gotten him during the confusion. If anyone asks, your stepmother was huddled in the corner, an innocent bystander. Otherwise, don't even mention her presence. Trust me, Temple— you don't want to deal with the heat that will come down on her, if it becomes common knowledge that she was the one to take him out."

He blinked, understanding settling behind his dark gaze. "Right. *Fuck*. You're right. Send Skye or Ryder to help me with her, when you can, okay? I'll keep her hidden in the cargo bay next door until then." He settled the woman's arm over his shoulder, and his voice turned tender. "Come on, Stella. I've got you. It's gonna be okay now, I promise—but we have to go now."

After a final, overwhelmed glance around the scene—first at the dead body on the ground, then at Martinez—Temple turned and eased his stepmother back toward the stacks of crates and barrels where they'd been hiding earlier. Beyond them, in the main part of the bay, the firefight sounded like it was winding down.

Once Temple was well away, Martinez lifted her hands to cup around her mouth like a megaphone. "The Premiere is dead!" she shouted at the top of her lungs. "He's been shot! D'you hear me? *Kovak is dead*!"

There was a pause in the sound of blaster fire and yelling. One of the last surviving security guards came running toward the hidden corner where Kovak had been sheltering, and Martinez cleanly picked him off with a blaster shot as he appeared. A few moments later, a scream rang through the cargo bay as someone else fell, and the echoing silence that followed showed that it had been the final guard.

"Is that all of them?" she called, to be sure.

"Yes," came Pax's flat voice, after a handful of seconds. "All of the enemy combatants have been neutralized. We're approaching your position—hold your fire."

More voices followed, as members of the Shadow Wing set the surviving protesters to securing the site—dealing with the injured and dead. Pax, Hunter, Ryder, and Skye appeared a moment later. Hunter had a nasty slice across one cheek. It was bleeding sluggishly, presumably the result of shrapnel from a cargo crate hitting him. Ryder was clutching an ugly blaster burn on her left forearm.

The Vithii medic looked around. "Where's Temple?" she snapped, fear kindling behind her light brown gaze.

"He's fine, don't worry." Martinez glanced around to make sure there were no eavesdroppers from the group of protesters they'd picked up. "He's making for the bay next to this one. There was a human woman with Kovak. A slave. Temple called her Stella—he said she was his stepmother."

Skye drew in a sharp breath, her face going pale.

"I told him to hide her there until I could send someone to help him smuggle her out of the compound," Martinez said. "She didn't seem to be injured, but she's in shock."

"Skye and I will go," Ryder said, eyeing the blonde woman as Skye struggled to regain her composure.

Pax had been peering down at the Premiere's broken body, but at that, he looked up at Martinez and raised an eyebrow. "This blaster wound was administered post-mortem," he said, as though discussing the weather or the results of a recent hoverball match.

Martinez met the cyborg's ocean-colored eyes and held them. "Yes. And if you want to protect the woman, Stella, you'll keep that fact to yourself. As far as the rest of the Seven Systems is concerned, Kovak was killed during a firefight between protesters and loyalists as he was trying to escape the Capital. End of story."

Calculations raced behind Pax's eyes, and a moment later, he nodded. "Logical. Such a cover story would be less inflammatory than allowing it to be known that he was killed by an enslaved human."

Skye's summer blue eyes glinted with grief and rage. "Kovak was keeping our stepmother as a... as a *seelaht*?" She swallowed hard. "And... she killed him?"

Martinez captured her gaze and held it. "He was killed during a firefight between protesters and loyalists as he was trying to escape," she repeated.

Skye took in a deep breath, and let it out unsteadily. "Right."

Hunter's hand rested on her shoulder. "Go, sparrow. Get Stella to the Haven, and make sure Ryder gets that arm wound treated, as well. We will meet you there as soon as we're able."

Skye nodded slowly. "Okay. I'll see you soon. Be safe, and don't let anyone do anything stupid."

Hunter let out a small breath of amusement. "It is, perhaps, a little too late for such a promise, beloved." He lifted her wrist to his lips and nipped it lightly.

She sighed. "Yeah, maybe so. Still... look out for each other, okay?"

"We always do," Hunter said without hesitation.

Ryder and Skye departed to collect Temple and his charge, leaving Martinez alone with Pax and Hunter.

"What about the others?" she asked, somewhat belatedly. "Are they all right?"

Hunter glanced toward the main part of the bay. "In addition to the blaster burn on his arm, Draven now has bruising across his back from a falling cargo container. Ash and Nahleene are uninjured. The three of them are directing the others. Several of the protesters were struck by weapons fire during the fight. It's likely that some were killed."

"Looks like we lost eight people," Draven said, approaching from the main area. He was moving stiffly, but didn't appear to be seriously hurt. "The rest should be stable enough to wait for help to get here."

"Then we need to move on the troops holding the main entrance immediately," Pax said. "They will not be expecting an attack from the rear."

For a moment, Hunter looked... exhausted. It was a look Martinez had seen in the mirror on more than one occasion, back in the dark days after the Badlands Rebellion—the look of someone who was having a hell of a hard time remembering why they were fighting, and who couldn't picture what 'afterward' looked like. She wondered how long this war had consumed the resistance leader's life.

Hunter rallied almost immediately, and nodded agreement. "You're right, of course. Come. Gather everyone still able to fight. Show them the Premiere's body so they know he's really dead, and then let's go end this for good."

⬥

The reason no additional troops had shown up during the firefight in the cargo bay became obvious as they snuck toward the terminal entrance. Under sheer force of numbers, the barricades that the loyalist forces had erected were nearly destroyed. The fire from outside was so heavy that it, rather than the guards themselves, was going to be the biggest danger as they made the final approach for an ambush from behind the lines.

In the end, they stayed back at the far edge of their weapons' useful range. Without Pax, the loss in accuracy might have made that a fatal tactical error, but apparently cyborg targeting software and cybernetically enhanced reflexes were everything they were cracked up to be, even for a rogue unit who'd regained his free will.

As the loyalist guards fell one by one, the confusion caused by the pincer attack allowed the mob outside to breach the barriers. It was all over rather quickly after that—but no less bloody for it. Hunter held their group back from the final hand-to-hand skirmish, with the iron control of someone unwilling to risk any more friends in a battle that was already as good as won.

As the mob swallowed up the last dregs of the Regime, Hunter directed their group to holster their weapons and raise their hands. Martinez was certainly thankful that they'd taken the time to don the resistance's characteristic white bandanas and armbands, but as the protesters who'd joined them for the assault on the side door merged back into the main group, there was no further violence inside the terminal.

Around them, excited chatter and cheering spread through the group, part of which broke off and headed further into the building. She was willing to bet that word of the Premiere's death was already spreading through the crowd like wildfire, thanks to the people who'd been there when it happened. Hopefully, they'd also help the wounded protesters get medical assistance, once they were done gawping at the blue-haired corpse.

Draven watched them go. "They'll be parading Kovak's body through the streets before the afternoon is over." He looked almost as tired as Hunter had earlier.

Ash clasped a hand around Draven's uninjured arm. "Let them," he said. "Just… let them. The Regime has fallen. We're still alive. Please—let's just go back to the safehouse, and… try to pick up the pieces, I suppose." His normally smooth voice was hoarse.

Hunter took a deep breath, and nodded. "Yes. With the allies in control of the government and the Premiere dead, our work is done. Let's go home."

Martinez swallowed against the heaviness in her chest. This wasn't her home, and the person she most wanted to talk to right now wouldn't be rejoining them at the Haven. She looked at the bodies littering the terminal entrance, and thought again of the ginger-haired boy they'd abandoned dead in the street with only a scrap of paper to identify him.

Despite Captain N'komo's tacit assistance in her quest to get here, there was no way to predict how her actions on Ilarius would affect her future on Terra Nova and Vithara. She'd gone rogue… thrown her lot in with vigilantes… killed police and security forces in the capital city of an allied world.

She'd done these things because what was happening on Ilarius was wrong, and couldn't be allowed to continue. But she'd also done them for

Kade, because this was the cause he'd dedicated his life to, and she'd promised to see it through on his behalf.

Now it was finished. And what would come next was a murky sea of uncertainty.

This is the way the world ends, she thought, the snippet from an old Terran poem slipping through the cracks of memory, echoes from some long-ago piece of childhood. *Not with a bang, but a whimper.*

NINETEEN

It took six full days before Martinez managed to wrangle passage to the Vitharan medical ship in orbit for herself, Hunter, and Skye. Ryder had already been there for four of those days, thanks to her exceptional expertise with Ilarian nanotechnology, along with her status as Kade's longstanding primary medical provider.

In the intervening time, Martinez had returned to the makeshift undercity clinic with the others, and done her best to be helpful while keeping a low profile. The allied forces had quickly consolidated their control in the Capital, quelling unrest and starting the laborious process of getting basic infrastructure and services back online. Communications were spotty, but Temple and Draven had managed to reach Jonah's relatives and confirm that they'd been able to claim the boy's body.

Martinez had joined the remaining members of the Shadow Wing at a small memorial service for him, held in a private home. It was a somber affair, and she didn't fit in with the people who had known the vibrant young man well. Yet she felt she owed it to him, somehow... so she stood with a bowed head as those around her grieved and did their best to honor his memory.

A tense peace reigned in the city, Kovak's remaining supporters correctly reading the public's sentiment and determining that silence was their best strategy for the moment. The race hatred and xenophobia would, Martinez suspected, crawl back into the darkness where it always lived when rationality held sway with the majority. The seismic fissures that had opened up between Ilarius' human and Vithii populations would take a long time to close. But all of the planet's citizens were once again protected equally by the law, and raising a hand against anyone you resented or didn't agree with was a fast track to arrest and incarceration by the allied forces.

The political upheaval that would follow was certain to be intense, as the allies and the natives tried to pound out a new system that would prevent the recurrence of such a nightmare in the future.

She couldn't help thinking that Kade should be there for it.

Martinez had spoken at length with Nahleene Veila'ana, during the stretches of time when both of them were busy doing mindless but necessary tasks in the clinic. It probably shouldn't have come as a surprise when Nahleene told her about the conversations she'd had with Kade regarding the planet's future. Of *course* Kade had been planning and scheming the whole time—preparing for 'what came after,' while the rest of them had just been scrambling to survive.

All of which made it even less fair that he was still comatose in a medical bed, orbiting the planet he'd fought so hard to save. Unsure what else to do, Martinez joined his friends as they gathered around him, exchanging desultory conversation as they waited for news from the team of doctors after the most recent experimental procedure he'd undergone.

She'd been mildly surprised when Hunter took a seat at the bedside and scooped Kade's limp hand into both of his, holding it tightly. Vithii men weren't generally known for being demonstrative with each other. If anything, she'd expected Skye to be the one expressing her emotions openly upon seeing Kade like this—but instead the human woman hung back, standing silently behind Hunter with her hand resting supportively on his shoulder.

Ryder wore a professional facade, though there was a definite brittleness to it. The Vithii medic had joined them not long after they'd arrived and given them a rundown of the groundbreaking procedure the doctors had attempted, along with the latest on Kade's condition. Then, she just sort of... *stayed*.

Martinez forced her way through the unspoken awkwardness inherent in being the only stranger among a group of people so tightly knit that they might as well be family. She grabbed a second chair and pulled it up to the other side of the bed, taking up a vigil across from Hunter. Though somehow, the idea of taking Kade's free hand and twining their fingers together seemed—*presumptuous*, in a way that it hadn't when she'd been alone with him.

Instead, she let the quiet, intermittent conversation flow over her. The atmosphere in the room made her ache, and not just because of the circumstances. She hadn't experienced this brand of closeness since she'd left the military... not even secondhand. Certainly not from her own family, who'd disagreed with her life choices for so long that they might as well not be family at all, these days. Not at university, where she'd often been someone that others came to for help and advice, but seldom received similar support in return. And not from her professional colleagues, either—her relationships within the diplomatic corps were generally cordial, but distant.

Her occasional one-night stands, she'd always kept at arms' length, using them only as a way to drown out her own thoughts when they got too loud. She'd had nothing more serious than that in the way of romantic relationships since before her military days.

Somehow, she'd become a loner, despite her measured circulation through the echelons of government. And... she hadn't done so out of conscious choice.

What had happened to her, anyway?

She'd received treatment for her PTSD after her honorable discharge, and she'd approached it in what she thought was a workmanlike matter. But even so, she'd turned into this person—this *being*—who never let anyone else in. At least, not until a crusty bastard of a Vithii had barged into her orbit and basically dared her to stand by and do nothing while his homeworld burned.

Meanwhile, these people—freedom fighters who'd spent years risking their lives to stave off a humanitarian disaster—had managed to find the kind of soul-deep bond Martinez had unknowingly craved. They could not have been more different from each other. Humans and Vithii, hailing from all walks of life, all education levels and personality types. Yet they'd supported each other to an unlikely victory against forces that were vastly more powerful than they were. They'd comforted each other through hard times. Even found love in the unlikeliest of circumstances.

Now, they waited to see if their friend would wake up.

The doctors were cautiously optimistic that the treatment they'd devised was successfully reversing much of the physical damage caused by the extreme swings in neurotransmitter balance Kade had suffered. They were unwilling to make any predictions about the timeline or likelihood of his waking up, however. Or about what sort of state he might be in if he did.

So, she and the others sat vigil.

At least the curtained-off area in the medical bay was relatively private, and reasonably quiet. Kade's medical sensors were currently tied to the nurse's station, rather than to the machines above the bed. That would change whenever medical personnel came in to check on him, but otherwise there was no point to having a beeping cacophony hanging over his head day and night.

Martinez studied Kade's haggard features. He no longer looked quite as deathly as he had at first, when the medics had arrived to save them from the unmanned space station where they'd docked after overpowering their kidnappers. After days of having fluids, nutrients, and drugs pumped into him, the dark, sunken circles beneath Kade's closed eyelids had filled in. He was pale for a Vithii, but no longer ghastly gray beneath his bronze complexion.

A section of his skull had been shaved for his last round of surgery, leaving him looking like either a guy exploring alternative lifestyles in his middle age, or the victim of an unfortunate prank. Silently, she urged him to wake up so he could bitch about it.

"How did all of you meet him, anyway?" she asked, to fill the silence that had descended over the curtained room.

"I tried to pick his pocket when I was fourteen," Hunter said. "*Tried* being the operative word."

Skye looked at him strangely. "Really? You never told me that story!"

Hunter gave a half-shrug that might have been called sheepish, had he been a less intimidating figure. "It's a mildly humiliating tale on my end… and he doesn't often care to speak of the past. Or to have it spoken of."

Ryder snorted. "Then by all means, spill. Maybe it'll piss him off enough to wake him up."

"Very well," Hunter said, with a hint of dryness. "It was when I was still living on the streets. As I said, I tried to pick his pocket. He looked rich—an easy mark. But he had me by the wrist the instant I reached for him, and he dodged my clumsy attempt to kick him so I could get free as though it were nothing."

He shifted in his seat, looking down at the hand he held.

"He should've called for the nearest police officer. Had me carted off for vagrancy, or attempted theft, or both. Instead, he looked me up and down, handed me fifty credits, and gave me the name of a man who would teach me some safer forms of street hustling in exchange for doing odd jobs. Then he walked away, and I didn't see him again for almost ten years."

"Wow," Skye said. "I had no idea."

"The next time we met, he'd only recently been released from prison," Hunter continued. "He was in terrible health, but he was still putting out feelers for other people who'd lost family members to Regime assassination. I hadn't… at least, not exactly—but I *was* looking for anyone with an ax to grind against the Vithii First movement, and the means to make some waves. Imagine my surprise when I recognized my new contact as the man who'd caught me red-handed and let me go with a fifty-credit chip a decade previously."

"Did he remember you, as well?" Martinez asked curiously.

Hunter huffed out a sharp breath. "Of course he did. He gave me that same head-to-toe sweep, and asked what my thoughts were on organized civil disobedience. I told him I didn't know what that meant, but if it involved making the Firsters pay for what they'd done, I was all for it."

"By the time I met Kade and Hunter, they were practically inseparable," Ryder said. "Hunter was already making a name for himself—not to mention making enemies in the Regime. Kade, on the other hand, was smart enough to keep a lower profile. I guess his family was rich as fuck to begin with, but he lost everything when his parents were killed and he was thrown in prison on trumped-up charges. Then he made his second fortune on the back of borrowed undercity money."

"So how did you meet him, exactly?" Martinez asked. She glanced down, and realized with a jolt that her hand had crept onto the mattress to cover Kade's when she wasn't paying attention—just like the last time she'd been here. None of the others commented.

"Ironically enough," Ryder said, "he stumbled into my back-alley medical practice in the throes of neurotonin withdrawal. I almost stunned him unconscious for barging in and acting like a raving asshole, but he managed to spit out the word 'neurotonin' before I pulled the trigger on him. He was just lucky that I had some of the stuff on hand."

"Afterward," Hunter continued, "Kade sent anyone who got sick or injured to Ryder, until eventually it just made more sense for her to join us. Draven was with us by then, and Kade had already hired Ash a few times when he needed a hacker. Then we found out that Ryder had been helping a rogue cyborg hide out in the undercity, and Pax joined us, as well."

It was quite a story. "How about you?" Martinez asked Skye.

"Me? Oh, I crashed a stolen shuttle on their doorstep, after fleeing Ilarius with the formula to the bioweapon antidote hidden in a piece of jewelry. Kade's first words to me were to accuse me of being a mad scientist's daughter, who daylighted as an accountant and played at being a spy on her nights off. *Badly*." Skye gave a rueful laugh. "And he was right."

The words trailed off into silence, only to be broken by a hoarse rasp from the bed.

"Well," Kade croaked. "In retrospect, I've seen people do worse."

TWENTY

This was a surprisingly nice dream, aside from the scratchy throat and the odd weight holding Kade's eyelids down. As a rule, he didn't dream much these days—not since his stint in the Capital prison. Mind you, that wasn't a bad thing, since what dreams he did have tended to skew heavily toward the nightmarish end of the spectrum.

All of which made *this* dream more than a little suspect. The setting was uncharacteristically saccharine, what with the whole 'surrounded by his friends telling stories about the past' thing. It was enough to make him wonder what sort of horror was hiding in the shadows, waiting to jump out from the depths of his jacked-up subconscious as soon as his emotional guard was down.

Certainly, there seemed to be a great deal of scrambling around and raised voices in response to his dry observation to Skye. Both of his hands also appeared to be restrained, but not by shackles—rather, they were held in tight, warm grips… one of them rather more crushing than the other, admittedly.

"*Tei'laal,*" Hunter said, and there was an unusual amount of tension in his familiar voice. "Open your eyes and look at me. *Now.*"

Kade had grown way too godsdamned used to listening to that voice over the past few years. He pried uncooperative eyelids open, though all he could make out beyond them was a blur of light that was *far* too fucking bright. He blinked a few times, a grunt of discontent slipping past his parched lips.

A hand lifted his head, supporting it a few inches above the surface of whatever he was lying on, and something brushed his lips. He identified the end of a drinking straw, and wondered—not for the first time—what the hell kind of dream this was supposed to be. It was growing more surreal by the moment.

"Small sips," Ryder said, settling the straw in place for him to drink.

He did, and immediately felt a bit better. Now if he could just clear the grit from the back of his eyelids…

Unbidden, a series of images presented themselves. Terra Nova. Vithara. The prisoner transport. The kidnapping. The escape. The broken neurotonin pump, hanging from his bleeding chest. He spit out the straw and tried to focus on the blur-that-was-probably-Hunter.

"Wait," he said. "Are we all dead? Because I was really banking on there not being an afterlife. Frankly, I don't have the energy for it."

Some of the tension in the hand crushing his bled away. "Not dead, *tei'laal*," Hunter said, sounding more himself. "Somewhat surprisingly, I'll grant you—but we're not."

That… sounded pretty unlikely, actually. And yet, if this *was* the afterlife, someone in the religious past had gotten things pretty badly garbled. But if it was real—

He tried to struggle upright, only to fall back ignominiously when his body failed him.

"Hang on… Isadora Martinez," he panted. "Is she—?"

The last thing he remembered was the stubborn woman refusing to stun him unconscious as he entered the final stages of neurotonin withdrawal. He'd been off his head… he could have done anything to her—

The blur across from Hunter shifted, leaning over him, and the grip on his other hand tightened. "Kade. I'm right here. I'm fine."

She sounded upset. Emotional. More commotion interrupted whatever else she might have been about to say—a new voice he didn't recognize cutting across the confusion with a pronounced Vitharan accent. "Please wait outside, all of you. We'll need to perform some tests now that he's awake."

"I'm not leaving." That was Ryder. "I'm his primary physician."

Kade wavered in and out of touch with the conversation for a bit, but when he checked back in, Ryder was still there—her shock of red hair distinctive even when his vision was blurry. His hands felt cold, now that they were empty. Other people were poking and prodding him, attaching sensors to his head and generally being annoying. If pressed, he would later claim that he'd lost consciousness at that point largely out of spite.

⚊⚊⚊◆⚊⚊⚊

The next time he became aware of his surroundings, it was easier to open his eyes and pull the room into focus. The lights were dim—standard ship's night. And this was definitely a ship. Now that he was a bit more awake, the sound of the engines and the smell of the stale, too-dry air were dead giveaways.

The others were clustered nearby, slouched on uncomfortable looking duraplast chairs in varying states of insensibility. Isadora was closest—right by his bedside—and she had slumped forward until her head and shoulders rested on the edge of the unforgiving mattress. The position didn't look remotely comfortable, but it did drive a sharp little spike of something straight into the center of his chest.

Ryder stirred, rising from her chair and crossing to him. "Back with us again?"

"Reluctantly," he managed, pleased to discover that the water he'd sipped earlier was still lubricating his throat enough for him to be able to speak without croaking. He must not have been out for long this time.

"Do you know where you are?" she asked, keeping her voice low to avoid waking the others.

"No clue," he said. "Not the afterlife, apparently. A ship?"

At his shoulder, Isadora Martinez snorted awake with a sound better suited to a barnyard animal than to an elegant human diplomat. Despite his best efforts, a wave of mild amusement assailed him, dispelling some of the heaviness crushing his chest.

"You're awake!" she exclaimed, groggy for only a moment before her attractive features sharpened. "How do you feel?"

"Like a bug under a microscope," he groused, as Hunter and Skye woke up and joined the knot of people around his bedside.

"Hmm," Ryder said. "I'm sorry to say, you'd better get used to it. For the moment, you're the sole test subject for a groundbreaking new medical treatment."

"Oh?" he asked. "That sounds tiresome. Is there more water?"

Isadora reached for a nearby table and retrieved a cup with a straw. "Here," she said. "Do you want me to—"

He waved off her abortive attempt to lift his head, and did it himself. His muscles felt nearly petrified with disuse, but at least they responded to his commands in a limited fashion this time. He drank a few sips and lay back.

Ryder regarded him closely. "What's the last thing you remember?"

He tipped his chin toward Isadora. "Trying to convince this stubborn human to stun me, before I lost control and hurt her in the throes of withdrawal," he said without hesitation.

Ryder nodded. "She *did* stun you, eventually. A medical ship from the Terra Novan fleet rescued both of you a couple of cycles later, and they transferred you to this Vitharan ship. You were in a coma for seven days."

"Only seven days? I'm surprised it wasn't permanent," he told her.

He watched as Ryder took a deep breath through her nose, as though to steady herself.

"It probably would have been, but the Vitharans are good at medicine... and Pax dropped by after arriving with the Maelfian fleet to donate some of his bots." She paused before continuing, "I hitched a ride up here as soon as I was able, and collaborated with the Vitharan doctors on a nanotech-based treatment to repair the damaged Roche nuclei in your brainstem."

He frowned, feeling an odd pulling sensation at the base of his scalp as he did. "What do you mean, 'repair'?"

"Your brainstem is now producing neurotonin normally for the first time since you were dosed in the prison."

He stared at Ryder blankly for a few seconds. When gawping at her didn't manage to twist the words into something logical, he looked at Hunter instead.

"The doctors here say that the damage done to you in the prison has been reversed," Hunter said.

Kade blinked, unsure what the hell he was supposed to do with that statement. Vitharan medicine was highly advanced, but they didn't have access to nanotech—or they hadn't before now, at any rate. Ryder was an expert on bots, but she hadn't been able to devise a treatment strategy for neurotonin imbalance that wouldn't also risk catastrophically altering other parts of his brain at the same time.

Had they truly managed to bridge the gap between the two technologies in a way that healed the damage he'd lived with for so long?

The question was too big. He set it aside in favor of something more immediate.

"What's happening on Ilarius?" he asked.

Logically, the ship they were on must be stationed near the planet, since Ryder and the others were here. Pax and Nahleene had apparently made it back with the Maelfian fleet. Knowing Ash and Draven as he did, he suspected they would have come along with the Vitharans rather than staying behind where it was safe—like *sane* people would've done. At least... he hoped his memory of the Vitharans joining the alliance was real.

"The Premiere is dead," Hunter said flatly. "The Regime is in tatters, and allied forces are keeping the peace while next steps are discussed. Pax, Nahleene, Draven, and Ash stayed behind on the surface to keep tabs on developments, since they've forged connections with the Maelfian and Vitharan delegations. Temple's there, too, trying to liaise with the humans who've been driven into hiding in the undercity."

A strange, lightheaded sensation made it feel like the medical bed was swaying, and Kade choked unexpectedly on his next breath. It was too easy. Too much like a fairytale ending, and he'd never believed in those. Maybe this really *was* some kind of intricate, fucked-up dream—

A small hand twined with his, and his eyes flew to Isadora, still seated in the chair next to him.

"That... can't be..." he began, aware that his heart was thundering as though he'd unexpectedly been dumped in the middle of a battle.

"It is, though," she said, confirming Hunter's words.

"It's all true," Skye chimed in. "Don't ask me how, but... we did it, Kade. It's over."

Ryder snorted. "Over? Hardly that. I imagine the fallout will be felt for years. But, yes—Kovak's gone, and so are most of his cronies. The planet is under martial law, but at least it's martial law enforced by civilized governments that aren't bent on genocide. And it's temporary."

"How did Kovak die?" Kade asked hoarsely, still trying to take everything in.

Isadora's face went flat and hard. "Aptly," she said.

Which… didn't really tell him anything, except that she'd been there when it happened.

"You kept your promise," he murmured, not sure whether that should surprise him.

A haunted edge crept into her expression. "Yeah. I suppose I did."

"She saved my life," Skye said. "We got caught in a firefight in the street. Jonah got killed. I would've been shot, too, but she pushed me out of the way."

Now discomfort joined Isadora's haunted look. "It was instinct, that's all," she said. "I'm… just glad I saw the shooter in time."

There were undercurrents swirling around her expression, but at this moment they just made Kade feel exhausted. The jolt of adrenaline from learning about everything he'd missed was wearing off, and he wasn't sure he could properly deal with any of it yet.

"So," he said slowly, "just to be clear, we're not currently under arrest, in immediate danger of death, or about to be embroiled in a space battle?"

"No," Hunter said in a solemn tone. "For the first time in quite a while, none of those things are a concern for us."

Kade nodded. "Good. In that case, all of you need to get out of my fucking room for a few hours, so I can rock quietly back and forth in the corner in private."

Skye huffed out a breath of rueful laughter. "I guess that means he's feeling more like himself."

Ryder leaned on the footboard of the medical bed and raised an eyebrow at him. "The doctors here seem satisfied with your medical scans for the moment. You're supposed to rest for a few days under observation, at which point they'll probably be willing to let you out of your kennel as long as you agree to take it easy for a few months. Though I have no doubt they'll be clamoring for frequent brain scans and blood tests to track the progress of the nano-repairs."

"Sounds lovely," he told her. "I can hardly wait."

Hunter leaned down and clasped callused fingers around the juncture of Kade's neck and shoulder, squeezing lightly. "Rest well, *tei'laal*. Everything is in hand, for once."

Kade's breath hitched as the untethered feeling of surreality returned, and he nodded rather than attempting to reply aloud. He clasped Hunter's forearm with his free hand and squeezed back, hoping that would be enough to convey what he wanted to. Hunter smiled at him, lopsided and sincere—the expression taking years off his appearance, until Kade could clearly see the echoes of the bright and promising young man he'd once been.

Hunter's hand slid away. He ushered Skye ahead of him as they left, both of them giving Kade a final look as they slipped through the curtains separating his bed from the rest of the medical bay. Ryder looked down at him from her spot at the end of the bed, poised as though to say something.

The silence stretched until Kade broke it with a quiet, "Thank you. And thank Pax when you get a chance... not that he'll understand why he deserves it, of course."

But Ryder looked troubled. "I can't help thinking that if I'd tried a little harder... researched a little more thoroughly…" She trailed off and shook her head. "Maybe I could have fixed this for you years ago."

He arched a brow, feeling the skin behind his ear pulling oddly again—a bandage, perhaps, or a surgical scar.

"Or you could have accidentally turned me into Pax's evil twin," he said. "Don't start with the what-ifs, Ryder. You of all people should know better than to entertain that kind of *greilo*-shit."

Ryder's lips twitched. "Foul-tempered ingrate," she shot back. "Never mind, then. I'm over it. I'll check back in a few hours to make sure you're still doing all right."

"Get some sleep, Ryder," he told her. "You look like I feel."

She made a dismissive noise and saw herself out, though she, too, couldn't seem to keep from throwing him a long look as she left. Kade's eyes moved to the last person remaining in the room. Isadora Martinez had been strangely silent through everything, though her fingers still tangled with his. When their gazes met and locked, she seemed to come back to herself, straightening in her chair.

"Sorry," she said, tugging at her hand as she made to rise. "I guess I should probably—"

He tightened his fingers around hers, halting her.

"No," he interrupted. "Stay. We need to talk."

TWENTY-ONE

Isadora looked cornered for a moment, but then she relaxed back into her seat, her hand still clasped with his. Kade studied her, taking in the dark circles under her eyes, along with the general sense of dishevelment that spoke of multiple days spent camped out at his bedside with the others. Despite the fact that he'd just chided Ryder for doing so, he thought about what-ifs and might-have-beens.

Not for the first time, either.

"You kept your promise to me," he repeated. "You saw things through in my stead."

"Yes," she said quietly. "I guess… I had some demons of my own that needed slaying down there."

He still only had scattered pieces of the puzzle that would form the picture of the last few days, but she'd as much as admitted that she'd been present when Kovak died.

"And did you slay them?" he asked.

She was silent for a moment before replying. "I… don't know." Her tone turned wry. "Though I suspect I've slayed my career, if nothing else."

He mulled that over. "Well—on the positive side, at least you're not wanted for murder on Vithara anymore." He frowned. "Assuming I didn't hallucinate that part of things, of course."

Her face softened. "No, that part really happened. We're both in the clear with the authorities. At least, we are as long as no one takes exception to the fact that I commandeered a damaged Terra Novan ship to get to Ilarius after the allied forces smashed through the planetary blockade."

"Oh, *did* you, now? I'm sorry I missed it," he said, meaning every word.

At that, she looked somber. "You should have been there, not me. You and the others were the ones who really made this happen."

He huffed out a breath. "I don't care who was there, as long as that bastard Kovak is dead and his sick Regime has been taken down. Trust me when I say, I wasn't in it for the glory."

"Yeah… I don't think there was much glory to be had."

"There never is," he agreed.

Silence filled the space between them, broken only by the subtle hum of the ship's systems in the background. He could feel her poised to speak, fighting with herself over whether or not to let the words escape.

Eventually, she gave in. "When things went south during the Badlands Rebellion, I was on my way to meet the rest of my team at the extraction point. I stopped to help a woman and her two kids, when I saw that they were in the path of the advancing Kritaani forces."

He searched her face, but it was a blank facade. Her hazel eyes were distant.

"You said you tried to save some people, but it didn't work out," he recalled.

She nodded. "I led them to a gap in the fence where people were trying to escape the rebel compound," she said, speaking in a low monotone. "Then I left to try to get to the rendezvous point, but I was too late. When I came back later, everyone who'd been caught at the bottleneck where I'd taken the woman and her kids was dead. I watched the Kritaani government forces haul her body off to a mass grave that was being dug nearby. Her children, too."

"Was it the rebels or the government forces who killed them?" Kade asked.

"I don't know," Isadora said distantly. "Just like I don't know if it was the riot police or a stray shot from a protester that got the boy, Jonah. And I've been thinking lately… does it even matter? They're just as dead, either way."

Jonah. Regret washed at the edges of Kade's emotions, over the loss of another promising young mind.

"No," he said, "I suppose it hardly matters now."

The haunted look in Isadora's eyes was back, and it made more sense to him now. Jonah's death was linked in her mind with the humans she'd tried to save on the Badlands colony. She'd already been struggling with the parallels between past and present, even before he'd selfishly demanded that she jump into the thick of it for him.

She rose abruptly, her hand sliding free of his as she abandoned his bedside in favor of pacing jerkily around the edges of the curtained space. And this… *this* was why he had no business pondering those elusive might-have-beens. He'd used Isadora Martinez for the Shadow Wing's ends. For *his own* ends. And he'd done all of it without a thought for how it might affect her.

Kade's miserable existence for the past decade-plus had been good for one thing, and one thing only—ending the Regime. If that goal had truly come to pass in the last few days, then he had some real questions surrounding what the hell he was supposed to do with the rest of his life now.

Martinez paced, trying to outrun the muddle of thoughts and emotions buzzing around her head like swarming insects. So much had happened in the past couple of weeks. She was struggling to catalogue the parts that were good, the parts that were bad, and the parts that were still up in the air.

Innocent people had died. But other people had lived, and something that would have been even more horrible had been stopped before it came to pass. Her eyes fell on Kade, and she realized belatedly that she'd practically yanked her hand out of his when she'd fled her chair in favor of prowling around the room like a caged animal.

She could see him closing off… pulling back.

And that wasn't what she wanted.

He looked up in surprise as she returned to his bedside and leaned over him—splaying her hand over the center of his chest, where his heart beat strongly against its cage of flesh and bone. His eyes were wary, as though he had no clue what to do with the gesture. And that was fair—she still had no idea how much of the connection she felt with him was her own wishful thinking, and how much was real.

"I keep thinking," she said, "that things should never have been allowed to get this bad. Not here.

Not on the Badlands colony. *You* didn't stand by silently while everything got worse and worse. You and the others stepped up and tried to do something. Why is it that the people in power—the ones who might have stopped all of this before it ever started—couldn't be bothered?"

He gave the question real consideration, even though he still seemed preoccupied by her hand on his chest.

"The Shadow Wing fought because we'd already lost things that were precious to us," he said. "I lost my parents. Hunter lost his guardians. Ryder lost her bondmate's loyalty, and her place in society. Ash lost a sister. Temple and Skye, a father. Draven lost a childhood. Pax lost his free will. People who haven't had anything valuable taken from them have no real motivation to risk themselves."

She stared into his steel-gray eyes, trying to put what she was feeling into words. "But they need to do it anyway. *I*... need to. Inertia and apathy aren't excuses for allowing atrocities to go unchallenged."

Something like regret creased his expression. "They frequently *are*, I'm sorry to say."

But she only shook her head. "They shouldn't be, though. I... thought I was making a difference in the military, but in the end, innocents still died. Then, I thought I could make a difference as a diplomat. But it took you and Jontalyss showing up on Terra Nova to jolt me into any kind of meaningful action, even though I already *knew* that what was happening on Ilarius was bad news."

Kade held her gaze, his brows drawing together. "It wasn't your job to police a planetary government you had nothing to do with. At least, not until we dragged you forcibly into the mess with us. It was sheer happenstance that Ash was able to infiltrate a household with a connection to an off-world diplomat. Even more so, that the diplomat in question was you."

Martinez took a deep breath, needing him to understand. "But that's not my point. *I* need to be somewhere I can actually make a difference. At first, I thought that meant the military. Then, I thought it meant an ambassadorship. I was wrong both times. But maybe those skill sets can be of use here."

The furrow between Kade's heavy brows deepened. "You… want to stay? On Ilarius?"

"I want to help," she said, feeling the truth of the words settle into her as she said them. "I want to make sure things here never again get to the point where innocent kids have to die in street protests, in order to change things."

Kade looked… stunned, as though he'd expected her to run for the hills the moment she got a chance.

She huffed out a rueful breath. "My old Special Forces commander tried to tell me I sucked at civilian life. I'm… pretty sure she was right about that, actually. But it's also fairly clear after the last few days that my PTSD won't let me go back to fighting with guns and fists. Not in situations where other people's lives are on the line if I have a flashback at the wrong moment."

Kade blinked up at her, evidently lost for words.

"So," she said. "How about it? Got any non-combat related openings for an ex-soldier with multiple advanced degrees and real-world experience in diplomacy? Or do Pax and Nahleene already hold the monopoly on that sector?"

He exhaled sharply. "I… suspect we can come to some kind of accommodation, if that's truly what you want to do," he said in a careful tone.

Okay. So, that was half of the battle won. Before she could talk herself out of tackling the other half, she grabbed her courage with both hands and softened her touch on Kade's chest, sliding her fingertips over hard muscle and sinew.

"Good," she said. "Although—I suppose this means I'll need to find someplace to stay on Ilarius… not to mention, a native guide." She let out an affected sigh, and purposely lightened her tone. "Preferably, this guide would also be someone rich. Since, you know, I'm technically unemployed now."

Kade was still looking at her like he thought he'd misheard her… or like he was worried that he was the butt of some kind of practical joke.

"Well," he said eventually, "you'll be happy to learn that I own several properties in various states of dereliction—many of which may or may not have been burned down by angry mobs in the last few days."

It was dangerously close to a joke, and something lurking behind her ribs grew infinitesimally lighter.

"Hmm. I suppose if we had to, we could wrangle lodgings in the secure government buildings where the allied leaders are staying," she mused. "Although, given the fact that you're still recovering from surgery, not to mention from being in a coma—I imagine you'll be needing someone to stay with you and look after you, at first."

He raised a skeptical eyebrow. "Are you volunteering to wipe my ass and give me sponge baths?"

Martinez snorted. "That depends heavily on how competent you want your ass-wiper to be." She gestured at herself. "I mean, do I even look like a nurse?"

Kade sobered. "No. You look like the woman who helped stop a genocidal maniac, and somehow managed to save my worthless hide in the process." He paused. Swallowed. "Look. I don't... know if I can give you everything you're looking for, Isadora Martinez. But... come with me to Ilarius anyway. Let's see if between us, we can make sure this kind of thing never happens again."

TWENTY-TWO

Twenty-three days after the official fall of the Regime, Ash peered into a cheery hospital room occupied by a single human figure. Stella Chantrell, widow of Dr. Zarian Chantrell, sat silently in a molded duraplast chair by the room's only window. She was wrapped in a drab robe, looking out across the cityscape beyond. No movement or shift of expression marred her perfect stillness as Skye led the way inside, followed by Temple and finally, Ash, who had come along for the visit at Skye's request.

Security was tight around the facility, even weeks after the government's downfall. Few people knew of Stella's presence here, much less that she had personally killed Xandrie Kovak. Nonetheless, the hospital administrators were taking no chances these days, and had instituted checkpoints for staff and visitors to ensure the safety of everyone undergoing treatment.

In many ways, tensions in the Capital were still running high.

Temple and Skye had been visiting their stepmother regularly since that fateful day at the freighter terminal, but so far there had been no noticeable improvement in Stella's condition. Ash could well imagine what the pale, slender woman must be going through after suffering months as a body slave at the hands of the now-deceased Premiere.

Before they came, Skye had taken Ash aside and privately shared the results of the medical screening Stella had undergone before being admitted to the hospital's inpatient treatment program. None of it was a surprise. All of it made bile rise in Ash's throat.

Malnutrition. Sleep deprivation. Physical assault. Sexual assault.

Just your average laundry list of damage for someone stuck for an extended period as the plaything of a sadist.

After she'd finished, Skye had looked at Ash with her huge blue eyes brimming. "I'm so sorry, Ash. I know this is probably… bringing everything back. But I don't know where else to turn. The doctors are doing their best, but the hospital is completely overwhelmed after the riots and the fighting."

She paused and caught her lower lip between her teeth before letting it slide free, visibly trying to keep a lid on her emotions. "It's been weeks, and she hasn't so much as spoken a single word. It's like she's retreated so far inside herself that nothing can reach her. Would you… come and talk to her?"

Ash had felt the weight of the last few terrible months pressing down on him like Sisyphus' boulder from ancient Terran mythology. But he'd only nodded and said, "Of course I will, Skye," before reaching out to swipe a tear away from her cheek with the ball of his thumb.

They were all complete psychological train wrecks—every last one of them. Ash wasn't sure if the others had truly taken on board the fact that the ten of them—a ragtag group of regular people, criminals, spies, and more recently, renegade diplomats—had saved an entire world from the depths of fascist horror. Eventually, it would hit them in the same way it had hit him. But in the mean time, Ilarius was still, in many ways, a planet filled with walking wounded.

From what he understood, neither Temple nor Skye had cared all that much for Stella as a stepmother. Not surprising, perhaps—while the events of the past several months had aged her, Ash estimated Stella to be in her late thirties at most. By all appearances, she'd been the embodiment of Zarian Chantrell's mid-life crisis... a much younger and very beautiful woman to distract him from the tragic loss of his first wife. The idea that such a marriage might have bred resentment with Zarian's grown children was practically a given.

Things had changed, though, and Stella was now the only remaining link between Zarian, Skye, and Temple. That Zarian had truly loved Stella seemed apparent—he'd done a horrific thing in a doomed attempt to protect her. Stella had been the primary leverage the Premiere used against Dr. Chantrell to force him to design the bioweapon that had nearly destroyed the human population in the Capital. And after Zarian followed his conscience and smuggled the formula for an antidote out with Skye, dying in the process, Stella bore the brunt of the Premiere's punishment—in the most personal and painful way conceivable.

"Stella?" Skye said tentatively. "Hi. It's Skye and Temple again. We brought a friend with us this time. I thought you might want to talk to him? His name's Ash. He... uh... he was a *veelaht* for a while, but he escaped."

Her stepmother, unsurprisingly, did not respond. Skye had explained that she'd been completely unresponsive since being admitted, refusing to speak or acknowledge her surroundings in any way. She sat staring unfocused into the middle distance for hours on end, and was completely reliant on the nurses and orderlies for her physical care.

The doctors had tentatively diagnosed catatonia, but it had so far been resistant to benzodiazepine. The next suggested step was electro-convulsive therapy, but Temple and Skye had been reluctant to pursue something so drastic until every other avenue had been exhausted.

Ash took a slow breath and let it out. Dragging a chair from the corner of the room, he set it at an angle to Stella's and sat, mirroring her as he looked out at the city. A curl of blue-gray smoke wafted upward in the distance—evidence of a structure fire that might have been either accidental or intentional. He was quiet for some time as he gathered his thoughts, aware of Temple and Skye hovering in the background.

"I've no doubt you're quite sick of people telling you that they understand how you must feel," he said eventually, not moving his gaze from the faraway plume of smoke. "But... for what it's worth, I killed my *Fei'graal* as well. You should know that there *is* life after enslavement, Stella Chantrell—I'm living proof of it."

Silence reigned for several long moments, but then Ash felt Stella's eyes drift to him and stay there. He turned to her slowly, watching as her brow furrowed in concentration. Gradually, her gaze focused until it was holding his properly.

"Stella?" Temple said hopefully. He and Skye crossed the room and crouched in the space between the two chairs. After another few minutes, Stella's attention wandered down to them. Her confused frown deepened.

"Where..." she rasped. After a pause to moisten her dry lips, she tried again. "Where's Zarian? Is he... all right?"

Ash's heart clenched in sympathy. Skye appeared to be at a loss as to how to respond, but Temple dipped his head before raising it again to meet Stella's dazed eyes.

"I'm so sorry, Stella," he said, his voice noticeably unsteady. "He died... doing something noble. Something that saved countless lives."

It was, perhaps, a manipulation of the truth. Or perhaps not, since the Premiere could have simply found another scientist to create his weapon if Dr. Chantrell had refused to do it—another scientist who might not have been brave enough or clever enough to devise an antidote at the same time.

Ash quietly vacated his chair and slipped away to stand near the door, giving the others space. Tears tracked down Skye's cheeks, and Temple's eyes were suspiciously bright. Stella's mouth worked for a few moments, forming words that only she could hear. Then, her expression crumpled, and her body bowed forward at the waist. Skye rose from her knees and caught Stella in her arms, holding her tight as the first ugly croak of a sob erupted from the older woman's throat. Temple stood and wrapped them both up in an embrace, the three clinging to each other as they grieved their lost loved one.

Staying silently out of the way, Ash poked at the tight knot of grief that lived in his own chest—a dull feeling of heartache for all that had been torn from them. Parents. Friends. Innocence. Trust.

He let himself out of the room, closing the door behind him with a soft click. When Temple and Skye found him sitting on a bench in the hallway with his face resting in his hands, some considerable time later, he realized he must have suffered his own minor lapse of dissociation in the interim. Skye sat next to him, half-turning to face him. Her eyes were red and swollen, but her expression was calm.

"One of the doctors is speaking with her now," she said evenly. "It won't be a simple road to recovery, but she seems to be aware of where she is and how she got here." Moving very deliberately so as to give him time to avoid it, she looped an arm around Ash's shoulders and drew him into an embrace. "Thank you, Ash," she murmured into his neck.

He swallowed and hugged her back, burying his face against her spun-gold hair for several moments before carefully pulling back. "I'm just glad I could help, Skye."

Skye gave him a watery smile, and nodded.

Temple cleared his throat. "So… can I get in on some of that hugging action without triggering a flashback and getting punched, stabbed, or otherwise debilitated for my trouble?"

Ash huffed out a breath of soft laughter and rose. "As your red-haired partner in crime always says, there's only one way to find out."

He accepted Temple's careful hug, patting the taller man on the back.

"We owe you, man," Temple said, before letting him go and stepping back.

Ash looked up at him fondly. "No," he said. "You really don't. Tell Stella I'm always available to talk, should she ever desire it. Who knows? Maybe it would do both of us some good."

After waving off Skye's offer to call him a ride, Ash left the two siblings at the hospital with their step-mother in favor of making his own way back to the old property at the edge of the city where they were currently staying. The place had served as one of the Shadow Wing's many safehouses off and on for years, and it was agreeably out of the way of much of the chaos currently taking place in the central areas of the Capital.

The house was still a falling-down wreck, but contractors had mysteriously begun arriving over the past several days, taking measurements and making notes on data padds. Ash suspected Kade's hand behind the sudden plans for renovation.

It was getting late by the time he arrived, and the place currently appeared to be free of plumbers, carpenters, or any other species of builder. This suited Ash quite well under the circumstances. He let himself in through the front door, making no attempt to be stealthy about it.

Hunter had chosen to go assist Ryder at her informal undercity clinic this evening, rather than mope around waiting for Skye's return. His presence at the hospital today would likely have been traumatic for Stella—given everything she'd suffered at the hands of Vithii males in the recent past.

Pax and Nahleene were embroiled in joint meetings with several officials from Vithara and Maelfius over the next several days, and were staying in the government district to save on commute time. Kade and Isadora Martinez were off doing… something. Ash was probably happier not knowing the details, since Kade seemed bent on ignoring the doctors' suggestions to take things easy for a few months.

As far as he knew, the pair hadn't given in to the raging sexual tension between them and slept together yet, for some strange reason. He'd considered starting a betting pool on the subject, but decided that the others wouldn't find the idea nearly as amusing as he did. Well… except for Draven. And maybe Skye and Temple, now that things with their stepmother were looking up.

Perhaps he'd have to revisit the idea after all.

But whatever the case, Kade and the ambassador weren't here right now. Someone else was, though.

"How did it go?" Draven asked, appearing from the direction of the kitchen.

He had a pale smear of what was probably flour across one sharp cheekbone, and he dusted his hands on the thighs of his trousers as he continued forward to meet Ash. With a sigh of loosening tension, Ash walked straight into Draven's arms and rested his weight against his lover's solid, comforting presence.

"It went well," he said. "Perhaps we can still wrest a happy ending of sorts from that particular tragedy."

Ash soaked up the noise of contentment he could feel rumbling through Draven's chest.

"That's great," Draven said, squeezing Ash closer to his body for a moment before loosening his grip. "Next question—how're *you* doing after digging up all that shit?"

"I've… been better," Ash replied honestly, still unused to this strange new world where he could admit things like that out loud.

Draven eased him back so he could look at him properly. "Okay," he said without judgment. "What do you think might help? Is there anything I can do?"

Affection so strong it took his breath away washed through Ash like a warm wave.

"Take me to bed," he suggested, "and remind me that all of this heartache and suffering is finally behind us."

Draven's hands cupped Ash's shoulders—a steady and grounding pressure.

"It is, Ash," he said earnestly. "Better days are coming for us. You'll see."

"I'm absolutely counting on it," Ash whispered, letting his eyes slide shut as Draven leaned down and captured his lips in a scorching, human-style kiss.

Everything else fell away as Ash gave himself over to the man he loved, letting Draven herd him gently backwards to the room they shared. Deft hands plucked at the fastenings of Ash's shirt along the way, baring his chest as they crossed the threshold into the darkened room. Draven's lips and hands never left him, even as he kicked the door shut behind them and walked Ash toward the welcoming softness of the bed.

Better days, indeed.

TWENTY-THREE

Hunter was doing his best to lose himself in the mindless, repetitive work of organizing donated medical supplies. While he mourned the fact that his presence with his bondmate would only have caused more heartache for the woman Skye and Temple called stepmother, there was something oddly satisfying about immersing himself in necessary but unskilled labor, while Ryder puttered around filing records and muttering under her breath.

The two of them were in similar straits—Temple had also gone with Skye to visit Stella Chantrell at the hospital. For now, the doctors were strictly limiting her exposure to Vithii individuals, in an attempt to prevent her from slipping deeper into whatever mental space she currently occupied. Since Ryder was always swamped with work related to her volunteer clinic here in the undercity, it made sense for Hunter to come with her and offer whatever help he could.

She turned, her gaze catching on him. He paused in the middle of counting the hypo-injectors he'd been unboxing, lifting an eyebrow in query.

A look of rueful amusement flitted across her features. "The notorious Rook, scourge of the Seven Systems, is doing inventory in my back-alley clinic," she said. "You know, sometimes I feel the need to pinch myself to make sure the last few weeks haven't been a dream."

The human nurse manning the front desk gave a barely audible snort. "If you're dreaming, then so are the rest of us, doc," he muttered.

"Is it truly so difficult to believe that good people have triumphed over those motivated by selfishness and cruelty?" Hunter asked.

For a moment, Ryder looked haunted. "Yes," she said quietly. "It really is. Honestly, I'd assumed we'd all be dead by now."

Hunter set the box of supplies aside, giving her his full attention. Many lives had been lost to the Regime, and they were still mourning those who hadn't made it. Skye's father. Kade's parents. Ash's sister. Jonah—a kind and loyal boy who had taken on the responsibilities of a man, only to die in a senseless act of random violence, just before the tide turned in favor of justice.

"We're still here, though," he told her. "We're not dead."

She scowled at him, using the dour expression to cover her disquiet. "No? Well, it wasn't for lack of trying, in your case." The scowl deepened. "Or in Kade's case, for that matter. Or in Ash's. Or *Pax's*. I'm surrounded by a bunch of suicidal idiots."

A fond smile tugged at Hunter's lips. "And yet, all of us are still around to make your life more difficult."

Ryder wrinkled her nose at the gentle teasing, and Hunter allowed his smile to spread until it crinkled the corners of his eyes.

"Have you heard from Kade yet today?" she asked, changing the subject.

Hunter let the evasion pass unremarked. He knew that Ryder was less than pleased with their mutual friend's insistence on diving right back into the thick of things despite having nearly died of neurotonin withdrawal. He also knew that if the frequent medical scans and tests Kade was undergoing had shown any sign of real danger, she would have immediately rounded him up and herded him right back into inpatient treatment, at blaster-point if necessary.

"Not today," he said. "As of yesterday, he and Martinez were still in talks with a group of Ilarian economic leaders about the possibility of funding a human-led business incubator in the outskirts of the Capital."

She raised an eyebrow. "And have the two of them gotten a room yet? I swear, the sexual tension leaks straight out of the comm-vid screen whenever I have a call with them. You could cut it with a knife."

Hunter let a breath of amusement escape through his nose. "Not as far as I know. At least, he still seemed as tightly wound as ever yesterday."

"Stubborn son of a *greilo* beast," Ryder muttered. "If he'd just *talk* to someone, instead of assuming his medical condition means he has nothing to offer a mate..."

"Talk to someone? *Really*, Ryder? Come, now—it's like you've never even met the man," Hunter said.

"Yeah, yeah," she grumbled. "Wishful thinking, I know."

"Probably so, yes. Though with luck, Martinez will turn out to be at least as stubborn as he is." He shot her a sidelong glance. "Or, I suppose you could always offer them free relationship counseling. I know how much you enjoy that sort of thing—the airing of complicated emotions… long, in-depth explorations of psychological pathology…"

She narrowed her eyes at him and drew breath to say something acerbic, but the sound of the clinic doors swooshing open interrupted her. Hunter tensed, having spent far too much of the past few years constantly watching for danger.

His fingers brushed the grip of the blaster at his hip—the Capital was still a dangerous place, even with the Regime out of power. But it was merely a human couple coming through the clinic's entrance… one obviously in imminent need of Ryder's services.

The dark-skinned woman leaned heavily on the curly-haired man, her free arm wrapped around her swollen belly. She was breathing fast through her nose, her shoulders hunched, and a rictus of pain on her face. Her male partner's gaze fell on the human nurse manning the reception desk. The nurse was already on his feet, coming around to the front to assist the pair.

"We need help!" the man said, sounding more than a little frantic. "Her water broke early, and someone said there was a medic here who will treat people even if they can't pay—"

Hunter saw the moment the man's attention caught on Ryder, wearing her doctor's scrubs and half-hidden in the back of the room. He froze mid-sentence, his mouth open. His arm tightened around the woman, and he took a step back as though considering making a run for the door. Fear and hatred twisted his pleasant features.

"Hang on, the medic's a *Vithii*? Oh, *hell*, no."

Ryder's chest heaved with a sigh, but she didn't respond otherwise.

"Pietre," the pregnant woman said through gritted teeth, fighting not to double over as a strong contraction rippled across her stomach. "The baby's coming! I don't know if I can make it to a different clinic..."

"Take a breath, buddy," the nurse advised, in a calm but no-nonsense tone. "If you don't want this woman giving birth in the middle of the street, you'd better calm down and let us help her. Ma'am, how far apart are your contractions?"

He reached forward as though to take the woman by the elbow, but the man shuffled back again, pulling her out of reach. "If you think I'm letting some Vithii butcher get anywhere near the woman I love—" he began.

Hunter had been following Ryder's lead, hanging back while the scene played out. The nurse, however, showed no such compunction.

"*Oy!*" he snapped, and stabbed a finger in Hunter's direction without turning around. "Look at that guy back there. You see those tattoos? That's Hunter Tarthasian, the bondmate of *Skye-fucking-Chantrell*. You've heard of Skye Chantrell, right? Voice of the Underground? Told people how to get the bioweapon antidote by drinking tap water after the Premiere tried to kill us all?"

The human man blinked, looking from the human nurse to Hunter and back again. Beside him, the woman let out a choked groan as another spasm rocked her.

"That's... Skye Chantrell's bondmate?" the man asked. "Seriously?"

"Yes, *seriously*," the nurse said sharply. His pointing finger moved to Ryder. "And *that's* their close friend, the doctor who helped manufacture the antidote and get it into the water system in the first place." He turned his full attention to the pregnant woman, helping to support her as she straightened from the contraction, still panting. "We're medical professionals, and we're *on your side*. Now, ma'am—will you please let us help you get this baby delivered safely?"

She looked up at her partner for a long moment, sweat beading her brow beneath the harsh overhead lights. "I… think we should trust them, Pietre. We can't just… hate half the population because they're Vithii. That's how it all started, you know? People hating other people because they're different, or because they've been told to hate them."

Reluctantly, Pietre released his grip on his partner, allowing the nurse to support her. "If…" He swallowed hard. "If you're sure, Vic. You know I just want to keep you and our baby safe."

Sensing that the drama was over, Ryder stepped forward. "Then let's get you both to a private room so we can meet this child of yours, shall we? Looks like he or she is pretty eager to meet *you*, so we'd better not dawdle."

Pietre nodded and squared his shoulders. "Okay. Yeah. I'm… look, I'm sorry about all that. Vic's right. I shouldn't have said those things. Let's go meet our kid."

The nurse urged Vic toward the interior door that led to the treatment rooms. Ryder ushered Pietre after them with a gesture before following behind. Just as she was about to disappear into the back, though, she turned and met Hunter's gaze for a long moment. An entire conversation passed between the two of them without the need for words as, quietly and without fanfare, the first tentative steps toward healing began on the battered colony where both of them had lived and wept, fought and bled for so many long years.

TWENTY-FOUR

Kade sat across the dining table from Pax, and considered how unlikely it would have been mere weeks ago for a rogue cyborg to openly show up for a meal in the heart of the Ilarian government complex. Some days, it was easy to feel like they weren't making progress fast enough on Ilarius, but moments like this one reminded him that, yes, things really were changing for the better.

Isadora was seated at Kade's right, finishing up her second helping of herbed rice and *fathaa* pods. She, too, had become gradually more comfortable with the idea of being in close contact with a cyborg.

Kade had received a recounting from Draven and Ash of the space battle at the edge of the Ilarian system, during which the ship the three of them were on was boarded by military cyborgs. Given that piece of background information, Isadora's earlier misgivings about Pax were understandable enough. Now, though, she was seated next to him and chatting amiably with Nahleene, who occupied the fourth and final chair around the square table in their borrowed quarters tonight.

"We do have some additional news tonight," Nahleene told them. "It's something that's been on the back burner for a couple of weeks, but we didn't want to say anything until we were sure."

"Oh?" Kade asked. "Do tell."

Pax twirled the stem of the wine glass he was holding between the fingers of his left hand, his gaze fixed on the play of light through the ruby depths. Nahleene's fingers brushed the top of his right hand, which rested on the table. She'd maintained the light contact throughout much of the meal, allowing Pax to experience the evening with the added benefit of second-hand emotion gleaned from his telepathic lover.

The cyborg lifted his eyes and took up the conversation. "After much discussion, the allies have agreed to fund a research project aimed at restoring the free will of the remaining cyborgs in the Ilarian military."

"They think that with more study, it may be possible to replicate what happened in Pax's brain," Nahleene explained. "It's all very theoretical at this point, but there's an entire new field of research opening up in regards to the interaction of nanotech and the sentient mind."

Kade raised his glass, still half-full of the wine that he was now allowed to have—in moderation—for the first time in years. "Hear, hear. I'll drink to that," he said wryly, drawing expressions of amusement from Nahleene and Isadora.

"That's wonderful news, you two," Isadora said. "Almost as wonderful as the news about the new breakthrough regarding the makeup of the re-formed legislature. Honestly, too much more of this, and I'll start to think we're making progress or something."

Kade snorted. "Don't worry—if you need to be brought back down from the clouds, you can always talk to Ryder about the state of social services in the human areas of the city."

"Ugh," Isadora groaned, sitting back in her chair and throwing one arm across her stomach theatrically. "Please… not after I've just eaten. Let me bask in the afterglow of a successful debate for this one night, at least."

And… just like that, Kade was hard—his cock swelling beneath the sheltering camouflage of the table solely in response to hearing that smoky voice uttering the word 'afterglow.' Because *somehow*, he'd thought it would be a brilliant idea to partner up with an intelligent, sharp-witted, tantalizingly seductive human woman who apparently wanted a relationship with him, despite the fact that he knew perfectly well he couldn't give her what she needed.

It felt vaguely ungrateful to say *'Fuck my life,'* when everything else was going so nauseatingly well. Of course, that was when the tantalizingly seductive human in question picked up a peeled slice of *daarlen* fruit, sucking on it with a contemplative expression for a few moments before popping it into her mouth.

All right. *Fine*, then.

Fuck his life. Fuck it right down to the depths of the humans' hell.

He blinked, and tore his eyes away. Unsurprisingly, the conversation had moved on without him while he was busy staring at Isadora's lips.

"The new plan to guarantee equal human and Vithii representation in all three branches of the legislature should go some way toward protecting both species' rights, going forward," Pax was saying.

"It's a solid idea," Isadora agreed, after she'd swallowed the thrice-damned fruit. "It might result in some additional gridlock as the different factions try to get things done, but maybe even *that* aspect will eventually end up resulting in more collaboration across the aisle."

"We can only hope," Nahleene agreed. With a sigh, she let her fingers slide away from Pax's, and deposited her napkin onto her plate. "Well, as lovely as this has been, I suppose we'd better head out. There's one more informal meeting on our agenda this evening, before we can call it a day."

"Indeed," Pax said. "Thank you for the meal, and the company. It was a most agreeable break from weightier matters."

"It certainly was," Nahleene agreed, rising from the table and stretching with a yawn. "And who knows? One of these days, maybe we'll get some proper time off."

Kade and the others rose with her.

Isadora chuckled. "Admit it—you'd go mad in the first thirty cycles, worrying about what was happening in your absence."

Nahleene let out an indelicate snort. "Yes, yes. Guilty as charged." She gave Isadora an assessing look for a moment, before her pale green gaze landed heavily on Kade. "Still, we all need to take what pleasure we can from the spaces in between. Life's too short—if we haven't learned that lesson by now, I don't suppose we ever will."

"Amen to that," Isadora muttered, coming around to wrap Nahleene in a brief embrace. "Have a good rest of the evening, you two."

Kade clasped Pax forearm to forearm, gruffly wishing him goodnight. To his mild irritation, the cyborg gave him a similar onceover to the one Nahleene had just given him.

But all he said was, "Goodnight, Kade. I look forward to speaking with you again soon."

Isadora showed the pair to the door, while Kade stared at the remains of their meal and sipped at his drink, trying to decide how important the subtext he was missing might be. When she returned, she leaned a hip against the edge of the table in front of him and picked up her unfinished wine.

"Well, that was nice," she said, pausing to take a sip from her glass before setting it aside. "So, in other news… rumor has it that Ash is threatening to start a betting pool around us sleeping together."

Kade choked on his wine.

Once he'd recovered himself, he gave a low cough to make sure his voice wouldn't betray him and said, "Do you want me to go yell at him? I have extensive practice."

Not that shouting at Ash ever *accomplished* anything, of course… but it was the principle of the thing.

She chuckled. "No, that won't be necessary. If I wanted him yelled at, I'm fully capable of doing so myself." Her head tilted as she regarded him. "Honestly, I'm more interested in your reaction. You can't really have missed the fact that the others have been gossiping about us since we got here, can you?"

The answer was yes—he apparently *had* missed it. Because prophets forbid his personal woes should stay, well… *personal*. Evidently, he'd given up that particular perk when he'd been sucked into a dysfunctional family of human and Vithii busybodies. Did Ash and the others truly have nothing better to do with their time than speculate on his non-existent love life?

"Doesn't it bother you?" he asked, partly to deflect, and partly because he was genuinely curious.

She shrugged one shoulder, and he tried not to focus on the way the wide neckline of her silk blouse shifted with the movement.

"Not particularly, no," she said, and he could hear the amusement behind her tone. "I mean... I was more or less attached to your bedside on the Vitharan medical ship, after all. And then there's the small matter of us sharing rooms here for weeks on end. Seems like a pretty logical assumption on their part."

She reached back and plucked another piece of fruit from the platter. It was only when she brought it to her lips again, licking off the juices without breaking eye contact, that the slow tide of realization washed over him.

She'd been driving him mad on purpose. This whole time, she'd been completely aware of the effect she had on him. His eyes widened, and he drew breath to say... something... only for it to stick in his lungs as he reached for words that weren't there.

Martinez had come to realize over the past few weeks that interpersonal communications weren't really Kade's strong suit. Oh... he was a competent enough communicator when it came to matters of politics and business, if a somewhat brusque one. But it was becoming increasingly clear that he hadn't unbuttoned and unlaced enough to have a meaningful personal exchange in... a very long time. Perhaps since before his parents were killed, as heartbreaking as that thought was.

He was *gaping* at her, for lack of a better word. She watched the realization crawl across his expression as she licked the section of *daarlen* fruit before popping it between her lips and swallowing.

"You…" he began. "You're…"

"Hoping that any betting pool doesn't have to drag on for very long before the payout?" she finished wryly. "Yes. Yes, I am."

… and then the walls slammed down before her eyes. Kade drained the contents of the wineglass in his hand and strode away, putting his back to her.

"I told you before we came to Ilarius that I wasn't in a position to give you everything you wanted out of this." The words were flat and gruff.

Right, then, she thought. *Looks like we're hashing this out tonight.*

It was as good a time as any. No immediate crises threatened. Things were on a generally positive course with the negotiations. No one was likely to bother them until tomorrow. And if Kade needed a good old-fashioned brawl to crack his defenses, she was up for it.

That wasn't the place to start, though.

"You're making an awful lot of assumptions about what I want," she said mildly.

He whirled and pinned her with gunmetal gray eyes. "Sex, based on the way you've been tormenting me these past few weeks. And some sort of romantic commitment, presumably. It's surprising to me that you haven't figured out I'm a poor candidate for either of those things." His voice lowered to a barely audible mutter. "Especially the first one."

"Hmm," she said. "So… no interest on your end, then? Funny how badly I misread you, in that case. I'm usually a pretty good judge."

He did the thing again where his mouth opened and closed a couple of times with no words coming out. She took a moment to feel bad for him.

"That's not what I said," he managed eventually. "I could harbor dreams of becoming the next system-wide hoverball champion, but that doesn't mean any coach with half a brain would recruit me to play. If you've a taste for Vithii men, you'd do better to find some handsome up-and-coming politician in the legislative chamber."

She gestured between them, encompassing the metaphorical gap that separated them… not to mention the thick tension curling through the atmosphere.

"This is about your impotence, isn't it," she said, gambling that he would have as little patience for dancing around personal matters as he did for dancing around political matters.

His hand closed around the edge of the sideboard he'd fetched up next to, fingers tightening until the knuckles turned white. "You certainly don't mince words, do you?"

"That's one of the big reasons we work so well together," she told him. "Now answer the question."

"Of course it's about my fucking impotence," he spat. "That's not going to go away just because my brain's full of nanobots pumping out neurotonin."

Martinez might or might not have had a private word with Ryder regarding Kade's condition shortly after they all returned to Ilarius. In Ryder's defense, she'd mostly stuck within the bounds of patient confidentiality… but she had at least been willing to speak in theoretical terms about the breakthrough research related to Kade's treatment with nanotech.

Yes, bots might someday be used for all sorts of complicated chronic conditions, including sexual dysfunction. Ryder herself had been using them for critical emergency medicine in extremely controlled and narrow circumstances for a few years now. But the Vitharan doctors were understandably reluctant to explore experimental applications for non-life-threatening conditions while the research was still in its infancy.

Cyborgs were able to utilize nanotech on a sweeping scale, but only thanks to the massive amount of technological hardware implanted inside them to maintain a standing population of repro-grammable nanobots within their bodies. Utilizing bots inside living bodies without machine implants to regulate them was an entirely different matter. And for now, treating impotence was low on the list of priorities for medical researchers.

"Again," Martinez told Kade, "you're assuming quite a bit regarding what it is that I want."

Kade visibly reined in his emotions, retreating further behind his wall. "Fine. What is it you think you want?"

She raised an eyebrow at the jab. "For a start, I want to see what's on the other side of that barrier you keep between yourself and the rest of the world. I only ever get glimpses, and I want more."

He continued to look at her, his grip still tight around the sideboard's edge. "I don't know if I have the key to unlock that door anymore."

Which… ironically might have been one of the most visceral and honest things he'd ever said to her. She nodded slowly.

"Okay. Then let me try first." She licked her lips, choosing her words with care. "I like sex. Which isn't to say I indulge all that often, in the grand scheme of things. Somewhere along the line, I realized that sex and intimacy were two completely different things—and I hadn't had the second one in a very long time. I realized... how much I missed it."

He didn't move from his position across the room, but she could see his chest rising and falling in an elevated rhythm.

"If I want orgasms, I can always buy a vibrator," she continued. "For intimacy, I need someone I trust enough to see me for who I am. Lost soul... part-time hypocrite... occasional PTSD basket case."

"You're not a hypocrite," he said.

She shrugged the words away. "I've been one in the past. I might become one again in the future. It would be nice to have someone around to call me on it, if it ever happens."

"So... what? We'll hold hands and gaze meaningfully into each other's eyes for a cycle or two in the evenings, after which you wish me a good night and go to bed with your rechargeable vibrating cock? Sounds lovely."

He was being deliberately provocative. Deliberately hurtful. She tamped down her irritation, fully aware that she'd been poking at a painful knot he'd rather have avoided altogether.

"That's not exactly what I had in mind, no." Lifting her chin, she pressed on despite the defensive signals he was sending out via the medium of his tightly controlled body language. "Rather than snipe at me, why don't you tell me what we'd be dealing with if we decided to give this a go? You're not exactly dead below the waist—I've already seen that much, at least."

"I can't believe I'm having this conversation," he said.

"You're not having this conversation, though—are you? " she pointed out. "Not yet. I mean… as conversations go, it's been pretty one-sided so far. Give me something to work with, here. You can become aroused, but… what? Not reach orgasm?"

"Orgasm isn't the problem," he said, as though she were being dense.

Martinez couldn't help her double take. "Umm. It's… not?"

Kade stared at her in turn. "I told you. I'm *impotent*," he said more slowly, as though he was concerned she hadn't heard him the first time, or didn't understand the words somehow. "I don't produce slick, I don't ejaculate, and more importantly, I can't form a knot. So, there wouldn't be much in it for you, which consequently makes it more of an exercise in frustration for me than anything else."

"You… do realize I'm human, right?" she asked.

He gave her a look of irritation. "I'd noticed, yes. And isn't the only reason human women sleep with Vithii men for the knotting? I can't imagine a minute or two of male rutting followed by a dry climax would be all that stimulating otherwise. Trust me when I say, it certainly isn't for female Vithii."

And with that final piece of information, connections started slotting together in her mind—followed immediately by a wave of exasperation laced with helpless fondness.

"Holy prophets above," she said. "For an intelligent man, Ehkadian Finisterre, you are one *hell* of an idiot."

Kade scowled. "I'm trying to be noble here. Could you maybe not insult me while I'm doing it?"

"Oh my gods, just shut up for a minute." She pressed fingertips against the bridge of her nose, rubbing at the corners of her eyes—not sure if she was trying to hold back hysterical laughter or tears. "No, on second thought, don't shut up," she said, lowering her hand. "Does arousal cause you any pain or discomfort?"

"Physically?" he asked with heavy irony.

And, yeah, she kind of wanted to cry for him right now, even though it was still mixed with a heavy dose of exasperation. She tried to keep both of those things out of her voice "Yes, physically."

"Pain, no. Frustration, yes," he growled.

Frustration… because he couldn't perform to Vithii cultural standards for sex, where knotting was more of a focus than orgasm. *Prophets.*

"When I tell you that I'm in it for the intimacy, but totally open to whatever kind of sexual contact would be reasonable and enjoyable for you, do you believe me?" she asked.

"I don't understand what that would even look like, Isadora," he said. "I don't see what you'd get out of it, beyond disappointment and eventually, resentment."

She reminded herself that he was Vithii, and Vithii weren't exactly known for their open-mindedness about sex. He was so focused on what he couldn't do that his mind genuinely didn't go to all the places hers did, once she learned that he could still experience arousal and release.

She took a centering breath through her nose. "*Do you believe me*?" she pressed.

His jaw worked. "I… believe that you believe it."

Pushing away from the table, she stalked toward him until she had him crowded up against the wall. He was breathing unsteadily, looking down at her from behind the hairline cracks in his barriers. She was sure she could hear the rapid thudding of his heart—a counterpoint to her own.

Martinez *ached* for him.

"Then tell me to stop if I do something you don't like," she told him. "And beyond that, let *me* worry about what I'm getting out of this."

With that, she stretched up, pressing their bodies together and burying her teeth in his neck, just below the sharp jut of his jaw.

TWENTY-FIVE

Wild need surged in Kade's belly as the infuriating creature before him closed her teeth around the tendon at the side of his neck and *sucked*. Godsdamnit—he'd tried to warn her off. He'd *tried*. Could he really be held accountable if she refused to be warned?

In an instant, he had their positions reversed, pinning her against the wall with a thump. A picture frame rattled off to her left—some generic, inoffensive piece-of-crap painting that he couldn't give two fucks about right now.

"Insufferable woman," he growled, and she had the audacity to laugh—a breathy sound that went straight to his traitorous cock.

"Thought I might enjoy a bit of a brawl with you," she said. "Looks like I was right."

Then she twisted improbably in his grip, somehow hooking his ankle with hers and levering him around until he was once more the one pinned. His shoulder bumped the painting, and the heavy frame crashed to the ground. Neither of them spared it a glance. In fact, he forgot about it completely when her fingers hooked in the collar of his formal shirt and tugged sharply. The front parted with a sound of ripping thread, buttons popping off and bouncing away.

A sound he didn't recognize rumbled up from his chest, and his fingers itched to return the favor on her silk blouse. She caught his hands in hers as he reached for her, though, pressing them against the wall next to his hips. His will to resist fled as her silk-covered breasts brushed against his bare chest, her fiery hazel eyes looking up at him with sly confidence.

"You'll get your turn," she said. "But for now, don't interrupt me while I'm unwrapping my present."

The maddening lips and teeth that had already sucked a mark into his neck worked the same magic on his collarbone, and the back of his skull thudded against the wall.

"*Fuck*," he said, more in response to her words and the sinful temptation of her mouth on his skin than the dull ache where his head had made contact with the hard plaster.

She lifted her face to grin at him, and it was all he could do to keep his hands where she'd put them rather than grabbing her and dragging her into his bedroom like an uncivilized savage. It grew even more difficult to resist when she bit her way down his chest and over his stomach.

His trousers were spared the same fate as the shirt, but she still made short work of the fastenings. Before his mind had really caught up to what was happening, they were down around his ass, she was kneeling in front of him, and her lips were wrapped around his aching cock.

The groan that escaped him felt like it traveled all the way up from his stones. His stomach sucked in as the urge to squirm away and the urge to thrust down her throat until she choked on him fought each other for dominance, leaving him frozen in place for an endless instant.

He was… aware of the human and Maelfian practice of fellatio, in the way most people were aware of miscellaneous weird sexual shit that other species were into—much of which didn't translate well across cultures. This kind of oral sex didn't really make sense for Vithii. Mostly, it just interfered with knotting.

What he'd failed to take into account, though, was that it also felt *amazing*. And… it wasn't as though he was going to be knotting Isadora whether she swallowed his length between her full lips or not.

Her tongue curled around him, delving into the slit, and he shuddered. "*Gods*—"

She pulled back, his length sliding free with a wet noise that should in no way have sounded sensual. He stared down at her, panting, as she steadied his hips in a firm grip and gazed up the length of his body from beneath dark eyelashes.

"I'm going to make you come like this," she said, as though that was the kind of thing people said to him every day. As though this were some normal, conventional occurrence between them.

"Why?" he asked hoarsely.

Something fell into shadow behind her bright gaze, as though his question had pained her.

"Because you deserve to feel pleasure," she told him earnestly. "And because I'm getting off on giving it to you. In fact… trust me when I say that whether or not you can produce slick is really pretty irrelevant at this point."

His nostrils flared, and he had to swallow another groan as the rich scent of female human arousal flooded his nose. It was different than a Vithii woman's scent would have been—less copper and musk, more seaweed and iron. Out of the blue, he wondered what it would taste like.

Was this what she had in mind? Would she be content with his tongue and fingers, after reducing him to incoherence with the lushness of her mouth? Rational thought fled as she swallowed him down again, choking a bit as his cock twisted and flexed, trying to get deeper. He could *feel* her throat constricting around him as she tried to take him all, and fuck fuck *fuck*—

There was no question of him lasting. In no time at all, a ball of liquid heat gathered tighter and tighter at the base of his spine—only to explode outward in shuddering bliss, his dick twitching and pulsing as it tried to shoot seed that wasn't there. His fingernails scrabbled at the wall as her wet, hot mouth slid over him, drawing out his climax before releasing him to the cool air.

His knees went rubbery, and he managed a semi-controlled collapse onto the floor as spots danced before his eyes. She climbed onto his lap, straddling him as he sat there crumpled and debauched—his clothing hanging open obscenely and his limbs in a tangle.

"Welp," she said, popping the 'p' in a way that might have been obnoxious, if Kade's body hadn't been swimming with a cocktail of lovey-dovey bonding hormones in the aftermath of his physical release. "Looks like you were right. Orgasm definitely isn't the problem."

She looked smug as hell, but in her defense, she'd probably earned it. He managed some sort of non-verbal grunt in response, and gathered her against his body tightly as he shuddered. The bite marks leading from his throat to his cock throbbed where his skin pressed against her clothing. In response, she wormed her arms around the small of his back and rested against him with every indication of contentment.

But… that couldn't be right. That wasn't how this sort of thing worked. Tension crept back into Kade's body as he tried to figure out what she expected of him now.

"Stop," she murmured against his neck. "I'm not waiting for you to read my mind. That's Nahleene's job description, not yours. I'm just enjoying the moment, and you can, too."

"I still don't know what you want from me," he managed.

"And I still don't know how you experience sex," she retorted, "So I don't know what the best way is for us to be together. The point is, it doesn't *matter*. I'm fine for now, doing whatever sounds most appealing to you while you recover. We can just hold each other. Or you're welcome to explore me however you'd like, either here or someplace more comfortable. You can get me off, or watch while I get myself off. If you get hard again later and want to try intercourse, we can do that. Just… *be intimate with me*. That's all I'm asking, Kade. Let me stay on this side of the wall with you."

But that was… too easy. Could it really be so easy? He felt overwhelmed with the choices she'd laid out, trying to integrate them somehow with the stunted remains of Vithii sexual imperatives—knot, protect, cherish.

Her lips pressed against the mark on his collarbone. "It's not a trick. I don't do coital trances, but I'm happy to do cuddling, with or without an orgasm first. Orgasms are good, but I kind of enjoy the slow burn of anticipation, too."

There was a beat of silence, then—

"I've wanted you so badly these past few weeks," Kade blurted, marking the onset of the uncontrolled verbal diarrhea that afflicted Vithii men after they climaxed. Ironically, *that* part of his sexual function seemed unaffected—never mind that he couldn't form a proper knot to go with it.

Typical.

"Mmm," Isadora murmured against him. "Looks like you're in luck, then."

Her teeth closed over the livid love bite she'd left earlier, and he jerked—some of his post-orgasmic disorientation draining away under the sharp jolt of sensation.

How could he best take care of this gorgeous alien creature who claimed she didn't need his knot? She'd said she would enjoy being held, and also that he could explore her body as he liked. To this point, she'd never lied to him or led him astray. If she would enjoy those things, he would try to do both.

"I want to touch you everywhere," he said, words slipping directly from his subconscious to the outside world.

She wriggled against him happily. "Be my guest. Let me know if you need me to move. Or you can just move me yourself. I do enjoy a bit of man-handling."

The conservative knee-length skirt she was wearing had hitched up around her hips when she straddled him. He swept one hand down the length of her spine and lower, his palm brushing over the ruched material. Grabbing the bottom, he lifted it even further, until his fingertips brushed the boundary between soft skin and lace.

Delving beneath the elastic top of her underwear, he explored the rounded globe of her ass. Smooth skin dimpled under his fingertips, but he could feel muscle lurking beneath the appealing softness of her curves. She shivered as he trailed a touch along the valley between her cheeks, feeling a tight pucker that fluttered lightly as he passed over it.

Exploring further, he encountered slick wetness that turned his touches into hot silk—frictionless and alluring. Was this what she'd meant earlier, about it not mattering if he could produce slick or not?

"Is this for me?" he asked hoarsely, pressing his fingers deeper as he sought out the source of the heat and slickness.

She moaned and went boneless in his grip. "Yes, it's all for you," she breathed, her lips still brushing the patch of flesh on his collarbone that she'd been abusing so deliciously.

A euphoric feeling washed over him, reminiscent of long ago, carefree days before everything went to shit. "I'm going to do everything to you," he told her, still floating in the hazy cloud where nothing separated thoughts from words. "Everything that either of us can possibly think of. I'm going to make you come so hard and so often that you won't care if I can't knot you."

She rolled her hips against his questing fingers. "I don't need your knot," she said breathlessly. "I just need you. Oh, *gods*—please keep doing that."

He kept doing that, while more words about how she looked and felt, how right it was to have her sprawled over him like this tumbled past his lips without his permission. His fingers explored her alien folds, and he hitched her a bit further up his body so he could reach better. She keened when a fingertip slid across a small, unfamiliar nub located near the apex of her lips.

"Here?" he asked, doing it again.

"Yes," she panted. "Yes, there, don't stop—"

He didn't stop... not as she writhed against him, and not as she shuddered apart under his touch. Not until she twisted her hips away, still gasping for breath. Suddenly, he needed to have her someplace more comfortable, and with considerably fewer clothes involved. Without giving it much thought, he hooked his hands beneath her thighs and used the wall at his back to lever himself upright, bringing her with him.

She made a punched out noise and wrapped her legs around his waist to steady herself, not protesting as he lifted her.

His bedroom, or hers? The beds were about the same size, and hers was closer... but some deeply buried part of him desperately wanted to drag her back to his den like the savage he'd compared himself to earlier. With no real reason to deny the impulse, he headed for the far end of the suite and scrabbled one-handed at the door handle to his room.

Opening the door might have been easier if his lips and teeth hadn't somehow found their way to the juncture of Isadora's shoulder when he wasn't paying attention—but he managed it all the same. A clumsy kick slammed it closed behind them.

The taste of her skin grew salty and metallic as he sucked his mark to the surface. He let go reluctantly so he could pour her onto the mattress. Her mahogany hair had fallen out of its stylish chignon at some point, and now it fanned across the pillow like a halo.

The skirt and blouse she was still wearing were in his way. He removed them without ceremony, gratified when she lifted her hips to assist his efforts. His own clothing probably looked ridiculous, hanging off him as it was. He removed it, as well, struck by the way her eyes darkened as she watched him disrobe.

Kade had few illusions about himself after a decade spent living under a premature death sentence. Gaunt, sharp-edged, whittled away until only muscle and sinew remained. Aged prematurely by his endocrine system's dysfunction, and the society he'd been fighting against. Grim tattoos of death and destruction covering a prison barcode inked irrevocably into his forearm.

"You're beautiful," Isadora said, her pupils blown wide and dark as she drank in his nakedness.

"You're still high on sex hormones," he told her.

"No," she retorted, only to blink and look a bit sheepish. "Well, okay, *yes*—but you *are*. That's not just the afterglow talking."

He shook his head. She was the beautiful one, with that combination of willowy strength and the delicacy shared by humans everywhere. The black lace of her bra and panties accented her golden skin and supple curves, but they still needed to go.

"Take those off," he said, his eyes playing over the offending items.

She fumbled behind her back for a moment and the bra popped open so she could shrug out of it. The panties followed, kicked to the foot of the bed. Kade inhaled as the smell of her arousal hit him anew. He picked up the scrap of lace and pressed it to his nose, unable to resist the impulse. It was so odd—her human pheromones should have meant nothing to him, yet once again, he was overcome with the desire to press his face between her legs and taste her nectar at its source.

Unlike fellatio, *that* kind of oral sex appeared occasionally in the lexicon of Vithii intimacy. While Kade couldn't lay claim to a vast reservoir of experience in such things—especially with a human—he wasn't a complete novice either. Isadora was still watching him with a wide-eyed stare, breasts heaving, and there didn't really seem to be a good reason to deny himself.

So he tossed the underwear away, heedless of where it landed, and prowled onto the bed until he could pull her legs apart, making space for himself. The smell here was even more intense than before. And when he dipped his head and ran his tongue along the length of her folds, the taste was even better.

TWENTY-SIX

Martinez basked in Kade's slow exploration between her thighs, enjoying the knowledge that he'd finally unbent enough to take such an initiative nearly as much as she was enjoying the act itself.

She'd harbored a suspicion over the last few weeks that Kade was his own worst enemy when it came to matters of the heart. She had eyes; she'd seen the love his comrades held for him. The memory of Hunter Tarthasian's imposing figure clasping Kade's hand in both of his as he lay in a coma conveyed all that needed to be said on the subject.

Kade was not unloved. Nor was he unloving, even if he wasn't prone to grand expressions of emotion toward those he considered family. Early in their acquaintance, she'd asked him about the reason behind his crusade against the Regime, wondering if it was some guilt-fueled attempt to redeem the legacy of his disgraced family.

"*While protecting the people I consider my family may in fact be part of my motivation, it's not remotely in the way you're thinking,*" he'd told her at the time.

He'd done what he'd done because it was the right thing to do. But he'd also done it in an attempt to protect the people he cared about. He could have bought himself passage off-planet years ago, and made a new life on one of the allied worlds.

Instead, he'd flung himself against the rocks of revolution until they had nearly broken him.

How lucky were they to be here, now, like this?

Kade's tongue rasped over her clit, sending a wave of pleasure sparking along her nerves.

"Oh, that's good," she moaned, letting her eyes slip closed.

She was rewarded by more of the same, pulses of warmth spreading through her belly. The sensation curled tighter inside her with each slow stroke, addictive and heady.

It was no lie that she'd had an utter lack of expectation regarding what form intimacy between them might ultimately take. Still, she found it hard to credit now that he'd been so deeply worried about his inability to please her. Perhaps cultural conditioning was to blame—the rigid rules surrounding Vithii masculinity, instilled since childhood. Or perhaps he'd spun his own narrative of personal inadequacy with no outside help.

It didn't matter, in the end—as long as he was willing to let old assumptions go in the face of new evidence to the contrary.

His tongue curled into her, rougher and more flexible than a human's. She came helplessly, clenching around him. His fingers dug into the meat of her hips, holding her in place. He lapped up her release, drawing fluttering aftershocks from her spent body.

Kade crawled up the length of her body and flopped down beside her. "All right?" he asked, pausing to swipe the ball of his thumb across his chin.

Gods above. He was covered in her juices, and the casual gesture nearly made her come again. "*Ngh*," she managed.

He regarded her, his head tilting. "Huh. Well, what do you know? I think I like you non-verbal."

She snorted on a laugh and dragged a hand across her face. "Ass."

Apparently, he was coming out of the bonding hormone 'stream-of-consciousness' phase, and returning to his usual acerbic self. As control of her limbs returned, she decided to indulge something she'd been itching to do since even before the disaster of a kidnapping—assuming he'd let her.

She nudged him in the side. "Roll over. I'm employing a fresh excuse to get my hands all over you."

He raised an eyebrow at her. "What's that supposed to mean?"

"Do it, and you'll find out," she retorted.

He held her eyes for a moment before shrugging and rolling onto his stomach. She scanned the bedside table and reached for a bottle of complementary unscented lotion that happened to be sitting there. After squirting some into her palm, she set it aside and hefted herself upright. The movement lacked much in the way of grace, mostly because half of her muscles still weren't returning calls from her brain.

Nevertheless, she managed to hitch herself around and straddle Kade's lower back. He made a questioning noise, trailing off to a low rumble as her hands closed on the muscles of his shoulders and started massaging them with long, slow strokes.

"Prophets," she said, feeling the rock-hard knots beneath her hands. "You need this more than anyone else I've ever met."

She took a few minutes to warm up the tight muscles with flat sweeps of her palms before really digging in. Kade trembled beneath her, small grunts escaping him now and then as longstanding spasms and adhesions in his fascia melted beneath her assault, one by one. She'd have to make sure he drank extra water before he fell asleep, she thought—and even then, he was probably going to feel like he'd been run over by a hoverbus tomorrow.

By the time she slid further back to sit on his thighs, and started work on the tempting curve of his glutes, he'd gone limp beneath her aside from the occasional flinch when she hit a new knot. Because she could, she spread his cheeks and slid lotion-slicked fingers along the valley in between, turning the massage intimate.

He tensed for an instant, only to relax again when she continued the same slow rhythm as before. She let her thumb play over the pucker of his ass, circling in decreasing spirals until the tip slid inside, then spiraling back out again, over and over. When she explored lower, delving forward until her fingertips stroked over the slight bulge where a human's testicles would be, his hips flexed into the mattress, and he groaned—low and filthy.

A fresh surge of answering desire throbbed between her legs.

"What's the matter? Would you be more comfortable on your back?" she teased, still stroking him intimately.

"That depends entirely on how smug you plan on being about getting me hard again so soon," he muttered into the pillow.

"Oh, I don't know," she said, letting amusement come through in her tone. "On a scale of one to ten... maybe a five? Six, tops."

He let out a put-upon sigh. "I suppose I can live with that."

She lifted her body enough for him to roll over, then immediately settled onto him again. He was, indeed, hard. His dick twitched and curved toward her heat... *seeking*.

Martinez leaned forward, catching her weight on her hands. The change in position brought him into contact with her slick folds. His cock moved restlessly against her, and they both caught their breaths.

"I won't last long enough to satisfy you this way," he said.

She smiled at him and lifted a hand to cup his cheek. "I'm already satisfied, you idiot. More than satisfied." Her thumb brushed over his lower lip. "But you never know... you might be surprised. There's a reason I sucked you off first."

His brow furrowed.

"It takes human men longer to come for a second time in one night, generally speaking," she explained. "Worth a try to see if that's the case for you, as well. And if not?" She shrugged. "We'll know for next time, and instead, you can get me right to the edge first, before you take me."

Kade seemed oddly bewildered by the observation. "You are... not like anyone else I've ever met."

Martinez huffed out a breath. "I should certainly hope not. Can I have your cock inside me now, please? The waiting is driving me a bit mad."

"I thought you enjoyed the 'slow burn of anticipation,'" he quipped, though he was already helping her lift her hips up to position him at her entrance, even as he said it.

"I do," she agreed. "In moderation."

With that, she sank down on him. It had been a while since she'd been with a Vitharan in this manner—she'd almost forgotten how their cocks seemed to act independently, burrowing inside with a little shimmying twist and settling deep. Nosing around… seeking out the places that made her shudder.

Kade arched beneath her, his head thrown back and eyes tightly closed.

"Look at me," she demanded breathlessly.

His eyes blinked open, dazed.

"You feel amazing," she told him truthfully. "I'm going to move now. I want you to let me take control. You just lie back and enjoy it. Don't worry about a thing, because this is perfect. You're *perfect*."

His chest hitched, rising and falling unevenly beneath her palm as she used his body to steady herself. She straightened above him, her breasts jutting out as his cock settled deeper. Keeping one hand splayed over his thundering heart for balance, she used the other to touch herself—palming her breasts, tweaking her nipples.

The cock inside her twisted restlessly. She let her hand wander downward, fingers seeking her clit and sliding circles around it. Beneath her, Kade looked undone, his chest still jerking in a rapid, uneven rhythm. His pupils were blown wide, surrounded by thin rings of steel gray. When she rolled her hips, he thrust up helplessly, a choked noise catching in his throat.

"So good," she said hoarsely, rising and falling above him as he met her stroke for stroke.

Her fingers moved faster, her inner walls clenching around him as she scaled the peak. Kade's hips snapped up sharply, his fists twisted in the bedclothes.

"Isadora," he rasped, his rhythm going sloppy as his body succumbed to its second release.

Martinez moaned as he went rigid beneath her, his cock twisting wildly against her G-spot... the tip brushing her cervix. A rolling, full-body climax took her at the same time Kade shook apart beneath her. She collapsed onto his chest, both of them panting like they'd just run a marathon.

It was some time before either of them spoke.

"I'm probably not medically cleared for something like this," Kade said, still sounding overcome.

Martinez settled herself more comfortably over his body. "Well... don't worry about it too much. You're still alive, right? I mean... hell, I can't actually feel my legs at the moment, and I'm not even under medical surveillance."

Kade swallowed. "Isadora, I..." He trailed off, before simply saying, "Thank you."

She wrapped her arms around him as best she could, tucking her hands under his shoulders and sighing happily.

"No need for that. But if we're going there anyway, then thanks for trusting me. Just think, though—we could have been doing this for weeks if you weren't so stubborn."

She felt the breath of a chuckle beneath her cheek, and smiled.

"What?" he asked. "And waste a perfectly good betting pool? Nonsense."

He was still nestled inside her, his questing cock gone soft and quiet.

"Can we stay like this for a bit?" she asked. "I'm not too heavy, am I?"

He scoffed. "Hardly. Go to sleep. That's what humans do, right? And I'll pretend you're in a coital trance, only with snoring."

Affection warmed her from her scalp to the tips of her toes. "Fair enough. Meanwhile, you can tell me all about my most sterling qualities, just like if we were knotted."

"Human vixen," he accused.

"Mm-hmm," she agreed. The silence stretched for a few moments before she said, "You know, I've been thinking."

"Always dangerous," Kade observed.

She roused herself enough to flick him in the ribs, but he was so relaxed he didn't even flinch. "I've been *thinking*," she repeated, "that you should consider getting in touch with the girl who was pregnant with your baby. See if she kept the child, and if she's open to contact with you."

Kade was quiet for a long stretch. "I... don't know. Maybe."

"Just something to consider," she said, and pressed a kiss to his chest.

His hand stroked through her tangled hair contemplatively. She was halfway to dozing when he started to speak again. "I never thought I'd be able to have something like this."

"I know," she said drowsily.

"I'm still not entirely convinced it's real."

She rubbed her cheek against him affectionately. "It is."

A pause.

"I want it to be."

"Good." She smiled again. "So do I."

The following evening, Kade sat in his office at the central hangar, checking the status of his various business accounts. His neck prickled, and he looked up to find Hunter staring at him with interest.

"What?" he asked irascibly, dragging his attention away from the file he'd been studying. Acquisitions had been a nightmare these past few weeks, with supply lines in chaos and interstellar trade at a near standstill.

"Nothing of import, old friend. Just wondering if anyone had warned Ash not to bother with the betting pool," Hunter said, deadpan.

Kade did his best to bristle. "Do I pry into your personal life, *tei'laal*?"

Hunter snorted. "Yes. You do. In fact, I seem to recall that you once considered stringing me up by my thumbs if I let my hormones get us all killed."

"That was different." He shot the younger man a hard glare. "Besides, what makes you so sure anything has happened?"

Isadora appeared in the doorway, looking decidedly amused. "At a guess, it's either the fact that you don't look like you've got a steel rod jammed up your spine today, or the giant hickey showing above your collar, lover."

Hunter swallowed a choked noise, and his response was almost irritating enough to cover up the flush of warmth that erupted in Kade's chest at the words.

Almost.

Isadora sauntered over and leaned on the back of Kade's chair, her forearms brushing his shoulders. "Here's a better idea, Hunter," she said. "Keep it on the down-low, and you can take the earliest betting date. We'll split the winnings."

A smile tugged at the corner of Hunter's lips—something Kade still hadn't grown used to seeing after such a long, bleak few years.

"Tempting," he said. "But ultimately a doomed plan, I'm afraid… unless you two plan on avoiding any contact with the others in the foreseeable future. I fear it will take more than a high collar to hide this new development from them."

"Ah, well," Isadora said lightly. "You can't say I didn't try."

"Perhaps we could return to the actual work that needs to be done today?" Kade suggested, not making any attempt to dial down the level of sarcasm. "Some of us have to be back in meetings tomorrow morning."

"Yes," Isadora said innocently. "And, you know, I'd hate to face those meetings without a solid night's rest first. We should probably call it a day, so we can go back to the suite. You know… *for sleeping.*"

Hunter burst out laughing—a pleasant rumble of amusement that Kade hadn't heard in… honestly, he couldn't remember how long.

"Ha, ha," Kade said in a flat tone. "Very amusing. Now, if we could just return to—"

Skye poked her head in the door. "Hey, what's so funny?" she asked. Then her eyes landed on him, and widened. "Whoa, *Kade*! Nice hickey!" She gave Isadora a thumbs-up sign and grinned. "Way to go, Isadora. So, has anyone told Ash yet?"
Hunter's laughter rang out around the room again, and this time, Isadora's joined it. Kade sighed heavily, but somehow, he couldn't bring himself to growl at them.

EPILOGUE

On an unnamed stellar cartography station, located on an unremarkable moon near the edge of the Ilarian system, a colony of slimy green space-mold continued its patient, months-long expansion through the outpost's plumbing system.

From a single spore that had made a lucky landing on the right-hand sink in the station's single lavatory, the mold had grown, reproducing at a painfully slow rate. The station air was dry. The condensation in the pipe barely provided enough moisture. The microscopic residue of dead skin cells and soap scum in the sink had scarcely provided enough raw nutrients for the mold's initial expansion.

In addition, every so often a noxious spray of chemicals or a blast of concentrated UV light threatened to undo all the hard-won progress it had made. The frantic search for a mutation that could successfully deal with each new stressor felt like a setback, but with every challenge met, the colony grew stronger.

Still, it was so *slow*.

Good things were nearby. Closer and closer the colony crept. Micron by micron. Cell by cell. Giving up and dying never even occurred to it. That wasn't what space mold *did*. Space mold grew. Space mold survived. Space mold found a way and *spread*.

The day when the edge of the colony finally reached the Slime Mold Promised Land came as a complete surprise—as much as anything could be considered a surprise to a collection of mindless eukaryotes. The shut-off valve for the sink faucet had been breached long ago, and past that single barrier, the only thing separating the colony from the station's water tanks was distance.

When the freshly spawned zygotes at the edge of the foremost cluster matured into plasmodia and extended their protoplasmic strands into the unknown, rather than bare metal, they touched an ocean of luxuriant liquid, free for the taking. A boundless supply of water, sufficient for all of the colony's needs and then some.

The precious moisture wicked along the interconnected plasmodia, slaking the mold's thirst and bolstering its strength. The colony had long ago stumbled upon a mutation that allowed it to gain nutrition from breaking down the metal of the pipe through which it was traveling. Now, with the addition of plentiful water, it had everything it needed for the next stage in its life cycle.

Within hours, hundreds upon hundreds of transparently delicate fruiting bodies had erupted from the main mass like tiny, cylindrical flowers. Always keen to keep its options open, the colony had also been growing outward from the lavatory sink, in addition to the focused expedition proceeding inexorably through the pipes. At this point, the green mass covered perhaps seventy percent of the available surfaces in the small room, which was, it thought, rather impressive given the less than ideal circumstances it had been dealing with up until now.

After a moment of pregnant possibility in which the entire colony stood poised, the fruiting bodies burst in unison, releasing billions of sweet-smelling spores into the station's recycled atmosphere.

It was something of a pity that no sentient beings were present to appreciate the accomplishment, really. In addition to the lovely smell, a long-ago mutation had also imbued the spores with a pleasant narcotic effect for many higher species.

The small group of beings that had been present intermittently through the colony's life cycle certainly seemed like they could have used a bit of chemically mediated relaxation, based on their frequent, unprovoked murder attempts using cleaning chemicals and UV rays.

Perhaps they would return at some point, and be able to appreciate the colony's accomplishment after the fact. And if not? Well, there would be other spore releases. There would be other moons, other stellar cartography stations, and other bipedal sentients with exciting new cleaning supplies to adapt to.

After all, life was persistent. Life held on, defiant in the face of impossible odds. Life knew that however bad things seemed, better days would come.

All it took was a bit of tenacity.

finis